**He married for money, not for love.
Fortunately, his wife did quite the opposite . . .**

Young and spirited, Glee Pembroke had always been secretly in love with her brother's best friend, Gregory Blankenship. So when she learned that this dedicated bachelor must marry by his twenty-fifth birthday or lose his inheritance, she boldly proposed a marriage of convenience, while secretly planning to win his love. Knowing of her new husband's reputation as a lover of loose women, Glee decided she must become "fast" herself—in order to capture his attention.

Though marriage to Glee did seem a sensible solution to his dilemma, Gregory had no intention of giving up his rakish ways, and he certainly wouldn't tolerate his bride gallivanting about Bath like some wanton female. Her outrageous antics were causing him no end of aggravation—and strangely—inspiring a jealousy he was not used to feeling. When did he become so possessive about his wife? Surely, he was not succumbing to the one condition he had so studiously avoided . . . love?

D0596417

Dear Readers,

In July of 1999, we launched the Ballad line with four new series, and each month we present both new and continuing stories set everywhere from medieval England to the American West—the kind of passionate, romantic stories you love best, written by the most gifted authors. At the back of each book, we tell you when you can find subsequent books in the series that have captured your heart.

First up this month is **With His Ring,** the second book in the fabulous new *Brides of Bath* series by Cheryl Bolen. What happens when a dedicated bachelor who marries for money discovers that his impetuous young wife has married for love—his? Next, Kelly McClymer returns with **The Next Best Bride.** A jilted groom marrying his errant fiancée's twin sister is hardly romantic, unless it happens in the charming *Once Upon a Wedding* series.

Reader favorite Kate Donovan is back with another installment of the *Happily Ever After Co.* This time in **Night After Night** a young woman looking for a teaching job instead of a husband finds the key to her past— and a man with the key to her heart. Finally, ever-talented Cindy Harris concludes the *Dublin Dreams* series with **Lover's Knot,** in which secrets are revealed, friendships are renewed . . . and passion turns to lasting love.

Why not start spring off right and read them all? Enjoy!

Kate Duffy
Editorial Director

THE BRIDES OF BATH

WITH HIS RING

Cheryl Bolen

ZEBRA BOOKS
Kensington Publishing Corp.
http://www.kensingtonbooks.com

This books is dedicated to the memory of two special women. First, my mother, Betty Appleton Williams Sills, who thought there was nothing I couldn't do. And to Professor Kathleen Bland Smith, who recognized and nurtured my raw talent. I'm also indebted to my grandmother, Vertie Byars Cheatham, and my aunts, Gloria Appleton DeCuir, and Marie Williams Gray.

ZEBRA BOOKS are published by

Kensington Publishing Corp.
850 Third Avenue
New York, NY 10022

Copyright © 2002 by Cheryl Bolen

All Kensington titles, imprints, and distributed lines are available at special quantity discounts for bulk purchases for sales promotion, premiums, fund-raising, educational or institutional use.

Special book excerpts or customized printings can also be created to fit specific needs. For details, write or phone the office of the Kensington Special Sales Manager: Kensington Publishing Corp., 850 Third Avenue, New York, NY 10022. Attn. Special Sales Department. Phone: 1-800-221-2647.

Zebra and the Z logo Reg. U.S. Pat. & TM Off.

First Printing: April 2002
10 9 8 7 6 5 4 3 2 1

Printed in the United States of America

ONE

The prick of a needle should have been so common an occurrence to Glee Pembroke—a most inferior needlewoman—that her stitching rhythm should have continued unbroken. But not today. Throwing her work down, she stomped her kid slipper and nibbled her pricked thumb into her little rosebud mouth. "I simply wasn't cut out for a life buried here at Hornsby Manor," she protested. "Why will my brother not allow me to live by myself in Bath? Other spinsters do."

Her elegant sister-in-law calmly set aside her own flawless needlework and directed a sympathetic gaze at Glee. "You're not a spinster. You're a nineteen-year-old maiden, and it's not acceptable for you to live alone."

"I prefer to think of myself as a spinster," Glee protested, her lower lip working into a lovely pout. "After all, I've two seasons behind me and still am not respectably wed."

Dianna shot Glee a scolding glance. "You failed to mention the eight offers of marriage you turned down."

"Eight and a half—if you count Percy Wittingham, whom I persuaded not to address my brother."

The impeccable Dianna gave a bemused smile. "I

know how very dull it must be here for you, with my recent confinement and with Felicity being on the grand tour."

Glee emphatically shook her head. "Nothing—not even a presentation to the queen—could have kept me away from Baby Georgette's birth." Her face softened and her voice grew sweet. "My niece is without a doubt the most precious baby ever to draw breath."

Dianna lowered her lashes, a glow of contentment suffusing her. "George and I think so."

Glee sighed. "You and George . . . and Felicity and Thomas . . . I'm surrounded by happily besotted married couples, and all I can ever aspire to is being an aunt." Despite the unrivaled success of her two seasons, the one man she had adored since earliest childhood, the only man she could ever truly love, remained as elusive as seraph's wings. Gregory "Blanks" Blankenship was so completely removed from her touch, she had never even given voice to her adulation of him. And if she could not have Blanks, she preferred to die a spinster.

Dianna's eyes softened. "Have patience, Glee. I'm two years older than you, Felicity's seven. If you had truly been desperate, you would have accepted one of those *eight and a half* proposals. And there will most likely be eight more. You're a very lovely young lady." A smug, mischievous smile settled over Dianna's normally placid face. "I know why you could not fall in love with any of those young men." The graceful young mother casually took up her sewing again.

"Pray, enlighten me," Glee said impatiently. Watching Dianna pick up her sewing, Glee was embarrassed to have her own meager snatches of embroidery in the same room with her sister-in-law's meticulous creations. How fortunate she was that Dianna was already married, for Glee compared most poorly to her beautiful sister-in-law's perfection.

"Whether you realize it or not, you have long been in love with a man who has not yet realized how eligible you are," Dianna continued.

Glee's brow arched. "Indeed?"

Dianna nodded. "A young man you've known almost all of your life, or at least since he and George attended Eton together."

"Blanks." The name tumbled from Glee's lips almost reverently. How had Dianna guessed? She met Dianna's gaze squarely. "You realize in Mr. Gregory Blankenship's eyes I will always be twelve years old."

Dianna nodded. "It is for you to force him to notice otherwise."

Glee pulled her shawl more closely about her and rose from the silk damask chair to stride to the fireplace and its crackling warmth. With her back to Dianna, she said, "Then, too, there's the fact that Mr. Blankenship has never been attracted to decent young ladies. Does he not keep a mistress?"

"You are not supposed to know of such things!" Dianna chided.

"Perhaps if I acted like a doxy, Blanks would find me appealing."

"Then you *do* care for him!"

Glee sighed, bit her lip, then met her sister-in-law's probing gaze with an embarrassed nod.

Had Dianna known that Glee compared every man to Blanks, and they all came up wanting? It was not just that he was taller and better looking than all the others. Or that he was enormously wealthy and displayed incomparable taste. Or that he was a noted whip. Though he was all those things, he was so much more.

He was uncommonly personable and solicitous of

all he met. It had been Blanks—not her own brother—who extracted her first tooth. And Blanks had been the one to console her when her favorite dog had died. And with a peculiar racing in her heart, she remembered a twelve-year-old Blanks proudly carrying her back to the manor house after she had tumbled from a tree and hurt her foot.

She remembered, too, that his ready smile could fill the gloomiest day with warm sunshine. She shuddered even now as she pictured his devastating grin.

Dianna smiled like the cat who caught the canary. "When Blanks is ready to settle down, he will want a good girl, not a doxy."

Glee turned around to face Dianna. "Despite that I'm five years younger than he, this red hair of mine could turn quite gray by the time Mr. Gregory Blankenship decides to settle down. To know Blanks is to know of his complete aversion to marriage and children—and his inability to admit he might be wrong about anything."

Dianna nodded. "But George had no intentions of settling down when he met me. Love, my dear, has a way of changing things—even a bachelor's toughest resolve."

How remarkably love had changed her brother, Glee thought. Not a day went by that Glee did not marvel over George's metamorphosis from heavy drinking, wildly gaming rake to besotted husband and devoted father. Of course, it had helped that he removed himself from his hedonistic friends in Bath and settled at Hornsby Manor.

"It's as likely that Blanks will suddenly fall in love with me as it is that faro and the races at Newmarket will cease to hold his interest. Not like George with you. I could almost see Cupid's arrow snare George's heart the minute he set eyes on you. And I assure you, my brother planned to stay a bachelor until he was thirty."

Glee's gaze dropped to the hearth where the flames leaped in a blaze of yellow and orange and blue. "Of course, I'm not adverse to offering Cupid a little encouragement—where Blanks is concerned." She looked mischievously at Dianna. "Tell me, does George have a book that tells one . . ." She turned her back to Dianna once again. "Tells one about sex. You know, how to go about it and all that."

She turned to face Dianna, who had suddenly colored, and watched Dianna intently for a moment.

Finally, Dianna answered in an embarrassed voice. "I'm sure I've never heard of such a book."

"Then how do you know what to do?"

Dianna avoided meeting Glee's gaze. Taking up her sewing again, she cleared her throat. "I suppose it's somewhat like breathing. It seems to come automatically—provided one is in love with one's partner."

The large door creaked open, and George came striding into the room. He was blond and burly and young and exuberant. And completely in love with his wife. His dancing eyes settled on Dianna. "What comes automatically?"

The two young women exchanged amused glances.

George planted a kiss on Dianna's cheek.

She looked up at him with adoring eyes. "Falling in love, my dear."

He glanced at Glee. "Is Glee in love again?"

With narrowed eyes, Glee faced her brother. "Please don't speak of the idiotic act I was party to when I was a child of seventeen."

"Yes, George," Dianna urged, "Glee's nothing like that girl who wanted to run off with her dancing master. She's ever so much more mature now."

"I'm utterly grateful no one outside our family knows of my former foolishness," Glee said.

"As am I," George agreed.

Glee's serious gaze nabbed her brother. "Surely you remember I was never in love with that moron dancing master."

George nodded sympathetically.

Glee strode to the door. "I shall leave you two lovebirds alone while I take a walk. The only thing better here than in Bath is that here I can walk without a maid."

Company was thin in Bath this winter, Gregory "Blanks" Blankenship lamented as he flipped a woolen scarf about his neck with one hand while maneuvering the reins to his gig with the other. How he missed good old George. There was nothing they could not persuade the pleasure-loving fellow to do—especially when he was in his cups. Gregory chuckled to himself as he recalled the time Appleton dared George to drink a tankard of hog's urine—which George promptly did, earning a fat five pounds from Gregory.

Remembering his solemn mission today, Gregory's smile vanished. He pulled his gig in front of his solicitor's place of business, eyeing a waiting young boy facing him from the pavement.

Coatless with a single toe poking through a hole of his well-worn shoes, the lad fairly bounced in front of Gregory, a wide smile revealing missing front teeth. He must be around six years old, Gregory decided.

"Morning, Gov'nah," the boy said.

Gregory leaped to the pavement and addressed the lad. "I'll wager you're a young man who has a way with horses. Keep an eye on mine, and there's a crown in it for you." Gregory knew a crown was an exorbitant amount to pay for so menial a task, but the boy looked as if he could certainly use it.

The lad's eyes rounded. "Right, Gov'nah! I ain't never seen a crown before." The little fellow took the reins and began to gently stroke the gray, speaking soothing words as Gregory mounted the steps.

Upstairs, Mr. Willowby's young clerk greeted Gregory. "Good morning, Mr. Blankenship. 'Twas sorry I was to learn of your father's death."

Gregory, who had had six weeks to become accustomed to the idea of his father's demise, acknowledged the man's condolences with a grim nod before withdrawing a guinea from his pocket and slapping it on the man's desk. "Be a good man, won't you, and see to it the little urchin who hangs about in front of your building gets a warm coat and new shoes."

The clerk took the coin, pushed back his chair and got up to walk to the window and peer out at the child. A light snow was beginning to fall. "His mum cleans for us, and I don't believe he has a father. Poor lad."

The door to Willowby's office opened, and a slender man with a pointed chin spoke to Gregory. "Won't you step into my office, Mr. Blankenship?"

Gregory followed him into the chamber and settled in a chair facing Willowby across an immaculate desk.

"I asked you to come today because I wanted to talk to you privately before we meet with the entire family," Willowby said.

Gregory cocked a brow.

Willowby cleared his throat and met Gregory's quizzing gaze with openness. "I wanted to prepare you."

Gregory's brows lowered. "Prepare me for what?"

Willowby expelled a deep sigh. "Your late father's will is a bit unusual."

Gregory shifted in his chair. His heart began to pound. Somehow, he knew this was not going to be pleasant. Not removing his eyes from Willowby, he said, "Go on."

"The last time I saw your father, he was somewhat out of charity with you. He kept mumbling that you were entirely too . . . ah, unsettled."

Gregory nodded.

"You'll have the opportunity to read his exact words, but they were something to the effect that he did not want you to squander away his money on your frivolous pursuits."

"So, he's cut me out of the will."

Mr. Willowby hesitated a moment. "Not exactly. According to your father's latest will, if you are not married by your twenty-fifth birthday, all properties will go to the next eldest, your half brother Jonathan."

"The good one!" Gregory interjected, his ever-present smile spreading across his face. Not that he was happy. The smile was to conceal his pain, a mask cultivated from years of practice with his stepmother who resented that he—not her own son—would inherit her husband's wealth. So, Gregory thought with sorrow, Jonathan would get the Blankenship fortune after all. Their sedate father had always preferred Jonathan, and probably with justification. Jonathan was just like their father. Serious. Frugal. And incapable of having fun. In short, totally opposite of Gregory.

Gregory scooted back his chair. "I'm grateful that you let me in on my father's scheme," he said, rising and striding toward the door.

Mr. Willowby cleared his throat. "How old are you now, Mr. Blankenship?"

Gregory stopped and turned to watch Willowby's amused gaze. "I'll be twenty-five in June."

"It's not too late for you to comply with the terms of your father's will."

"To get married?" Gregory's eyes narrowed suspiciously.

Willowby nodded.

"But I've got less than four months and no prospective bride." Nor did he desire a bride. Ever.

"I should think any number of women would be more than happy to accommodate you, especially with such a great deal of money at stake."

"My brother would see through such a scheme readily and challenge such an action."

"It is possible to actually fall in love in a very short period of time. Take Mrs. Willowby and me. I offered for her a week after we met."

Gregory, who had never met Mrs. Willowby, suddenly pictured the sharp-chinned solicitor with an equally sharp-chinned bride leading a trail of little pointy-chinned youngsters. A sure reason to avoid matrimony. "Would that I could be so fortunate," Gregory murmured.

He stepped toward the solicitor and placed a firm hand on his shoulder. "Thank you, Willowby."

Willowby's clerk was gone when Gregory passed through the chamber again, drawing on his gloves before braving the day's chill. He hoped the clerk was off procuring a coat and shoes for the wretched lad now tending his horse.

The boy stood faithfully beside Gregory's mount, despite the snowflakes which settled into his blond hair. Gregory patted the lad's head. "I see you're as good as your word." He tossed the boy a crown. "It's much too cold for you to be outdoors without a coat. Be a good lad and go warm yourself in Mr. Willowby's second-floor office." Gregory shot a glance toward the building.

He watched the boy, clutching his coin, enter the building; then Gregory took a seat on the box and directed his conveyance down Bath's Milsom Street. Despite the bitter cold, he had no desire to return to his town house. He did not feel like making polite conversation or flashing smiles he did not feel. Though he had presented a stoic front to Willowby, Gregory felt lower than an adder's belly.

Once more, his father had played him cruelly in favor of Jonathan. Gregory wanted to hate his half brother as he hated his father, but he could not. Jonathan was younger and smaller and always evoked a sense of protection in Gregory despite the fact that his brother looked upon him as an opponent. Though they were just over two years apart in age, they had never been close. Jonathan resented it when Gregory was better at his sums or when Gregory's mount went faster than his. And Jonathan coveted whatever Gregory had, even though their tastes were vastly different. Gregory would weaken and give his brother the toy sword or the silver spurs or the book of poems Jonathan hungered after, only to watch dust cover them once they were in Jonathan's possession.

Gregory rode across Pulteney Bridge, noting that the River Avon was nearly frozen. He was too angry to take note of the chill in his bones. Never had it occurred to him that he would not live out his life in the extravagant style he had lived it these first twenty-four years.

It was different with Jonathan. Not only was he not raised with such expectations, he would never know what to do with such vast sums of money. Jonathan's life's passion was squeezing as much as he could out of a shilling. At his own lodgings in London, he denied himself what other young men of his class considered necessities. He kept no horse, nor a fire in his chamber, and he substituted inferior tallows for the better quality wax candles—and these used only sparingly. Gregory suspected his brother saved a goodly portion of his three hundred a year. Jonathan frequently put up at Sutton Manor to spare himself expenses.

Gregory could not understand Jonathan's frugal obsession. What good was money if it could not be used to purchase what made a soul happy? In one bleak second the full force of how perilously close he was to losing his fortune walloped Gregory. Good lord, would he have to give up his horses? And his tailor? And his gaming? His heart tripped. Would he have to dismiss Carlotta?

How was he to get along? He remembered when his best friend George had lost the little bit of fortune that was left him by his viscount father. How had George managed before he married the sister of the fabulously wealthy Mr. Thomas Moreland?

Perhaps George would have some timely advice to offer. Damned if he wouldn't just ride over to Warwickshire and visit his viscount friend.

From the second-floor window adjacent to Willowby's office, Jonathan Blankenship watched his brother get on his gig. With a satisfied smile on his face, Jonathan continued watching until Gregory crossed the River Avon. Now, to remove himself from the building without old man Willowby seeing him and knowing he had listened to everything.

TWO

Dianna was always right. Glee's merino pelisse would have offered little protection against the afternoon's dank chill. Even the emerald cloak Dianna had suggested barely warmed Glee as she trod through the sodden land surrounding Hornsby Manor. Then there was also Dianna's astute observation about Blanks. Her own subsequent admission liberated her from years of secret devotion. Glee's insides roiled and shook and settled into sweet anticipation as she contemplated Gregory Blankenship and her ardor for him.

The feelings which currently swamped her had always filled to capacity the innermost chamber of her heart. It had just taken Dianna's sage observation to unleash them, drenching Glee in feelings she could not put a name to. Thoughts of Blanks aroused her in ways she had never before experienced. A bittersweet longing surged deep within her, a longing only Blanks could satisfy.

She lifted her skirts and crossed the brook over a submerged stone path, feeling feather-light and not at all distressed over her wet slippers. She felt unaccountably womanly, ripe for the love shared by a man and a woman. A love that encompassed body and soul. Now she knew what had been missing from her life.

Until she could capture Blanks's prurient heart, she could never be complete.

But how did one go about snaring such elusive love? Blanks's life had been little more than a series of playful pranks and illicit love. If only Blanks had admired a lady, then Glee might have some idea what type of woman appealed to him. She would have something to emulate. Instead, she had no clue. Never had he been attracted to a woman whom he could bring home to the stern man who had been his father.

Perhaps, she thought hopefully, his father's death—and his own subsequent position as head of the house—would force him to mature, to want a wife and family. After all, he was four and twenty. The same as George. And look at how happily George had embraced matrimony and fatherhood.

Blanks's father's death also secured for him a fortune. Her heart hammered as she thought of how such blessed circumstances would attract lovely fortune hunters. As if his powerful good looks had not already made him one of the most desirable men in England. *Drat.* One more obstacle to her only happiness.

After leaving the thicket, she glimpsed a clear view of Hornsby Manor a half mile away. Its three stories of gray stones nearly blended with the murky skies of the same color. She heard the pounding of hooves from behind and turned to see a young man, great coat flapping behind him, galloping toward the manor. Had her thoughts conjured up Blanks? The man's mahogany hair and the elegant ease with which he sat his horse most certainly looked like Blanks. As he came closer, she realized the rider was, indeed, her secret love.

And her heartbeat accelerated. She ran her fingers through her tussled hair and turned to face him, biting into her lips to render them rosier. Now she was sorry she had taken Dianna's advice and worn the ill-fitting voluminous cloak.

When he was within ten feet of her, a smile of recognition lighted his ruggedly handsome face. Unconsciously, she returned the smile as he dismounted and began to lead his bay behind him.

"Ah, Miss Pembroke, a pleasure to see you again," he said.

Though conversation had always come easily between them, Glee found herself at a loss for words. She stood stone still facing him, her teeth chattering. "Was George expecting you?" she finally managed.

He shook his head, impish doubt on his beguiling face. "Is that a problem?"

"Of course not," she reassured. "George will be utterly delighted to have you here, and I confess I, too, am glad of the company."

He fell into step beside her. "Devilishly cold, is it not?"

"Indeed it is," she managed.

He began to remove his many-layered woolen coat and drape it across her shoulders. "Can't have your lovely teeth chattering."

She looked up at his darkly handsome face as he was looking down at her. The tip of her head barely came to his shoulders. She felt utterly feminine. "I cannot take your coat, Mr. Blankenship."

There it was. His bone-melting grin. She could swoon.

"Mr. Blankenship?" he asked with mock indignation. "Since when did you decide to stop calling me Blanks?"

"You addressed me as Miss Pembroke first. Then there is the fact you *are* the head of your family now, and neither of us is a child any longer." There! Let him think on that.

He took her hand, patted it, and tucked it into the crook of his arm. Suddenly she was no longer cold, but warm and as content as a kitten in the sunshine.

"I must confess," she said, "I do prefer calling you Blanks."

"And I prefer to remember you as that charming little sister who snuck away from the schoolroom to follow George and me about in the wood." He let out a little chuckle. "Are you still afraid of frogs?"

Of course she was, but she was not about to admit it. "I'm not a silly child anymore," she said haughtily.

"How could I forget? The ravishing Miss Pembroke, Belle of Bath. Pray that your rejected suitors do not do themselves in."

He had noticed her success! This was very good. She still reveled from his compliment on her teeth and his gesture of shedding his own coat for her comfort. "While I'm languishing on the shelf, another younger lady will be sure to supplant me." This was good. Let him think of her as old enough to be on the shelf.

A hearty laugh broke from deep within his powerful chest. "I would hardly say you're on the shelf."

This was not at all what she wanted. "I suppose I'll have to take a husband next season whether I love him or not. I wish to be a married lady with a home of my own."

He stroked her arm. "Your prince will come. Give him time. After all, you're not yet twenty."

So he remembered her age. This, too, was good. "I cannot tell you how wonderful it will be to have your company at Hornsby Manor. It's been dreadfully dull here. As you know, George and Dianna are so perfectly besotted over each other, they make for most tedious company. You must promise to be my partner for whist tonight."

"You now play whist?"

She scowled again. "I will have you know I can beat George half the time."

"Then I will be happy to be your partner."

They walked along the gravel path that would place them at the front door of the manor house in less than a moment's time, and Glee slowed her steps to keep Blanks with her longer. "What brings you to Hornsby Manor?" She looked up into his manly face, admiring his dark, flashing eyes. For once, he was not smiling.

"I've had some rather bad news."

Her brows plunged. "No!" First, his father's death. Now what?

"It seems my financial expectations are not to be fulfilled. I need advice from George on how to live with reduced circumstances."

"Are you saying your father squandered away his fortune as our father did?"

"No, nothing like that. He apparently feared *I* would squander away his fortune."

"Then he left it to your younger brother?" she asked, her voice incredulous.

He nodded solemnly. "He did, indeed. Or close to it. His will stipulated that if I was not wed by my twenty-fifth birthday, the money and lands would go to Jonathan."

"Your twenty-fifth birthday is in June, is it not?"

"The sixteenth day of June."

"Then you'll simply have to marry by then." Her heart somersaulted. He was here surely for a few days. No other woman could get her clutches into him. Oh, she had her work cut out for her.

Keeping her mind on the card game proved difficult when Glee felt the solidness of Blanks's knee briefly touching hers under the table. An overwhelming envy of his current mistress seized her. What would it be like to lie with him? To have his long, brown body stretched out beside her? She could picture his muscled torso, firm and strong. She could imagine trailing her fingers through a mass of hair on his rippled chest, for she instinctively knew dark hair would mat there. She ached to feel his arms come around her, pulling her into him. She grew hot and throbbed low in her belly. She longed to feel his firm mouth settling over her own. When he looked up and met her gaze, her face flushed.

It was terribly difficult to concentrate on her cards. His solemn face proved far more enticing. When he studied his cards, she studied him. She couldn't remember Blanks without that devastating smile of his revealing perfectly even, chalk-white teeth. When he grinned, a dimple pinched his smooth brown cheek on one side only. But now as she watched him, he seemed somber, his jaw tightening, his mouth firm. She watched the flickering candlelight play with his closely cropped, slightly curly mahogany-brown hair. Brows in the identical shade of brown hooded eyes the color of deep amber. His dark lashes lifted, and he shot her his familiar heart-stopping smile. Like an image reflecting off the pond, she instantly returned the smile.

She forced herself to keep her mind on the game. After all, she had to convince him she was mature and intelligent to purge his mind of memories of a childish Glee. She counted trumps diligently. She defended her hand cunningly. She bid intelligently.

And she and Blanks won the first rubber. With his devastating grin dimpling his bronzed skin, he met her gaze. "It seems our Glee has grown up to be an admirable whist player."

Our Glee. Could she dare hope? She only smiled demurely and concentrated on the next hand. At least she gave the appearance of concentrating. Men did not desire to share their lives with talkative misses. And the only person in the world she wanted to share her life with faced her across the table. She dare not appear to be a talkative miss.

"She's a devilishly good whist player," George snapped. "I wish I could be smarter than one of my sisters. Daresay they're wise because they've always got their heads in a book."

"You're very wise," Dianna assured her husband. "I doubt that Felicity or Glee could have turned the estate around as you have." Dianna gave Glee an embarrassed look. "I mean no offense, dear sister."

"You only spoke the truth," Glee said.

"A good thing Dianna forbade me to wager on the game," George said.

"Speaking of wagers, Blanks," Glee said, "you owe me a sovereign."

"Why?"

"Because I wagered that Jason Pope would marry before the year was out, and you insisted he would never be . . . *snared.* I know it's terribly difficult for you to admit you were wrong."

His eyes hard and cold, Gregory tossed her a sovereign, still incapable of admitting he had been mistaken.

Glee turned back to her brother. "Shame on you for saying Dianna forbade you to wager. "I daresay my sister is not so forceful as to forbid you anything."

"She has merely fooled you," George said. "My wife commands most sweetly."

"And George jumps happily through her hoops," Blanks declared.

George laughed. "You wait, my friend. Before the year is out I expect to find you shackled."

Dianna's lovely face went solemn. "Shackled?"

Glee watched as George set his hand on his wife's, stroking it tenderly. "For Blanks, it's shackled. For me, it's heaven."

How Glee envied the love that bound her brother and Dianna as eternally as the tide. She was almost embarrassed as Dianna pursed her elegant lips and sent a kiss across the table at her beloved.

It was apparently more than Blanks could stand. "Whose bid?" he asked.

"I think it's yours, pet," George said to Glee. He never called his wife *pet*. She was always *my love*.

They played in relative silence, with Glee and Blanks winning the next rubber before the foursome retired for the night.

Sleep eluded Gregory. The solution to his dilemma had seemed so obvious to everyone. To Willowby. To Glee. And to George. Only Gregory knew how useless it was for him to contemplate marriage. He had long ago vowed never to marry. All of his sexual intimacies had been conducted with experienced women who knew how to prevent pregnancy. He had no desire to impregnate a woman he valued and loved to lose her in childbed as he had lost his mother.

He had grown to hate his father for his mother's death and forcing an uncaring stepmother on him. Aurora had always despised Gregory for usurping her precious Jonathan from their father's vast fortune.

And now she had won. The fortune would be Jonathan's.

Sleep was the last thing Glee wanted. This all-encompassing love she felt for Blanks demanded contemplation. She could almost curse him for disrupting her heretofore placid existence, yet the sweet rapture of her love was intoxicating. It seemed her entire nineteen years had been but a prelude for this. *This*. This brink of fulfillment. This delicious arousal. This yearning to intertwine her life with his.

If only she knew more about him. Then she could commence on her plan to snag his heart. But he guarded his feelings as securely as a vault. That smile she had come to love so dearly was but a mask. Even his extravagant pranks and excessive living must conceal a man of deep feeling. If only she could penetrate the armor he had erected around his heart.

She bolted upright in her bed. How foolish she had been to expect to win his love! Never would that be freely given. No, she must not even try. He obviously feared such a commitment. What he needed now was a wife, not a love. For he was not ready for love. She must learn to take her happiness in feeble increments. First, she would have to convince him to marry her.

A marriage in name only.

Like a general with a battle plan, she would conquer his heart later.

One thing seemed clear. He had no desire to marry, even if it meant forfeiting his fortune. What was there about the state of marriage that could repulse him so?

THREE

Blanks was alone in the breakfast parlor when Glee came down the following morning. George had persisted in coddling Dianna since her confinement and insisted she take breakfast in bed. It was just as well. Glee intended to hoard Blanks's company. Her heart did an odd flip when she stole a glance at him sitting at the walnut table, stirring his tea unconsciously while gazing out the window. Smoky half-moons rested under his eyes, and he seemed not at all the Blanks he carefully revealed to the world.

But when he heard her footfall and turned to face her with his dazzling smile, she felt the deception of his persona. "Good morning," she said, shooting him a smile she did not feel and pouring hot coffee from a sterling urn on the sideboard. He sprang to his feet as she walked toward the table, and he began to pull out the chair on his immediate left.

Yesterday's voluptuous clouds had reneged on their promises of rain, and the warm sun now revealed itself for the first time in days. "A good day for a ride," she said.

"But I thought you were terrified of horses."

She sighed. "My dear Mr. Blankenship—"

"Blanks," he reminded.

She ignored him. "Must I continually remind you I am no longer that child you persist in remembering me as?"

His slow, sensuous grin dissolved her. "Are you not still waiting for your prince?" he asked.

"The past two seasons, yes, but I assure you I no longer harbor such childish illusions."

"A pity," he said with a bit of moroseness, his warm chestnut eyes studying hers.

She selected a scone from beneath the covered salver on the table. "I admit being surrounded by the boundless love of George and Dianna and Felicity and Thomas is a bit daunting. I suppose being party to such devotion would be pleasant, but I cannot aspire to such."

His brows lifted. "So jaded at nineteen?"

She placed her scone on the dish and directed an icy glance at the man she loved. "I am not a child, *Mister* Blankenship, but a woman with realistic expectations."

"Somehow I miss the girl who believed in happy endings."

His words cut through her like a rapier. She did so believe in love and happy endings, but she knew Blanks wanted no part of them. She had to convince him she shared his abhorrence of being shackled. Only then could she cultivate his love.

"Please say that you'll ride with me this morning," she said, looking up at him with hopeful eyes.

"It will be my pleasure."

After breakfast, she took great pains with her toilet. With help from Patty, her abigail, Glee donned her emerald green riding habit. Emerald was most definitely her best color. A good match for her eyes. For years she had lamented that she was not blond with periwinkle eyes like her sister Felicity. But after two seasons of unequalled success, Glee had discovered that her auburn hair and ivory skin were as appreciated as her sister's blond fairness.

She hoped her success had nothing to do with the fine wardrobe she had been able to acquire since Felicity had married a man with the means to restore to them the lifestyle of a viscount's family. How she had detested wearing Felicity's well-worn hand-me-downs and having no funds for abigails or slippers without holes. Most of all, she hated having no money for subscriptions to the lending libraries. Now, thank heavens, she was able to read whatever she liked whenever she liked. At least when she was in Bath.

Patty gingerly placed the green velvet hat askance on Glee's swept-back hair, then plunged in a hat pin to secure it. She stood back to appraise her charge. "The master's friend is sure to swoon when he takes a look at you."

Glee's brows lowered. "What makes you think I care a fig about what Mr. Blankenship thinks?"

" 'Cause I know you, too well," Patty said.

"Is it that obvious?" Glee asked, her lips puckered into a pout.

"To a woman, yes. But men don't think of the same things we do. I'm sure your Mr. Blankenship will never notice any change in you."

Glee sighed with relief, then dabbed rosewater on the soft side of her wrists. She cast a glance in her looking glass, satisfied with her reflection. Riding habits revealed her trim waist far better than the dresses dictated by fashion. She smiled mischievously at Patty. "I should like it excessively if Mr. Blankenship swooned over me."

With a wink, she disappeared through the door.

* * *

They had not spoken as they rode through the thicket, Blanks considerately lifting low-hanging tree branches to clear her path. When they entered the glen, still bleak from winter's cold, he spoke. "I return to Bath tomorrow."

Her heart stampeded. When it stilled enough for her to speak, her voice was low and not without disappointment. "So soon?"

He smiled and nodded. "George is much too busy to entertain me in the ways he once did."

While George's new responsibilities diminished the pleasure he had once given Blanks, Glee took pride in her brother's transformation from reckless rake to happy family man. But obviously, he was not a man Blanks wanted to emulate. If Gregory Blankenship did not know his own heart, Glee most certainly thought she did. With the right woman, he, too, could put to pasture his irrepressible quest for amusement. He, too, could become the son his father had wanted him to become. He could settle at Sutton Hall, have children, and continue to steer the thriving estates as his disciplined father had done before him. Glee was convinced she knew Blanks's heart better than he. In time, she could bring about the changes in him. With true love to bolster him, his smiles could be windows to his soul, not screens covering his torture.

For she instinctively knew Blanks was tortured, but she knew not why. George said Blanks had been the most popular lad at Eton. He excelled in sport. He grew bigger and stronger than his classmates—and far more handsome. His income was enormous, and as the first son, promised to be extravagant. What in his life could have caused him to shun love and commitment?

"George had to meet with his steward this morning," Blanks continued. "He plans to work me in this afternoon. We had decided on billiards if it were raining, but now that it's sunny, we'll shoot."

"I confess I've enjoyed having you all to myself, but I suppose it's been far too tedious for you—for you obviously think of me as a silly chit."

He scowled at her. "A lady does not use the word *chit.*"

"Then you think of me as a lady—and not a little girl?"

"Of course. I realize, too, that were we in Bath, you and I would be prohibited from riding alone together."

"Thank heavens we're not in Bath!"

Once they had ridden through the glen and came upon a small pond, she asked if they could stop for their picnic.

They rode to the edge of the shimmering green water, then Gregory dismounted and helped her from her horse before unloading his saddlebags of their luncheon fare. There were hard eggs and newly churned cheese and bread that had been still hot from the oven when Cook packed it. Gregory had seen to it that a bottle of Bordeaux had been stashed in the saddlebag, too. As he tethered the horses, Glee spread out their repast. He watched as she gracefully sat beside the food and removed her hat. Her magnificent tresses had come loose and twirled along the slender marble column of her neck. His breath caught, and he had to remind himself Glee was no temptress but George's little sister.

It was difficult. With her fragile porcelain beauty and that glorious head of hair, she was quite possibly the most beautiful creature he had ever beheld. And though she was small, he noted that her figure curved pleasantly in the right places.

She poured his wine and silently handed it to him as he sat down. His fingers brushed across her delicate hands, and he fought the urge to envelop her hand in his, to settle his lips on her rosebud mouth. Good lord, what had he been thinking to steal her away without benefit of a chaperon? A moron could determine that Glee Pembroke was a lovely young woman whom no man could resist.

And Gregory was indeed a man. Despite that he had vowed to never sully a lady. For George's sake—and for Glee's—Gregory would honor that vow.

He watched as Glee spread soft cheese on a chunk of bread. When she finished, she looked up at him, dazzling him with deep green eyes framed with long, dark lashes. Had the scamp colored them?

"Is anything as good as fresh country cheese?" she asked, offering him the bread in her hand.

He took it, bit in, and agreed heartily with her as she prepared another piece for herself. They ate all they had brought and languidly finished the wine.

His belly full, Gregory dug his dusty Hessians into the brittle grass, leaned back on his elbows, and allowed the sun to warm the length of him.

"You know, Blanks, I've been thinking about your problem," Glee began. "Your father was a positive ogre to raise you to vast expectations, then withdraw them once you've had a quarter of a century to grow accustomed to them."

"My thoughts exactly."

"You could never manage as your brother does. You must have a valet and tailoring by Weston. You must have the purse to allow the deep play you enjoy so dearly, and the fencing and boxing with the best masters and the finest mounts Tattersall's has to offer." She placed her willowy hands on her waist. "You simply must get married."

He grinned and let out a harrumph. "That would be as detestable to me as being poor."

Her face grew serious. "Of course, you're right, but I wasn't thinking of a real marriage. I think you should have a marriage in name only. You'd be free to cavort as you always have. In fact, I've given it considerable thought, and I've decided we should suit each other's needs admirably."

He choked and jerked up, casting a suspicious glance at Glee. "We?"

Her lovely eyes round, she nodded. "I am precisely what you need, Gregory Blankenship."

"Thank you for your generous offer, but I must refuse. I have no desire to marry—even to one as *perfect* for my situation as you."

"Now don't be so hasty," she said, lifting her chin petulantly. "You don't want a real wife, and I don't want a real husband. However, I should like excessively to be a married woman, especially to a man of means. I could have my own house in Bath—well, it would actually be our house—and I could buy new gowns whenever I wanted. I could even keep a carriage."

He started to protest, but she shooed him to silence.

"Just think, Blanks, we've known each other forever. I find nothing at all offensive in you, and I hope you will be able to tolerate me."

He merely nodded as he listened to her lunacy. After all, he couldn't hurt the girl's feelings.

She babbled on. "Since I discovered that I could not seem to fall in love, I have determined it is far better to unite myself to someone whom I enjoy being with. And I've always loved being with you." She stopped long enough to take a breath. "So there you have it."

Good lord, she was serious! He saw it in the earnestness of her lovely face. He would have to let her down with consideration. "It's most kind of you to sacrifice yourself for me, but I cannot allow it," he said. "You deserve a man who will cherish you as George cherishes Dianna."

"Fie," she said. "I'd far rather link my life to one who enjoys a rollicking good time, not a stuffed shirt like George has become. We'd have great fun, Blanks, and I promise not to tie you down."

He began to pick up the leavings of their lunch, avoiding contact with her spectacular eyes. "You have done me a great honor, Miss Pembroke, but, nonetheless, I must decline."

Now he allowed himself a glimpse into her face. Her eyes moistened. Poor lass, she really had been serious. Marrying him had actually appealed to her. He hated like the devil to hurt her. Tossing aside his bundle, he scooted to her side and took her slender hand into his brown one. Like the rich texture of the thick velvet she wore, Glee was softness and beauty and sweet smells of rose petals.

She swallowed hard and began to speak, her voice quivering. " 'Twould be a marriage in name only. You could . . ." she gulped, "keep your mistresses."

He muttered a curse under his breath and let go of her hand. "You're not supposed to know of such things."

She looked up at him, her face sorrowful. "I am a woman."

"Precisely why I cannot marry you. I don't want a wife, and I don't want children. To deny you the love of a husband and the satisfaction of bearing fat babes would be a heinous offense."

She sat up straight and ran her fingers through her wind-blown curls. *He didn't want children.* How very odd. "I knew you didn't want a wife, but no children?"

His dark eyes piercing into hers, he nodded.

"I thought all men wanted an heir."

"Not me. Never have."

It had not occurred to Glee that Blanks did not want children. She had never imagined she would not give birth to a bevy of babes. Now, she must rethink what it was she wanted from life. Blanks, most assuredly. But no babes? If that was the only way she could have him, she might have to settle for being childless, but Glee had every confidence she could change Blanks's ideas on the subject once they were married. The trick was to get him to marry her.

She smiled and spoke lightly. "Dianna's birthing was unmistakably the most horrid experience of my life. I daresay I'll not be disappointed to be spared such torture."

She had been unable to look him in the eye as she spoke, for she had lied when she said she did not want children. Actually, she hadn't lied. She had not said she didn't want children; she said she didn't crave the birthing experience.

Glee stood up and tried to be flippant. "If you won't marry me, I'll have to throw myself away on someone else." Then she strode to untie her horse.

He got to his feet, cursing under his breath. He silently gave her a leg up, then mounted his own bay. They rode back through the glen, and he cleared her way through the thicket, but they did not speak.

Even when they rode up to the manor house, and a footman took charge of their mounts, no words passed between them.

During the afternoon, Gregory hunted with George, and they nearly rekindled their former intimacy. They wagered on whether it would take twelve minutes or fifteen to reach the wood. They wagered on which of the two would be the first to bag a dove. They wagered on which dove would weigh the most. And they tipped a flask of Scotch whiskey to ward off the gathering chill.

Despite the ease with which the two men conversed on trivialities, Gregory could not apprise George of his sister's unusual offer. *'Twould be a marriage in name only* . . . It was a proposal which dominated Gregory's every thought.

I'll have to throw myself away on someone else kept ringing in his ear like a death knell.

FOUR

When she heard the servants stirring early the next morning, Glee rose from her rumpled bed and began to dress herself. After she pulled her soft muslin dress over her head, she shot a glance into her looking glass. Though the chamber was dimly lit at this early hour, she saw well enough to plunge into a foul temper. Lack of sleep embedded itself on her face. Her last hope of ensnaring Blanks had been to dazzle him with her beauty today. She stomped her bare foot, cursing the fact she had lain awake all night and cursing the man who caused her lack of sleep.

She flung herself on the cushioned bench before her Venetian dressing table and propped her face on her fists, her thoughts once more flitting to Blanks. Throughout the wee hours of the morning, lying in the darkness of her room, Glee had planned to the last detail what she would wear this morning and how Patty would arrange her hair. Now, with the puffiness around her eyes, Glee would never attract Blanks.

During the night, each tick from the ormolu clock on her mantel had painfully reminded her that Blanks would be leaving today. With each passing second, he slipped further from her grasp. He would return to Bath, her clever plot to ensnare him a failure.

Oddly, she had felt no embarrassment over her own forwardness with him. She had but a few hours in which to capture him before he departed, and she meant to do everything in her power to convince him to marry her. She did not regret any of her actions, only their failure. Was there something else she could have done or said that might have persuaded him to marry her? She had turned this question over and over in her mind, but no better plan presented itself.

Glee was sliding on her kid slippers when Patty quietly entered her chamber. "My, but you're up early, Miss Glee." She walked to her mistress's dressing table and took up Glee's brush. "Is it because Mr. Blankenship leaves today?"

Glee nodded solemnly, then shot a hopeful look at her abigail. "Patty, it's imperative that you fashion my hair lovelier than you've ever done before. This is my last hope with Mr. Blankenship. I have a terrible feeling he will find someone else when he returns to Bath."

Patty stood back to survey Glee, then nodded slowly. "We'll sweep that thick hair of yours back and allow some curly tendrils to spiral about your fair face. You'll be quite the most beautiful girl he's ever seen." She ran her eye over her mistress's soft ivory dress, then began to brush out Glee's coppery tresses.

"Woman, not girl," Glee corrected. "I want Gregory Blankenship to think of me as a woman."

A deep smile brought out the dimples on Patty's thin, fair face. "The gentleman will assuredly think of you as a hot-blooded woman in *that* dress." Her glance flicked to Glee's white breasts that barely tucked into the bodice of her gown.

When Patty was finished, Glee gushed with admiration over her maid's accomplishment. Her hair looked so lovely the bags under her eyes quite possibly might not be so very noticeable after all.

Since none of the servants would be prepared for breakfast at this early hour, Glee decided to take a turn around the park. If she were lucky, one last scheme to capture Blanks would present itself to her as she walked. Hopefully, the mist would not saturate her hair too much. She had to look her best at breakfast. Breakfast with Blanks.

Gregory's heels jabbed into his mount, and the bay streaked through the wood surrounding Hornsby Manor, swooping winds at his back. He lifted his face to the gathering clouds and frowned. They had deuced better clear. He felt low enough already without the weather threatening his departure.

Why did he feel so wretched? Lack of sleep, of course, contributed to his malaise. Throughout the night visions of that blasted Glee Pembroke flashed through his mind. He kept picturing her as she looked when she had told him she would have to wed *someone else.* Bloody hell. The girl deserved her prince charming but would likely settle for something considerably less.

He thought on how keenly the vile William Jefferson had lusted after the girl last season. Because Jefferson was possessed of wealth, something Glee indicated she would like in a husband, Gregory's stomach turned at the thought of Jefferson defiling Glee's innocence. Though purported to be shopping for a wife, Jefferson had little regard for the female sex. He bragged about his liaisons with married women, he left his mistresses with no settlement, and he took perverse pleasure in deflowering virgins. That he fancied whores meant he was likely disease-ridden. Worst of all was that busi-

ness in London year before last. The man would never
do for Glee. *He'll get Glee over my dead body,* Gregory vowed. He spurred ahead even faster, cursing under his breath.

Something else had robbed Gregory of sleep the night before: Glee's bizarre proposal. Why in heaven's name had he turned her down? Wasn't her plan exactly what he needed? A wife—and his fortune—both on his twenty-fifth birthday? A "wife" who would not really be a wife. He would be able to keep his mistress, cavort with his bachelor friends, and would not have to dance attendance on his youthful bride. A perfect solution to his dilemma.

Then why *had* he not accepted her offer? His initial reaction to her bold proposal had been to reject it immediately. For as long as he could remember, he had vowed never to marry, never to sire children. Then once he had firmly rejected Glee, other reasons for denying her came to mind. He hated like hell standing in the way of the happiness she deserved with another man. With himself as her husband, she would never be able to fulfill her dreams.

Her announcement that she would settle for a loveless marriage to another, though, put the situation in an entirely different light. At least if she married Gregory, Glee would be under the protection of a man who valued her. Who had done so for most of his life. If he let her get away, she might throw herself away on the beast William Jefferson. And that was completely unacceptable.

Beset by his disturbing thoughts, Gregory absently turned his sprinting mount back toward Hornsby Manor. Just beyond the wood, he saw that Glee circled the park. An unfamiliar nervousness squirmed in his belly. He dismounted and, leading his bay behind him, covered the spread of winter-brittle grass that separated him from Glee.

When she looked up and smiled at him, his stomach once again behaved in a most uncharacteristic manner. She did not look like a girl, but a woman. A beautiful woman ripe for matrimony. A vision in white. Unaccountably, his gaze riveted to her expanse of alabaster-white breasts that dipped into the soft ivory muslin of her gown. Then his eyes traveled up her slender neck to her pretty face and magnificent hair the color of cinnamon. For a sliver of a second, the man in him took over, and he almost forgot the ravishing creature was George's little sister.

But his serious side showed its rare face, immediately squelching his own manly desires. *She is George's little sister. A lady and a virgin.* Such thoughts only made him realize he could not allow Glee to fall into the clutches of a man like Jefferson.

"You're out early this morning," she said by way of a greeting.

"I was going to say the same to you." Now that he was beside her, he realized from her eyes that she had not slept. He fell into step beside her, the manor house to their backs. "I take it you slept no better than I," he said.

Her eyes widened. "How did you know I didn't sleep?"

" 'Twas the same with me," he admitted. "May I hope I was not the cause of your wakefulness?"

She stopped and put fists to waist, looking up at him with flashing eyes. "Of course you were, you odious man." Lifting her chin haughtily, she strolled forward. "An idiot could see how good it would be for both of us if you were to marry me."

"While it might be good for me, I fail to see how

the marriage would be advantageous to you—other than the money, of course."

"I told you, I'm tired of being a spinster. I hate being buried at Hornsby Manor. I crave a home of my own—preferably in Bath—and the freedom to do as I please." She stopped and gazed up at him. "I vow, if you don't marry me, Blanks, I shall marry the first man who offers."

What if that man was William Jefferson? Gregory cleared his throat. "We can't have that."

Their flaring eyes met and held. His stomach was most unsteady. "What of your prince on the white horse?"

She turned and glanced at the horse trotting behind them, tethered to Blanks's right hand. "Bays suit me just fine."

He winced silently. "I've been around you long enough to know that you wished for a love match."

"Fie!" she said. "Love matches are nothing more than childish dreams. Real marriage is about two people who *like* each other and respect one another's independence. I believe it's a business arrangement of sorts between two adults of the same class."

They entered the wood along the same path they traveled when on horseback. He proffered his crooked arm, and they trod on under the canopy of barren branches. No words passed between them the first five minutes, then Glee broadsided him with a startling question. "Why do you not desire children of your own?"

It took him several seconds to dismiss his astonishment and formulate an answer. He had never told anyone the truth. Fear of losing a beloved wife on childbed seemed a weakness, and he had spent his life carefully chiseling himself into a man who had no weaknesses.

No Achilles' heels. "Why must I have a reason?" he asked.

They had now entered the glen and walked in the direction of the pond as if its shimmering water were calling them. The wind had gotten stronger, rippling the water and tossing Glee's hair errantly about her face.

She squeezed his arm. "I'm sorry. It was a personal question I had no right to ask."

But she must be troubled by his aversion to fathering children. He had known she would want the little rascals. He had been so caught up in her question, he had been unaware of the darkening skies. As seemingly gradual as a man's hair turns gray, the clouds had turned a menacing black. The air was heavy with mist. He could not deny that a rainstorm was imminent. The problem was they would never be able to make it back to Hornsby before the clouds burst.

Then he remembered the folly where he and George had played as youngsters. It was atop the knoll on the other side of the pond. He turned to Glee and spoke with urgency. "Come, let's make it to the folly before the rain comes."

Hand in hand, they began to sprint across the barren land, past the pond and up the knoll to the folly. It looked like a round Greek temple. Ionic columns ringed it to form an outer wall that was not really a wall. At least the domed roof there would keep them dry.

With rain now dropping in a staccato rhythm, they began to run toward the folly. By the time they ducked into its dryness, the rain was falling in buckets. Thunder cracked, and lightning flashed off in the distance.

He could see that Glee was shivering, and though she put up a brave front, he knew she was frightened.

He draped his arm around her. She moved as close as she could to him without touching.

He glanced at a low stone bench in the middle of the covered structure. "Let's go sit on the bench," he said. "It looks as if we could be here for quite some time."

They sat down, and she looked up at him. "It doesn't look as if you'll be able to return to Bath today. I hope that doesn't terribly disappoint you."

'Twould be difficult spending one more night sitting across the whist table from Glee, knowing she was a lady and George's little sister, and he could never assuage his lustful needs with her. "How could I begrudge anything which keeps me in George's company longer? I have missed him greatly, to be sure."

Shivering, she wrapped her arms around herself as the great swooshing winds swept moist air all around them. "I didn't think it would rain today," she said with disbelief.

The relentless pounding of rain was so loud he was surprised he had heard her soft voice. "So you didn't dress appropriately," he said with a smile, putting his arm around her and pulling her into his embrace. He had known she was small, but he was totally unprepared for how delicate she actually felt. 'Twas rather like squeezing a raw egg. He was afraid he would crush her.

When she looked up at him, he saw the rainwater that still clung to her long lashes, making them darker than normal—like her wet hair.

"Do you remember that day when we were children and we found refuge from a wretched storm here?" she asked.

He gave a little laugh. "If I recall correctly, we were here for hours."

"You recall correctly," she said, her face lifting into a smile. "I thought you were terribly gallant."

He gave her a puzzled look. "Why?"

"Because you had insisted that George not bar me from the folly. My brother was going through one of those stages where he was always saying *no girls allowed*. You said I wasn't a real girl. I was a sister, and that was something altogether different."

Gregory threw his head back and laughed. "There is no doubt now. You are every inch the girl."

She looked up at him, a serious look on her face. "Not a girl, Blanks. A woman."

Good lord, did she have any idea how seductive she could be? He swallowed hard. "Yes, you are that." He must think of a way to change the direction of his thoughts. "So tell me, when is your sister due to return from the Continent?"

"Her last post indicated they would be in Rome several more weeks, then return by way of Paris, where they would stay for a few more weeks. Then they will return to England for the birth of their first child."

"She is . . . increasing? I did not know."

"She and Thomas are ecstatic. George wants the babe born here at Hornsby, but Thomas says it's to be born at Winston Hall."

Ecstatic. In the normal course of things, a firstborn child brought great joy to a loving couple. He knew Glee would desire a child—no matter what she said. He was the one who was not normal. He was the one who could never marry.

He thought of the wealthy Thomas Moreland and of how deeply he loved Glee's sister, Felicity. What would the man do if he were to lose his beloved wife on childbed? "Are the women in your family good breeders?"

"Oh, yes. Mama did not die in childbed. In fact,

Papa said he could scarcely keep her down during her confinement. Unfortunately, she was not a good rider. She died from a fall from my father's horse."

"So that explains why you were so terrified of horses when you were small."

She nodded. "You know, Blanks, you have something with me you won't have with other women."

"And what is that?"

"History," she said pensively. "I cannot remember a time when I didn't know you. I remember when you first came to Hornsby. George had written us so much about you and your athletic prowess. He was most enamored of you. So when our family finally made your acquaintance, I thought you were a dashing Lancelot."

"How disappointed you must have been."

"Not at all. I used to wish you were my brother, instead of George, because you were always so very kind to me."

"I daresay that was because I had no sisters of my own. Having a little sister was a pleasant novelty."

There was a faraway sound in her voice when she spoke. "Yes, we *did* used to pretend I was your little sister." Then she turned to him. "I don't think of you at all as a brother anymore."

His stomach clinched. "I wonder if Felicity's babe will be a boy or girl."

"Of course, they are hoping for a son, but I think it would be fun if they had a daughter. Then she and Georgette could be the best of cousins. More like sisters, really."

"I have to say I never pictured George with a little girl, but I've never seen a more besotted father."

Glee thought of how a child of his own would soften Blanks, too. He didn't yet know how good a father he could be. But she did.

Instead of passing, the storm strengthened. The

fierce rains gave no sign of letting up. Thunder crashed
and lightning bolted all around them. Though she was
damp and miserable physically, a contented warmth
spread throughout her insides. Sitting within the circle
of Blanks's protective embrace, she felt invincible.
Comfortable. Happy.

With no discernible changing in the sun, she was
not able to judge how long they had sat there in the
center of the folly, surrounded by menacing weather,
but it had now been several hours. She wondered if
George knew she had gone outdoors. Would he be worried about her?

Her eyelids grew heavy and her head dropped to
Blanks's chest. His hold around her tightened. Though
she was not asleep, she decided to pretend to be, for
nothing had ever felt as wonderful as sitting here so
close to Blanks.

Within a few moments, his breathing changed, and
his head nestled next to hers. He had indeed gone to
sleep. That he felt that comfortable with her despite
the chill wind which cut into them and the rampage
of wretched weather that swirled around them told her
he, too, was comfortable with her.

Why could he not see that they were so very good
together? His refusal to marry her, though, she found
oddly admirable. His own principles kept him from
marrying, even if he would lose a sizable fortune. That
he would not waver from his resolve was oddly satisfying. He felt strongly about avoiding marriage and
fatherhood and was not easily led from his resolution.
How could she not respect such a man?

While he slept so utterly close to her, the rain abated.
The dark skies moved to the south and the thunder and
lightning along with them. George was sure to come
looking for her now.

Which gave her a wicked idea.

So gently as not to wake Blanks, she untied her hair and spread it wildly about her. Then she lowered the bodice of her gown until the top of her pink nipple showed.

Now she would wait for her brother to find them.

FIVE

She saw the top of George's blond head as he climbed the knoll toward them, and she quickly turned her face away. With scorched cheeks, she softly wound one arm behind Blanks and settled the other on his sizable shoulder. He stirred, at first resting one possessive hand at her waist.

She had to act with haste. She began to plant soft kisses on his mahogany hair, his rugged cheek, then his mouth.

"What the deuce?" Blanks mumbled. He grabbed her by the waist and, by leaning back and studying her with a puzzled look, lengthened the distance between their upper torsos. She solemnly watched, her cheeks hot, as Blanks's shocked glance fell on her exposed breast.

At the very same instant George called his greetings to them.

That was her signal to make a great scene for the sake of her brother. Her glance swung to her brother as she shrieked and in great, exaggerated sweeps crossed her arms in front of her to hide her breasts, each hand hugging the opposite arm.

George mounted the steps to the folly. She gazed up at him, her cheeks still scarlet. He glanced from her to Blanks. There wasn't so much as an inch separating Blanks from her as they sat on the cold stone bench. "Blanks . . ." George trailed. "She's my sister, for God's sake."

Blanks shot her a hard stare, then glanced back at her brother. Strangely, he made no effort to defend himself.

Like an actress on center stage, she turned her back to both of them and gathered up the bodice of her moist gown to cover her breasts. Then she turned back to look remorsefully at her brother.

His flaring eyes were on Blanks. "My sister's a virgin. A mere babe where such matters are concerned."

There was no sign of Blanks's perpetual smile, only grim acceptance of his fate. "I sincerely beg your pardon," he said in a contrite voice. "It's only that Miss Pembroke has done me the goodness of consenting to be my wife." His angry eyes shifted back to Glee.

Anger still flashed in George's eyes as his gaze settled on Blanks. "See me in the library when you return." Then he spun on his muddied boots and stormed from the folly.

Gregory watched until George was out of his vision. Without facing Glee, he spoke. "So you've succeeded in trapping me."

Her voice was soft, pleading. "Please don't be angry, Blanks. I did it for you. I knew you'd never relent. You'd lose your fortune and come to regret that you had spurned marriage."

"So you did it for me," he mocked bitterly. "Why is it meddling women always think they know what's best for men? They always believe they can change us."

She faced him defiantly. "I'm not going to say I'm sorry."

"So now my best friend is to believe I'm using his

baby sister. A fine kettle of fish you've put me in."
He had an overwhelming desire to wring her graceful
little neck. To think, he had actually been softening
toward her and her bizarre proposal! Until this.

Miss Glee Pembroke had made her bed, and he
would see to it that she lay in it. No love match. No
lovemaking. No children. How was she going to like
that? He got to his feet.

She scurried to catch up with him as he left the folly,
and silently fell into step beside him, two of her steps
to every one of his.

When they got to the thicket, he spoke to her. "If
I'm to be burdened with you for a wife, you're to understand the rules."

"What rules?" she asked in a voice breathless from
trying to keep up with his hurried pace.

He slowed. "First, it's to be a marriage in name only.
You will not share my bed. We will not have children."
He looked down on her. The afternoon sun highlighted
her emerald eyes.

Her cheeks hot, she gazed up at him and cleared
her throat. "Does that mean I'm free to take lovers?"

Rage swept through him. "It does not." The very
idea set his blood to boiling. But how could he expect
to keep his mistress and not allow Glee to enjoy other
men? Especially when he had no plans to exercise his
conjugal rights. "For the first year we'll make every
effort to assure others the marriage is a love match.
Most of all, my brother is to be convinced. If he were
to suspect I married only to collect my inheritance, he
would undoubtedly challenge me in court."

"And my brother?" she asked.

"I shall attempt to convince him I've fallen in love
with you. George would not relish his sister being a
pawn in a ploy to get my inheritance."

They trod silently along through the muddy mire.

Filled with anger, first at Glee then at himself for not exposing Glee's scheme, Gregory pondered his unwelcome predicament. He would have to make the best of it. After all, now his inheritance was secure. He thought of all the reasons Glee had cited to encourage the marriage. There were worse fates. Yet this was not the fate he had striven for all these years. *Damn Glee.*

The poor girl would never have her prince. Never bear a child. "I propose to allow you to select the house of your choice in Bath. You'll have *carte blanche* in its furnishings and decorations." Merely a crumb he was tossing her way. Women liked that sort of thing. "You also will have a carriage." Such materialism compensated poorly for depriving her of a loving husband and the children he knew she wanted.

She nodded solemnly. "I wanted this marriage because we are . . ." she swallowed, *"were* friends. Can we not still be?"

He strode ahead. They came to the park in front of Hornsby. They had been friends. Always. Far better for Glee to marry a friend than a man bent on wringing her innocence from her, on using her. But, he somberly reflected, wasn't he to be using her? He tried to shake away his feelings of guilt by reminding himself of her shameless trap to ensnare him. She was only getting what she had asked for. Finally he glanced down at her. "We'll continue to be friends." It suddenly occurred to him the chill had been absent from his voice.

As they drew nearer the manor house, he took her hand. "Remember, everyone is to think we're in love. You're to tell no one the truth."

"From this day forward, I'll do whatever you ask," she said in a soft voice. "When can we marry?"

Even if it were not to be a real marriage, Gregory meant to cling to his bachelorhood for as long as he could. "We can post banns this week."

Her face fell. Of course, she would have preferred the quicker special license. Why was the girl so eager to marry? God knows he was in no hurry.

Gregory's stomach knotted as he faced his dearest friend across the Turkish carpet of the library, steeling himself to lie to George for the first time in the seventeen years they had known one another.

From his silk damask settee, George spoke somberly. "Despite that you're my best friend, I must tell you I would be excessively displeased were you to use my sister merely to gain your inheritance. Glee needs a man who will love her and take care of her for the rest of her life. She wants a happy home bursting with children." He stopped for a moment. "I would be extremely surprised if you can offer her any of the things she needs."

Gregory felt the knife turning. He came dangerously close to calling the whole thing off. Then he remembered Glee's pledge to marry the first man who sought her out. And with rising anger, he thought of the scoundrel Jefferson. Gregory coughed. "You must know I have had a soft spot for Miss Pembroke since she was a little girl. It wasn't until this stay, however, that I realized how much I truly cared for her. It was Miss Pembroke herself who pointed out that a match between us would be a most fortunate connection. And since my feelings for her were rapidly changing from that of a brother to that of a lover . . . I came to realize how very much I wanted to marry her." His voice lowered and he spoke somberly. "That is, if you have no objections."

How had he ever found the words? Gregory thought of the times when he had been alone with Glee in the meadows and the unexpected feelings of lust she summoned within him. Those feelings must have rushed through his memory as he spoke. Good lord, would George think him a cradle robber? His heart pounded as he waited for George to make some kind of comment.

The expression on George's face was solemn. Was he angry at his friend's desire for the unspoiled Glee? Was he remembering all the wicked things Gregory had done which would render him unsuitable to marry his sister?

Finally, George spoke. "I hope you understand your declaration has been rather a shock for me. First, for as long as I've known you, you've insisted marriage was something you meant to avoid. Then there's the fact you've never been remotely attracted to a girl like Glee."

George, of course, was alluding to all the tarts Gregory had been involved with since he lost his virginity at sixteen. "The lightskirts who have gone before her make Miss Pembroke's innocence completely refreshing. She's the first—the only—lady of quality I have either desired or wished to marry. I suspect you must have felt the same way over Miss Moreland—before she became Lady Sedgewick."

George nodded. "Like you, I had scoffed at the idea of marriage."

"Then Miss Moreland stole your heart as Miss Pembroke has stolen mine."

A wide smile crossed George's face. "Forgive me if I'm a bit taken aback. 'Tis hard to realize the elusive Mr. Blankenship has lost his heart to that scamp of a sister of mine."

Gregory's heart pounded. "But I have most assuredly."

"Then I'm glad of it, even happier to have you for a brother."

The two men stood up and embraced, then moved to the desk to arrange settlements. When they were finished, George leveled a serious gaze at his friend. "I must tell you I'm rather happy my sister is the means by which you will secure your fortune."

Dianna would be the test, Glee thought as she nervously strolled toward the morning room after changing from her wet clothing. Her stomach plummeted. She mentally kicked herself. Isn't this exactly what she wanted? What she had prayed for? Hadn't she told herself if she could just capture Blanks, she would make him fall in love with her? Never mind that he had long ago vowed never to marry. Never mind that he didn't love her. And what if he had always been as immovable as a mountain? Mr. Gregory Blankenship had met his match in Glee.

She casually strolled into the room.

Dianna looked up, then began to pour tea for Glee. "I thought you would be with Blanks," she said.

Glee took the proffered cup and saucer, then sucked in her breath. "He's in the library with George."

"A pity he has to leave today," Dianna said as she continued with her sewing. "George would love for him to stay longer."

"As would I," Glee said softly. "We have just become betrothed."

Stunned, Dianna's mouth gaped open, her sewing flung aside. "Did I hear you correctly?"

I have to be convincing, Glee told herself. "I confess, I've never been so surprised in my life. Please don't tell George, but I was the one to tell Blanks how advantageous it would be for him to marry me. He was aghast at first, but the longer we've been together, the more sense my proposal made. Especially in light of his growing ardor for me." Glee continued stirring her tea long after it was necessary.

"It doesn't seem that you two have been together very much," Dianna countered.

"You forget the mornings when you've been taking a tray in bed. Blanks and I have breakfasted together every morning and have spent a great deal of time outdoors with each other." Glee sighed happily. "I wonder what it is about the fresh air that makes gentlemen so amorous?" She felt guilty for misleading her sister, but there was nothing she wouldn't do for Blanks, and he had told her to convince everyone theirs was a love match.

Dianna smiled smugly. "Then you two have kissed?"

Glee's heart tripped. "Any number of times," she said casually. *Would that it were so.*

"Oh, Glee," Dianna exclaimed, rising from her chair and throwing her arms around Glee. "I'm truly happy for you."

The door to the morning room opened and the gentlemen entered. George went to stand behind his wife and lovingly put his hands on her shoulders. "I am, too," he said, looking at Glee. "You've made me a very happy brother."

To her utter surprise, Blanks came to stand behind Glee and, obviously taking a cue from George, put his hands on her shoulders. "Me, too, my love," Blanks said to her.

Glee's heart melted. She didn't know which made her the happiest. His hands on her or hearing him address her as *my love.* Even if such actions were nothing more than a sham, she relished them. She fully realized, albeit with disappointment, he didn't care a fig for her. But Glee Pembroke, soon to be Mrs. Blankenship, had a great deal of confidence in herself. *I will make him love me.* A pity Blanks was so very stubborn.

"When is the date to be?" Dianna asked.

"Four weeks from Sunday," George said. "In our village church."

Dianna looked puzzled but said nothing.

"In the meantime, love," Blanks said to Glee, "you have much to do. You must select a house for us in Bath and set about furnishing it."

"And you'll need a trousseau," Dianna reminded Glee.

Glee bit at her lip. "I don't suppose, Dianna . . ."

"Georgette will be fine with her nurse and wet nurse," Dianna finished. "I'll be delighted to accompany you to Bath."

Bless Dianna! "You're a jewel," Glee said to her.

Blanks bent and kissed Glee on the top of her shining auburn hair. "It pains me to tell you, love, I return to Bath within the hour."

Really, he could have made his fortune on the stage! He sounded so convincing. To think, he even kissed her on the top of her head! A pity he avoided her lips for she very strongly desired to receive a *real* kiss from her betrothed.

That afternoon Blanks returned to Bath. The four of them paraded through the manor's impressive front doors to see him off as the groom brought his horse around. Before he climbed on the mount, Gregory took both of Glee's hands. "I shall miss you dreadfully, my love."

She smiled up at him. "It won't be but three days until we're reunited, my darling."

As Blanks stood there gazing upon her with a decidedly forlorn look, Glee's heart fluttered. Then he bent to kiss her, and her stomach vaulted as she rose on her toes to taste him. The touch of his lips was

magical. It was as if the birds chorused louder when
their lips came together, stopping her pulse. She quite
forgot there were any other creatures on earth, save
Blanks and her and the happily singing birds. She
smelled his musky scent and delighted at the sturdy
feel of him. The man was a positive paradox. So very
large and so excruciatingly tender.

Then she nearly unraveled when his arms came
around her. She felt unbelievably feminine. And ripe
with womanhood.

He managed to terminate the kiss but continued to
hold her—even more tightly. "I'll miss you," he said
throatily.

He sounded so convincing! *I shall miss you, too.*
She wanted to say the words but found she had lost
her voice.

Then he pulled away and mounted his bay. Looking
at George, he said, "I thank you and Lady Sedgewick
for your hospitality—and for making me the happiest
of men." Then he rode off without a backward glance
at Glee.

Look out, Edmund Kean, Glee mused. The greatest
actor in England now undoubtedly was Gregory
Blankenship. Anyone watching that parting scene
would be thoroughly convinced of Blanks's deep affection for her.

During the next few days Glee was so busy with
wedding arrangements and packing for Bath that she
had little time to think of Blanks. Until her last night
at Hornsby Manor. Exhausted from her preparations,
she sank into bed, fully intending to sleep, but she was
unable to do so. Blanks kept intruding on her thoughts.
It was hard to believe she would be Mrs. Blankenship
before the month was out.

She was fully aware that marrying the man she adored would not guarantee any happily-ever-afters. She knew the road ahead would be difficult to navigate. It would be uphill all the way. But she had confidence in her abilities to snare his affections—given time. It wasn't as if they didn't already like each other. She expected Blanks would be solicitous of her. That was a start. And he *had* said she was pretty. Which assured her that she did not repulse him. Thank goodness.

But now that she was embarking on marriage with him, she realized her *hopes* to ensnare his heart weren't good enough. She needed a plan. Like a general in battle. For the unbudgingly stubborn Blanks was a mighty opponent.

The rest of the night she assembled in her mind the weapons that would carry her to victory. The most important of these was her love for him. Because she cared so deeply for him, she wanted to learn everything she could about him. Her mission in life would be to see to his happiness. If haddock was what he desired at dinner, haddock he would get. If he desired to stay out every night with his friends, nary a criticizing word would come from her.

From little things he had jokingly said over the years, she had come to realize that his stepmother held no love for him. Since his mother had died when he was but a babe, he had likely never known the love of a woman. True love, that is. Her heart ached for the lonely child he must have been. Glee was prepared to swaddle him in love and drench him with affection.

She had other plans, too. Not only would she not interfere in his pleasure pursuits, but she also meant to join him. They would continue to be the best of friends.

Friendship, she had observed, was the foundation of

all good marriages. If her schemes came to fruition, Blanks would grow tired of his hedonistic ways and long for his own estate, complete with loving wife and children. Then he would know true happiness.

Children. Surely Blanks would want them someday. She could not imagine life without them. Somewhere down their uneven road, she and Blanks would start a family. Even if she had told her betrothed she would be happy without them.

If, in the coming years, he was still opposed to fathering children, she told herself she would respect his feelings. As much as she wanted children, she wanted Blanks more. She would love him to her dying day.

She had one last weapon to employ in her battle to win Blanks's heart, but she wouldn't use it until after they were married.

SIX

Having checked into Bath's Sheridan Arms Hotel and overseen the unpacking of her bags, Glee now hastened to Number 7, Dianna's chambers. They had decided against staying at Dianna's brother's estate because its location three miles from the city would be less convenient than the hotel.

Dianna, now changed from her traveling clothes, opened the door herself and stepped into the hallway, closing the door behind her and slipping a shawl around her shoulders. "I was just leaving to go to your chambers," she said with a laugh.

The two women descended the stairs to the ground floor, speaking all the while. "According to Blanks's letter there are three prime town houses on the market and I am to take my pick of them," Glee said. "The Harrison House on Queen Square, I am sure, will undoubtedly outshine the others. You've been there, have you not?"

"A lovely home," Dianna answered, "and such an excellent location."

Glee nodded her agreement. "Between the Upper Assembly Rooms and the Pump Room. Even if it weren't one of the finest houses in Bath, I believe I would choose it for where it's located." They strolled through the opulent lobby and out the door to High Street. Glee fastened her pelisse and braced against the chilly wind that greeted them outside.

"Are we going there first?" Dianna asked.

"Yes, I thought we'd walk since it's so near the hotel."

Soon they walked along the pavement on Milsom Street. Glee felt somewhat guilty that she hadn't let her betrothed know she was already in Bath. Somehow, she had thought he might be displeased to learn she was coming a day early. His insistence on posting banns instead of marrying by special license as did others of their class, told her he wished to cling to his bachelorhood every extra day he possibly could.

A pity he was not as anxious to be with her as she was to be with him.

She and Dianna lifted their skirts as they crossed the street where last night's rain had puddled. They barely squeezed between a hay cart and a hansom before making it to the other side of Milsom. Glee glanced at the front window of Mrs. Simmons's Millinery Creations. She was surprised the crippled lad who was always in front of the shop was not there. Then she remembered this was the time of day he would be riding the pony given him by Dianna's brother.

Next, her thoughts turned to Blanks. Glee decided she would not see him until that night. She would wait until late afternoon, then send along a note to his lodgings informing him she had come early. Her stomach somersaulted at the thought of seeing him again. Her own Blanks. Would he hasten to the hotel to see her? Would they go to the Upper Assembly Rooms together tonight? Would he hold her in his arms as they waltzed?

"I hadn't realized how much I missed Bath," Glee said.

Dianna nodded. "I love it here. It's my favorite place."

Glee was aware of how well-traveled her sister-in-law was. "Really? Why is that?"

"Can't you guess?"

A smile broke across Glee's face. "Let me see, would it be because Bath is where you met, fell in love with, and married my brother?"

"Correct answer. I can see that you come from intelligent stock."

"Undoubtedly. And I am sure my baby niece is already in possession of remarkable brains. As to her father, though," Glee said with a smile, "I am not so sure."

Dianna playfully swatted at Glee. "How could you malign such a wonderful creature?"

"My brother a wonderful creature? I fear some supernatural power has cast a besotted spell over you. What else could explain such devotion a full year after you two began to live as man and wife?"

Dianna rolled her eyes. "If you're going to be wed, you must be aware that many married people are devoted to one another." Dianna's voice gentled. "Like George and me."

Yes, that's the kind of marriage Glee wanted, too. *If only.*

At that precise moment Glee saw her betrothed and Carlotta Ennis strolling along the pavement on the other side of the street. If she hadn't so recently crossed the street, Glee would have come up to him face-to-face. The flamboyant widow he was with had been acquainted with Glee's family for many years. She and Glee's sister Felicity had accompanied their first husbands to Portugal, where both men were killed during the Peninsular Campaign.

"Look, Dianna, there's Blanks and Mrs. Ennis! Let's cross the street."

Dianna stiffened, and her eyes went cold. Her fingers dug into Glee's arm.

Why was Dianna acting like this? Had she taken a sudden aversion to Blanks? Glee's eyes followed Blanks and Carlotta as they entered a tea shop. Were they going to nuncheon there? How peculiar. "What's the matter with you, Di?"

Dianna shook her head. "Nothing. It's just . . . just that we really must hurry to Queen Square. You do have an appointment to look at the house."

She's lying. Why did Dianna so strongly wish to avoid Blanks? Surely he hadn't—

All of a sudden, Glee's heart thudded. And she knew why Dianna was acting so peculiarly. Dianna was privy to information that was withheld from Glee. George shared everything with her. *Including the fact that Carlotta Ennis was Blanks's mistress.*

Gregory had been putting off this meeting with Carlotta for as long as he could, but with Glee arriving tomorrow, he could postpone it no longer. He had wanted to delay the voluptuous Carlotta's anguish, to delay the tears he knew would come. For Carlotta clearly loved him. She had craved his every touch at the expense of her good name.

She had lured him into her bed despite that he had told her from the beginning he would never offer marriage. When it became clear she could not bring him to the altar, she banished her pride and begged to be his mistress. In the year since she had been under his protection, there had been no occasion when she had not eagerly welcomed him into her bed no matter what time of day or night. *I live to be in your arms, my darling,* she had often huskily whispered to him during their heated lovemaking.

From across the small, linen-topped table, Gregory watched the lovely Carlotta with her radiant black hair, his eyes travelling to the rising and falling of her generous breasts that spilled into her purple gown.

"What's the matter, my love?" Carlotta asked with a trembling voice.

"What makes you think something is wrong?"

"Your actions," she said decisively. "I've never known you to prefer a tea room to my bed."

The serving lady brought their tea and set it and two cups and saucers on the table.

Gregory's heart pounded. He would have to tell her. "I have some news to share."

Her lashes lifted seductively to reveal lavender eyes wide with fear.

"I'm afraid it's not very good news, my dear." Had he ever called Carlotta *my dear* before? He fleetingly thought of Glee. Whom he had called *my love.* In both instances, his words were far from the truth. "First, I shall tell you about my father's disappointing will. I get nothing, unless . . ."

"Unless what?" Carlotta asked, not able to remove her frightened gaze from him.

"Unless I'm married on my twenty-fifth birthday."

Now a smile hitched across her exotically beautiful face.

He frowned. "I'm to marry Glee Pembroke."

An anguished gasp broke from her throat. "No! You can't!" Her eyes quickly filled with tears which began to spill down her ivory cheeks. She did nothing to check them. "Why can't you marry me? You said yourself we suit very well. And best of all, you don't want children, and I abhor the sniveling brats. Don't you see that Pembroke child can never love you in the ways I have?"

He was stunned over her hatred of children. After all, she had a child of her own. 'Twas fortunate the poor lad did not reside with his mother.

Then Gregory remembered Carlotta's question. Why had he never considered marrying Carlotta? She was the most compatible bed partner he had ever possessed. She was beautiful and of good birth. And without a doubt, she loved him.

The thing of it was that he honestly had never wanted to marry any woman. His aversion to matrimony had been schooled by years of staunch avowal.

Had he to make his decision over again, though, he would still choose Glee Pembroke over Carlotta Ennis. Even if Glee proved to be a cold fish in bed. Now why had he gone and thought about Glee in bed? Hadn't he firmly decided he would never touch her? Resisting Glee's charms could prove most difficult, he realized, as he remembered the intensity of their farewell kiss. Oddly, it had stirred him in ways Carlotta's kisses never had.

His reasons for deciding on marrying Glee had nothing to do with sex and nothing to do with her nobility of birth but everything to do with William Jefferson and others of his ilk. Throwing Glee to the likes of them was akin to coaxing lambs to slaughter.

Unlike the innocent Glee, Carlotta could easily handle herself—with or without his protection. Though he clearly meant to settle her well.

How could he explain all this to Carlotta? "I have made it clear to Miss Pembroke that our marriage is to be a marriage in name only. I have no intentions of relinquishing my ties to you, my lovely Carlotta." He picked up her icy hand and brushed his lips across it.

Still, her tears flowed unchecked. Now that the tea had steeped, she poured it into their cups, but instead of drinking hers, she wrapped her hands around the cup for warmth. "Why her?" she asked in a low voice not devoid of pain.

He shrugged.

"It's because I bring shame now that I've allowed myself to become your mistress. You've lost all respect for me. And now—" she broke off, sobbing, "you've lost your desire for me."

"No, that's not it at all!" he protested. "I'm here today with you. Would I be doing that if I were ashamed of you?"

"You're throwing me crumbs to assuage your conscience."

He shook his head vigorously, though her words rang true. His big hand covered hers. He felt the warmth from the steaming cup. "You must understand how important you are to me," he said.

She laughed a bitter laugh. "All you want is my compliant body because your wife won't be able to satisfy you."

"There's much more to you than a compliant body, Carlotta," he said in a deep, low voice.

Her long, black lashes lowered. "Why couldn't you have asked me?"

He shrugged. "I honestly don't know."

"I never thought you would be so snobbish that you would marry for rank."

"I'm not marrying Miss Pembroke for her family's rank," he protested angrily.

"Then why? She's a mere child—and not the innocent you think her. What can she do for you?"

It's not what she can do for me as much as what I can do for her. Why had Carlotta maligned Glee? He didn't like it above half. He picked up his cup and downed his tea in one gulp. "We can talk on this from now until doomsday, but it won't change the fact that I've offered for Glee, she accepted, and the banns have been posted. There's nothing we can say or do now that will change anything."

Carlotta shot him a puzzled glance. "You want to marry her, don't you?"

"For God's sake, Carlotta, I've never wanted to marry *any* woman. You know that. Now, drink your tea."

She shook her head. "I no longer want it." Her eyes flashing in anger, she picked up her cup and slung its contents at him.

His temper scorching, he scooted back his chair and stood up. "I suggest we leave," he uttered in a voice shaking with anger.

They strolled silently along Cheap Street and turned onto Milsom. Her tears had finally stopped. When they got to her door on Queen Street, she turned to him. "This will be goodbye, Gregory," she said.

His brows lowered.

"I will use what little pride I have left to sever my illicit ties to you," she said. "I shan't allow you to slake your hunger in my bed." Her voice broke on the last few words; then she opened the door and entered, slamming the door in Gregory's face.

Glee would never know how she made it to Queen Square. Her heart raced, and she felt as if the blood had drained from her body. *Blanks and Carlotta!* It made her sick to think of the beautiful widow lying within his arms, allowing Blanks to love her like he would never love Glee.

And there was no way Glee could ever compete with Carlotta and her buxom beauty. How sadly she compared to Blanks's mistress. *Blanks's mistress*. The thought was like a dagger to the heart.

Since her refusal to allow Glee to cross the street to meet Blanks, Dianna had not uttered a word. Even when a passing horse kicked water on her pink gown.

Finally, Glee broke the silence. "She's his mistress, isn't she?"

"A young maiden is not supposed to know of such things," Dianna recited.

"Oh, but I do know," Glee said forlornly.

Dianna's glance shifted sympathetically to Glee.

"Why couldn't it have been a woman from the lower classes?" Glee mused aloud.

"Or one with a wart on her nose?" Dianna added.

Glee tried to summon a laugh. Sweet heaven, she had known Blanks kept mistresses, but never had she supposed such a woman would come from her own class. Or be so very beautiful.

When they got to the Harrison House, Glee moved through the lavish ground floor chambers completely without emotion. When she was informed that all the tasteful furnishings were to be included, she made no comment for her every thought was on Blanks.

Upstairs, she viewed the mistress's and master's chambers and dressing rooms, still without comment. When she beheld the olive-green bed in the master's chamber, she realized this is where Blanks would sleep. Just steps from her own bed. With a dull pain in her heart, she wondered if she would ever share the bed with the man she loved.

When the tour of the house was concluded, she said, "I shall tell my husband-to-be to purchase this house." *My husband-to-be.* At least she would have something Carlotta would never have. His name.

And hopefully she would one day have his heart—if her battle strategies were successful.

SEVEN

What a black day it had been for Gregory. First, the unpleasantness with Carlotta, which left him feeling bloody low. Then the unwelcome missive he had received from Glee informing him she had come to Bath a day early. And now at the Upper Assembly Rooms, he was being besieged with well-wishers offering felicitations upon his upcoming nuptials. Since Glee had decided on the Harrison House earlier in the day, word had spread through the city like leaves scattered on the wind.

Gregory's stomach knotted when he saw Jefferson—a devilish smile on his face—strolling across the ballroom floor toward him.

"I say, Blankenship, quite a conquest you've made with Sedgewick's beautiful sister."

Gregory's eyes swept over Jefferson. Why had he never before noticed how dandified the man was, with his colorful waistcoats and elaborately tied cravat? "I am a most fortunate man," Gregory responded.

Jefferson clapped a hand on Gregory's shoulder. "And I was foolish enough to believe you would never be caught in parson's mousetrap." He leaned closer and spoke in a hoarse whisper. "It is to be hoped your decision was not forced because you've compromised the lady."

The air of detachment Gregory so carefully cultivated crumbled as rage swept through him. He brought himself face-to-face with the much-smaller Jefferson. He grabbed Jefferson's lapels and spoke in a guttural voice. "If you ever again impugn Miss Pembroke—or even *think* about casting doubt on her character—I swear, Jefferson, I'll call you out." His hands fisted, he looked into Jefferson's pupils. "Have I made myself clear?"

Bravado replaced the fleeting look of fear on Jefferson's face. "Of course, I meant no offense." His glance flicked across the room to Glee, who was being led onto the dance floor by a gangly youth. "Miss Pembroke is quite above our touch, you lucky devil."

"Devil is right!"

Gregory spun around to match the familiar voice to the speaker, Timothy Appleton. Next to George, Appleton was Gregory's oldest friend.

Jefferson excused himself, leaving Gregory to Appleton's chastisement.

"Why, pray tell, am I a devil?" Gregory asked.

"Because you failed to mention your betrothal to me, one of your oldest and dearest friends," Appleton said.

"Oh, that." Gregory brushed a speck of lint from his black coat. " 'Tis three weeks off still, and I mean to enjoy every last day of bachelorhood."

"You're as bad as George. Remember, he swore off marriage until his thirtieth birthday, and he upped and married at twenty-four. And now you," Appleton said forlornly. "What's a fellow to do for pleasure anymore?"

A smile stretched across Gregory's face. "I can think of any number of things."

"Fact is, it's never the same after one weds. I long for the good old days. Oh, the times we've had," Appleton said wistfully. "Never was a chap more fun than George when he was in his cups. Remember the night he stretched out and went to sleep in front of Carlton House? And what about that trip to Newmarket when Elvin lost all his money and donned his groom's clothes to beg for dinner?"

"Melvin," Gregory corrected. Appleton was forever getting the twins mixed up. "The things that meek fellow will do when in his cups!"

Appleton shook his head sadly. "All the fun will be gone once you're wed."

Gregory patted his friend's back. "Not at all. Miss Pembroke assures me I can continue on as I always have."

"That's exactly what Miss Moreland—before she was Lady Sedgewick—said to Sedgewick. Look at him now. He's lost all his desire for enjoying a rollicking good time." Appleton shook his head. "Fail to understand what could be so amusing at a country estate with no one for company but a wife and babe!"

"Nor do I," Gregory said. "I assure you, I have no plans for my marriage to Miss Pembroke to change my activities in any way."

This comment failed to elicit the desired response in Appleton. "Can't understand why you're getting shackled then at all. You were the last one I ever expected would marry. Especially after all your avowed denials."

If only he could tell Appleton the truth. But he could never allow his brother to learn the marriage was a sham. "Have you not noticed Miss Pembroke's many excellent qualities?" Gregory asked.

" 'Course I have. I know of half a dozen blokes

whose hearts she broke. It's just that *you* have never been attracted to *ladies*."

"At least not until I was ready to settle down," Gregory defended.

"Never been so shocked as I was this afternoon when Melvin informed me you was to wed. Thought he had bats in his belfry. Told him so, too. Bet a pony he was wrong. So of course I came straightaway to your lodgings where Stanley informed me you'd gone off to see Miss Pembroke at her hotel."

"Sorry I missed you," Gregory said, wishing like anything he could get Appleton off the subject of his nuptials. Demmed well wished *he* could get them out of his mind, too, and thoroughly enjoy his last weeks of utter freedom. Why did Glee have to come a day early? "Say, after I take Miss Pembroke home from the assembly, what say you we descend upon Mrs. Starr's gaming establishment?"

"I'm told the new dealer there's as fine a looking bit of muslin as there is." Appleton winked. "Fair and buxom."

"All the more reason to go," Gregory said with a mischievous smile.

"Go where?" said one of the twins who now joined them. Gregory was fairly certain the speaker was Elvin. Though the two, with their Roman noses and prematurely receding dark hairlines, looked exactly alike, their facial expressions differed vastly. Melvin was excessively shy and reticent while exuberance marked his brother's manner. The twin addressing them was undoubtedly exuberant.

Gregory's gaze swept over his three companions to settle on Elvin. "We go to Mrs. Starr's tonight after this dull affair."

Elvin's glance flitted to Glee, who was still dancing. "Will your betrothed allow you such freedom?"

So he had heard, too. Was there anyone left in Bath who was unaware of his forthcoming nuptials? "Of course she will, and my freedom shall extend to my married life as well."

Elvin shook his head mournfully. "Blackest day in me life. Blanks bespoken for. Whatever shall we do?"

Melvin nodded his agreement. "Daresay it's a pity."

Gregory shot his friends a stern look. "Everyone here tonight has offered felicitations, except the three of you."

"Sorry," Melvin said. "Wish you all the best and all that sort of thing."

"Naturally we want the best for you," Appleton said. "That goes without saying."

" 'Tis just that we'll miss the good times we've shared," Elvin said.

"I've been telling Appleton that nothing has to change just because I'm getting married. Miss Pembroke has no desire to usurp my friends. She's a great sport. Says it's perfectly acceptable with her that I continue on as I always have." *'Twas the least she could do.*

"So the gel is to call the plays?" Elvin challenged.

"Never," Gregory snapped. He was aware that the orchestra had quit playing and looked to see Glee making her way across the ballroom toward him.

If only I'd stayed in Warwickshire another day, Glee lamented. Then she might not have learned the sad news about Carlotta nor would she have had to endure Blanks's wrath for robbing a day of his precious bachelorhood. He had been a positive ogre since visiting her at the hotel late that afternoon. Was he comparing her to Carlotta, bereft with disappointment that she was not the lovely, raven-haired widow? No doubt he was wishing Glee to the devil.

Were she truly benevolent, she would release him of obligation to marry her. But she was not benevolent. And she was as stubborn as he. Nothing would prevent her from marrying Blanks and being given the opportunity to earn his eternal love. And nothing would ever quench her thirst to love and be loved by Gregory Blankenship.

She smiled and greeted Appleton, then the twins, whom she was forever getting mixed up. George, too, had been unable to determine which twin was which. The only person who could tell them apart was Blanks.

Glee moved to Blanks's side. "I had hoped for a dance with you tonight."

"You've not lacked for partners," he said with an air of indifference.

"But none of them has been the man I'll wed," she countered. "We simply must satisfy all the wagging tongues, my dear Mr. Blankenship."

His dark eyes flashed with some emotion she could not name; then he excused himself from his friends and offered Glee his arm as the violins signaled a waltz.

Though she had danced with Blanks many times, she had never waltzed with him. She was completely unprepared for her reaction to being held so closely to him. 'Twas as if the dance floor were a cloud. She felt so light and utterly feminine. And so wholly aware of his masculinity as he lightly held her, his sandalwood scent rushing to her blossoming senses. Her heart accelerated and she hoped she would not be called upon to speak, for she feared her trembling voice would betray her.

She need not worry that he would address her. Mechanically conducting the dance steps, he had no desire to converse with her. She wondered if he was thinking of Carlotta.

With mere inches separating the length of their bodies, Glee unexpectedly drew the parallel that their position in relation to one another was not unlike that of two lovers sharing a bed. She fleetingly wondered if a man and woman could perform the sexual act standing up. Then she thought of Blanks making love to Carlotta. Had he enjoyed Carlotta's body today? The thought brought pain. For the virgin Glee hungered to feel Gregory inside her.

"You're not pleased that I came early," she said.

"Why would you say that?" he asked in mock outrage.

"Because I've known you all my life."

"Then your knowledge extends to clairvoyance?"

"Not to clairvoyance. To reality. I know you, Blanks, as no other woman ever will. I vow to make your life as happy as I possibly can."

"You have a most peculiar way of doing that."

Her heart sank. Of course he was referring to her entrapment of him.

They spoke no more for the rest of the dance.

The last dance of the night Glee granted to William Jefferson. It was a waltz. When he placed his hand to her waist, she felt none of the raw emotion she had felt when Blanks had done the same thing. Mr. Jefferson was much shorter than Blanks—and though not as handsome as Blanks, he was considered one of the finest-looking men in Bath. It was said that his dress was all that was fashionable in Paris and London. Whatever was the latest rage from the Continent, Mr. Jefferson eagerly adopted. He was the first man in Bath to sport long, white pantaloons. He flaunted his costly snuffboxes as some women did their bonnets. And the man prided himself on the fact he wore a different colored waistcoat every day. Tonight's was kelly green.

Glee preferred a man with more subtle taste. A man like Blanks.

"Mr. Blankenship is a most fortunate man," Jefferson said.

Glee feigned ignorance of what he spoke. "Pray tell, why?"

"Because he has stolen the loveliest girl in Bath. You must know you have broken many hearts."

"Fie, Mr. Jefferson, you will turn my head."

"I speak the truth. I'm one of the men who would wish to do harm to Mr. Blankenship."

Even though she knew the man jested, his statement caused her heart to trip. "I beg that you not say that."

"I would never knowingly distress you, Miss Pembroke."

With surprise—and not without a trace of disgust— she suddenly realized the man was flirting with her, even though she was engaged to be married to a man standing no more than twenty feet away.

Perhaps she could use his flirtations to her own advantage. After all, Mr. Jefferson was possessed of some social standing and attractiveness. Let Blanks know that *other* men found her desirable. Knowing that Blanks avoided dancing tonight—except the one dance with her—she decided to play up to Mr. Jefferson while Blanks watched.

She tossed her head back and laughed playfully. "Really, Mr. Jefferson, you are much too kind."

"Truthful, not kind."

"Since we are being truthful, you must tell me why it is you have never married. You are older than my betrothed, are you not?"

He nodded. "I'm two and thirty."

"Two and thirty!" she exclaimed. "How is it you have avoided matrimony for so many seasons?"

He tightened his hold on her and spoke in a low, husky voice. "It seems that every woman who appeals to me is someone else's wife."

"Oh, dear."

"I'm giving you fair warning that I will not let a wedding ring stop me from showering attentions upon you."

"Oh, dear."

Though he continued to chat with his friends, Gregory never let Glee stray from his vision. He did not at all like what he saw. The dandy and Glee looked good together. He showered her with the attentions Gregory had failed to give her. And he held her far too tightly. And why did the neckline of Glee's blasted dress have to be so wretchedly low?

Gregory decided it was a very good thing, indeed, that he would not allow Glee to escape his scrutiny. Glee was far too innocent and trusting for the likes of William Jefferson. Gregory would have to be her protector.

Oddly, it was a role he was not adverse to.

EIGHT

During the well-lit walk from the Assembly Rooms to the hotel, Gregory had few words for Glee and Dianna.

"Does the location of the Harrison House suit you, Blanks?" Glee asked, looking up into his inscrutable face.

He nodded. "It's a very fine location. Most convenient. But you must stop calling it the Harrison House. It will be our house in a matter of weeks."

Our house. This was the first time she had thought of anything as *ours.* Her heart tripped. "Yes, the Blankenship House. I like the sound of it very much," she said. "Have you begun to make the necessary arrangements for its purchase?"

"I'm talking with my solicitor tomorrow. I shall tell him we desire to occupy it immediately upon our marriage in three weeks' time."

Our marriage. At least he was no longer afraid to say it. "Then I take it there's to be no honeymoon." She stated it matter-of-factly, hoping disappointment did not creep into her voice. She should have known there would be no honeymoon, since the marriage was not to be a real marriage in the accepted sense. Of course, Blanks would be anxious to return to his friends in Bath. After all, she had encouraged him to continue as he always had. Hadn't she told him their marriage would alter nothing?

He turned to her. "I had not given any thought to a honeymoon. Does that disappoint you?"

"Of course not," she said cheerfully. "I'm looking forward to setting up *our house*. It will be great fun." She must never initiate anything—even a desired honeymoon—that would be unpleasant to Blanks. She'd already delivered enough unpleasantness upon him. Now she would spend her life making it up to him.

When they reached the hotel lobby, he said his farewells, then met Glee's gaze. "Will you do me the goodness of meeting me at the Pump Room in the morning?" Then, as an afterthought, he glanced at Dianna. "You and Lady Sedgewick, that is."

Glee looked at Dianna, then back to Gregory. "We should love it."

"Nine o'clock?"

He grimaced. "Nine o'clock it shall be."

Glee turned to Dianna. "I'll have a private word with Blanks, if it does not offend you."

Dianna gave the couple a knowing smile. "I should be offended if the two of you do not have a private moment together." She turned and entered the hotel.

Blanks shot Glee a quizzing look.

Her heart drummed. "I just wanted you to know I saw you with your mistress today. You don't have to hide anything from me." Her seeming acceptance took a good deal of bravado she was far from feeling.

"Bloody hell, Glee! I know ours is not to be a real marriage, but really, you can hardly expect me to discuss so delicate a subject with you." Frowning, he added, "Nine in the morning." Then he spun on his heel and departed.

* * *

Once he left the hotel, Blanks angrily stormed the two blocks to Mrs. Starr's establishment, where the twins and Appleton were just walking up.

"I say, Blanks, we've made a wager which involves you," Appleton said.

Gregory came abreast of them and stopped, lifting a single brow.

"Elvin wagered five quid you could sample the new dealer's charms this very night."

Gregory leveled a gaze at Appleton. "And you?"

"I said fleeting trysts weren't your style. Always concerned about disease, you are."

That much was true. One unpleasant experience at Oxford had taught him to be careful. "I cannot possibly answer your challenge until I see the lady in question."

"She's blond. You used to be partial to blondes before . . . Mrs. Ennis."

"Have you not noticed my affianced is possessed of red hair?" he asked with a smile.

A liveried butler let the four of them into Mrs. Starr's parlor, where play took place at five different tables. Elvin elbowed Blanks and spoke softly out of the side of his mouth. "She's at the faro table."

"Then it's faro I play first," Gregory said, strolling up to the table, where the buxom dealer was playing with an older, bald-headed gentleman. While Gregory watched and waited for the hand to end, a servant soon brought brandy, which Gregory—like his friends—consumed quickly. Mrs. Starr, ever the wise businesswoman, made sure her servants kept her customers plied with liquor.

Gregory used the idle time to study the dealer. Though she was fair like Glee, she was a good bit larger than Glee—especially in her bosom. He decided the woman must have had the neckline of her gown cut even lower than the current fashion in order to display her most notable feature. Or features.

Substitute purple for the peach dress color and view her only from the neck down, and there was no difference whatsoever between her and Carlotta.

He thought back over his meeting with Carlotta that afternoon, remembering her words. *Because I allowed myself to be your mistress, I've lost your respect.* He had vehemently disagreed, but now he wondered if there was some truth to her charge. Carlotta was not a woman he would choose to marry. He would never wish to bring her home to his father, were his father still alive.

Yet she had been the perfect mistress. He even cared about her as one would a friend. And he would see to it she received a generous settlement.

Perhaps the dealer would make a good mistress. Her face was pretty. Her voice was melodic—even cultured. Her taste in clothing suggested she knew quality. Though she was pretty, she was not as pretty as Glee. And for some unexplainable reason, that bothered him.

Now why had he gone and thought of Glee? He had the rest of his life to be saddled with her. *Damn it!*

When the game was finished, Gregory pulled out a chair and sat down in front of the dealer. She looked up at him and smiled coyly. "I'm Sheila. I don't believe I've seen you here before."

"Nor have I seen you. You cannot have been here long."

She lowered her lashes seductively. "This is my fourth week here."

"I can see I've been away far too long."

She shuffled the deck and put it into the faro box, turning up the top cards.

Faro wasn't Gregory's favorite game. In fact, it held little interest for him. He was far more interested in the *vingt-un* being played at the next table, where Appleton sat. Then why had Gregory come here? *For Sheila*. What a fool he was being. All to prove to his friends Glee meant nothing to him.

Now he would have to play up to Sheila. Because he had been blessed with good looks and large fortune, his friends thought there was no woman in the kingdom immune to his charms. A heavy burden, indeed, for him.

His friends would be proven right once again. First, Sheila allowed him to win. Then, she took his sport away when she asked him to see her home when all the patrons left. He smiled a bitter smile as he realized that within a few hours he would see her magnificent body unclothed.

Then, completely unsummoned, he wondered what Glee's slender body would look like unclothed. He slapped his counter on the queen of spades.

As the last of Mrs. Starr's patrons was taking his leave, Gregory and his chums gathered in the foyer to collect their hats and coats.

"Excuse me, gentlemen, for not leaving with you, but Miss Sheila has asked me to accompany her home," Gregory said.

Appleton turned to Elvin. "I'll have to owe you. Mrs. Starr was very inhospitable to me tonight."

Melvin grinned and spoke with slurred words. "But I must say her liquor was quite good."

"And plentiful," his twin added.

For all he knew, Gregory could be slurring his words, too, for he had consumed a great deal of brandy. He watched as his friends left; a moment later

Sheila—wearing a fox-trimmed cloak—joined him, tucking her gloved hand into his bent arm.

Her lodgings were only a ten-minute walk away. When they arrived at her door, she turned to him. Light from the street lantern fell on her face. "Should you like to come up?" She moved closer to him until he felt her most intimate parts rub against him.

A smile on his face, he put his arms around her.

She lifted her face to his for a kiss.

Though brandy made him randy, he could not bring himself to kiss her. The last woman he kissed had been Glee. This doxy's kisses would violate the sweet innocence left by Glee's tender lips.

Actually, he didn't want to bed Sheila. He too vividly remembered the *illness* he had contracted at Oxford. There was also the fact that he was growing weary of buxom women. He fancied his next mistress would be petite. Like Glee. *Damn!* Why did he continue to think of her? Hadn't she done enough to make his life miserable?

"I'm afraid I've had too much to drink," he said apologetically. "If I went up to your place I'd likely fall asleep and miss my assignation with my affianced tomorrow morning." He inwardly rejoiced. There were advantages to being affianced, after all. Sheila held the promise of becoming besotted like so many of the others, a prospect he did not relish in the least. One purple-hued, lovelorn woman was quite enough for him right now.

Her face fell, as did her voice. "Next time, perhaps."

He bid good night, knowing there would be no next time.

By the time he arrived at his lodgings, the sun was rising over the River Avon. He had to meet Glee at nine o'clock. Bloody hell, he thought as he fell into slumber, forgetting to leave a note for his valet to wake him before nine o'clock.

Standing waiting for the attendant to fetch her second glass of water, Glee tapped her foot impatiently. Her betrothed was not the only one absent from this morning's social hub at the Pump Room. Timothy Appleton was not here, nor were the twins. Her heart drummed. Neither was Carlotta Ennis. Was Blanks with Carlotta? Had he spent the night with her? Good God, would he sleep with Carlotta after they were married?

Glee had thought she couldn't wait until they were married and she could be with him always. It now occurred to her that might not be the case.

Dianna came up to stand beside her. "Don't be so morose, pet. Blanks and his friends likely stayed out excessively late last night. You know how it is with young bachelors. He's merely sleeping. I daresay he'll show up at the hotel this afternoon—all apologetic."

Glee took her glass. "A pity I won't be there. I desire to return to Hornsby Manor at once."

Dianna raised her brows in concern. "What of the furnishings for your new house?"

"I can just as easily select those once I'm married." *If I marry,* she thought with disappointment. Blanks may want to cry off now that he was back in Bath with his friends. And back with Carlotta.

Dianna put a gentle hand on Glee's forearm. "Don't be angry with him. He's only enjoying his last days as a bachelor."

Glee harrumphed. *But he'll continue as a bachelor even after we marry. If we marry.* "I shan't be angry with Blanks. I only desire to return to the manor house in order to prepare my trousseau."

"But I thought there were several more things you wished to purchase for it in Bath."

Glee moved to leave the Pump Room. "I can purchase those now, before we leave."

Before returning to the hotel, Glee purchased a half-dozen delicate night shifts. Once in her chambers, she sat down to compose a letter to Blanks.

> *My Dear Blanks,*
>   *I hope you are not disappointed to learn I have returned to Hornsby Manor to prepare for our wedding. My mission in Bath was accomplished far sooner than I had expected.*
>   *I'm sorry to have missed you at the Pump Room this morning but am looking forward to our wedding day, when I will see you again at the chapel in Duncaster for the ceremony which will make us man and wife.*
>   *It is to be hoped you enjoy your waning days of bachelorhood, though you and I both know those days do not have to come to an end with our marriage.*
>
>   *With love,*
>   *Glee*

Signing the letter had taken a great deal of thought. She thought of signing simply *love,* but did not wish to scare him off. The same went for *yours.* She finally deemed *with love* appropriate. It was something the sister of his friend would sign—which, after all, was exactly what he expected her to be. Nothing more. Also, it conveyed affection without the possessiveness of *your fiancee* or *all my love.*

Satisfied, she sealed the letter and gave it to a page to deliver to Blanks's lodgings.

It was well into afternoon when Gregory awoke, cursing himself for having missed the morning meeting with Glee at the Pump Room. No sooner was he awake than Stanley brought him the note from Glee. Cursing as he read, he wadded it up and threw it into the smoldering fire.

"Hurry, Stanley, my clothes!"

His valet quickly gathered up his master's clothing, but by the time he returned, Gregory had fallen back into his pillows. "Never mind. She's likely gone by now."

Stanley murmured his apologies.

" 'Tis just as well," Gregory said. He bloody well planned to do as Glee bid and thoroughly enjoy his remaining days of bachelorhood. With no Carlotta. No Sheila. He didn't need any women. He'd get his bloody fill of them—or one of them—soon enough.

He might even pop over to London, go to Jackson's salon. For some reason, he wanted to pound something.

"What day is it, Stanley?"

" 'Tis Thursday, sir."

"No. I mean what is the date?"

"It's the twenty-seventh day of February."

Blanks did the mental calculations. "Only nineteen more days of freedom."

NINE

'Twas a dreary day, much like it had been the day Glee's irrational act had forced Blanks to become betrothed to her. Under stone-gray skies she walked to the folly and sat upon its marble bench to ponder her predicament. She had left Bath more than two weeks ago and had not heard a word from Blanks since then.

She chided herself for not staying there, but she had instinctively known Blanks needed total freedom the last weeks of his bachelorhood. As she gazed around the barren stone edifice where Blanks's fate had been sealed, she came to realize he was not going to marry her after all.

And it served her right. She had gone ahead and thrust him into a marriage he wanted no part of. All of this she had orchestrated, knowing full well that being married was something he found onerous.

That as a spurned bride she would be the laughing-stock of Bath caused her no concern whatsoever. That much, she deserved. What really hurt was worrying about Blanks and the eternal emptiness which he would now be unable to escape. His perpetual quest for pleasure was merely a substitute for a meaningful, loving relationship. Her own shattered dreams and the unfulfilled love she had planned to lavish on Blanks caused her considerable pain. She physically ached from the void losing Blanks would create, a bleakness reaching deep into her soul.

Even her sister's return from the Continent to be present at her wedding had failed to bring Glee out of the doldrums. She had flinched when Felicity told her, "I've always known you were in love with Blanks."

Had Blanks, too, known Glee had misrepresented her intentions? Was she as transparent as glass?

Her sister's presence made Glee's suffering even more acute. For Felicity had the undying love of her husband and the promise of the child she now carried in her womb.

And Glee would have nothing.

As Glee sat there in the folly, the skies overhead had turned darker. Since she had no desire to be stranded there alone, she picked herself up from the bench and dusted off her skirts to return to the manor house before the rains came.

She was almost back to the house when she saw Blanks walking toward her.

"I was worried you'd be caught in the storm," he said, as she came abreast of him.

A smile widened across her face. "I cannot tell you how very good it is to see you. I had begun to fear you were going to leave me stranded at the altar."

His smile reached his dark, flashing eyes. "I couldn't do that to you, Glee."

No lover's murmurs could have been more welcome. "Despite your great aversion to marrying me," she said with a laugh. She looked up at him as he fell into step beside her, and she slipped her arm through his, sighing. "I promise you, Blanks, you'll not regret our marriage. We'll make a good team. A fun pair." She could not tell him her life's mission was to immerse him with her love.

"If I had to get shackled, I'm glad it's to you," he said with a laugh.

Glee was quite sure she floated all the way to the front door of the manor house.

Throughout dinner that night Glee continued to feel as if she were buoyed by clouds. She could not remember ever being so happy. Her gaze swept around the table, where everyone present was someone she loved. George and Dianna. Felicity and Thomas. And Blanks. The only thing marring her complete happiness was the knowledge Blanks did not love her as George loved Dianna or as Thomas loved Felicity, but that was all right. Blanks had said he would rather marry her than anyone else. That was enough for now.

She would win his love one day. One day he would be happy that he married her.

After dinner, Blanks asked her to accompany him to the conservatory. They strolled down the length of the dimly lit west wing and came to the glass-enclosed room. No servant had thought to light a candle in the room.

"The moonlight will suffice," Blanks said in a low voice, taking her by the hand.

Glee's insides quivered in anticipation. Was he wishing to kiss her? Oh, but she would like that excessively. She followed him into the conservatory. Blanks was right. Moonlight bathed the room. She looked up into his face.

"I have a wedding present for you," he said in a husky whisper.

Her heart fell. 'Twas not to be a kiss, after all.

From his pocket, he pulled out a silken box that was the size of book. He opened it to reveal magnificent emeralds. There was a dazzling necklace and an emerald ring clustered with oblong diamonds.

" 'Twas my mother's and her mother's before her," he whispered, offering it to her.

Glee was overwhelmed as much by the tenderness in his voice as by the generosity of the gift. Without thinking, her arms flung around his neck. "They're beautiful!"

He patted her on the back—a gesture she was certain he had never done with Carlotta.

She removed her arms from him. "I shall wear them with great pride."

A smile flashed across his face. "I want you to wear the necklace at our wedding. There, I'll place the ring on your finger."

"I'll never take it off," she whispered. She really was going to marry him, her heart's desire. She was deeply touched.

She took the box. "Do you remember your mother?"

He shook his head almost angrily. "She died in childbed when I was less than a year old. The babe died with her." His eyes went cold, and the ever-present smile vanished from his face. "I'm afraid I've always held my father rather responsible for killing her."

Surely his wife's body hadn't healed from giving birth to Blanks when the man impregnated her again. What a brute! Glee gave Blanks a puzzled look. "But . . . your brother is so close to you in age . . ."

His voice chilled. "Yes, my father remarried the day his year of mourning was up." His eyes narrowed. "My stepmother delivered him another son eight months later. Jonathan and I were born twenty-eight months apart."

He held his father responsible for his mother's death! Immediately upon hearing his words, Glee understood how his mother's death must have preyed on the motherless boy throughout the years of his childhood. Was that why he abhorred marriage? Why he did not want children? Did he fear the pain of losing a wife as he had lost his mother?

He offered his arm as he began to stroll from the room. "We had best join the others, or your brother will come looking for me with a pistol."

She laughed. "Silly, it's permissible for us be alone together. We'll be husband and wife in two days."

He winced. "Must you remind me?"

At least he was now able to joke about it in front of her. That was a significant improvement. She laughed, then stood on her toes and reached up to kiss him. It was a chaste kiss, one he did not return. "Thank you for my wedding present."

Gregory had come to realize Glee's leaving Bath had allowed him to ease into his acceptance of the inevitability of their marriage. He had actually adjusted to the idea. Perhaps their marriage would be for the best. At least now his fortune was secure, and he would gladly bestow the lion's share of it on Glee. And Glee had assured him she would not interfere with his pleasures. It wouldn't really be like getting shackled. After all, they weren't going to share a bed. They would remain good friends. Nothing more.

If only Jonathan doesn't get suspicious, Gregory thought. He had written to both Sutton Hall and to Jonathan's lodgings in London to inform his brother of his upcoming wedding. It was a courtesy he did not extend to his stepmother. There was no love between her and Gregory, and only Gregory's sense of obligation kept the roof of Sutton Hall over her head. Of course, Sutton Hall would be his and Glee's once they were married. A pity Glee was too kindhearted to throw the mean-spirited woman out. He had little doubt were the tables turned, Aurora wouldn't hesitate to give him the boot.

But she was his father's widow, his brother's mother. And it wasn't as if there was not an abundance of room at Sutton Hall. He supposed he would always be saddled with the dreadful woman.

But he didn't have to invite her to his wedding.

To Gregory's great surprise, Jonathan showed up at Hornsby Manor late in the afternoon the day before the wedding.

"I'm honored that you've come for our wedding," Gregory said, putting an arm around his much-shorter brother. "I must introduce you to my lovely Miss Pembroke." If he ever were going to be convincing of his devotion to Glee, it had better be now, Gregory thought. Jonathan must never get wind that his and Glee's marriage was to be a sham.

He found her in the library, where she was reading. She glanced at them, then stood up and came forward. Oddly, Gregory was proud of her. She looked particularly delicate in her mint green dress as she glided gracefully toward them, her hand outstretched, a smile on her lovely face.

"You must be Jonathan," she said to his brother. "Even though you and Bl— . . . Gregory are just half brothers, I would know you anywhere. You have his chin, as well as his coloring. I cannot tell you how happy I am that you have come to our wedding. Come, Jonathan," she said, "let's sit and talk. We've so much news to share with you."

They sat on the facing brocaded sofas before the fire, and Glee rang for tea.

"You'll have to come visit us after the wedding," she said to Jonathan. "Blanks—forgive me for not calling your brother by his Christian name—he's purchased the Harrison House in Bath for us."

Jonathan's eyes widened. "The one on Queen Square?"

She nodded.

"I should have known. My brother's not one to settle for less, though I fail to see why you need a house that size for just the two of you."

Gregory's stomach dropped. Why must Glee flaunt his extravagance to his pinchpenny brother? "It's not so large as you think," Gregory snapped.

"And you must see the lovely new carriage Blanks has presented me," Glee continued, her eyes sparkling with mirth.

"I daresay he's got the blunt," Jonathan said coolly.

Gregory fought his strong desire to stuff his handkerchief in his affianced's mouth.

After tea, Glee stood up and said, "Come, dear brother," as she began to stroll from the library, her arm tucked into Jonathan's. "I must make you known to my family."

Somehow, Jonathan had not been prepared for Miss Pembroke's uncommon beauty. She was fair and petite and at once elicited a protectiveness. She was, quite simply, a diamond of the first water. Any man would want to marry her. Any man but his brother. He had not lived his life with Gregory not to know how strong his brother's aversion to marriage was and to fathering children.

Clearly, Gregory meant to gain his inheritance, whatever the cost. Nothing more. Which was not at all what his blessed father had in mind when stipulating that Gregory must be wed by his twenty-fifth birthday. Their father wanted Gregory to lay to rest his rakish ways, to care about the running of his estates more than the outcome of the races at Newmarket. He wanted his firstborn to sire an heir.

Jonathan was certain his brother would continue down his corrupt path, taking Sutton Hall with him. And if Jonathan had to earn his brother's eternal contempt to prevent that from happening, so be it.

A marriage wasn't a marriage if it was not consummated. Jonathan would wager his year's income that Gregory had no intentions of consummating the marriage. Not that Gregory didn't like bedding beautiful women. He just didn't like bedding beautiful women of respectable pedigree.

First, Jonathan would do everything in his power to prevent his brother's marriage from occurring. And if that failed, he could at least gain Miss Pembroke's confidence and learn enough to prove in court that his brother's marriage was never consummated.

The problem was that Miss Pembroke, like so many others of her sex, was clearly in love with his brother. The way she looked at Gregory with love in her eyes was no sham. She could no more conceal her love than she could camouflage her fiery tresses.

How fortunate that Gregory did not fancy decent women.

Jonathan kissed Miss Pembroke's dainty white hand. "Now that I see you, I shall be very jealous of my brother."

She smiled and looked up adoringly at Gregory, who, uncharacteristically, lifted her hand to his mouth for a tender kiss. 'Twas all an act to fool him, of course. But he knew his brother far too well to be taken in.

Miss Pembroke's beautiful sister and sister-in-law were in the nursery cooing over an infant child. Jonathan could not possibly have determined if the

babe was a girl or boy. As far as he could tell, all
babies looked the same. As he watched the three
women—who were the three prettiest women he had
ever seen in one gathering—lavishing attention on the
babe, it became clear to him that Miss Pembroke genuinely cared for her baby niece or nephew. It was also
clear that she was cut out to be an adoring mother.
Like his own. A pity his brother would starve Miss
Pembroke's maternal instincts.

Jonathan turned to Gregory. "Even with your marriage imminent, I cannot fathom you as a father."

The smile on Gregory's face fell. He swallowed. "I
admit I have never longed for an heir as other men do,
but if that is what makes my dearest wife happy, I shall
oblige her." Gregory looked at Glee, whose cheeks
grew scarlet.

"I daresay my sister will tell you all the pain and
discomfort of lying-in quickly fades from memory
once you hold your child in your arms," Glee said.
"Of course, I was present at Georgette's birth, and I've
yet to recall the ordeal without a strong desire to avoid
such pain." She flashed a smile. "My sister, Felicity,
will become a mother by All Souls' Day. She and her
husband are most excited, are you not?" she asked,
turning shining eyes on Felicity.

The girl loved his brother so dearly she feigned an
aversion to childbirth she was far from feeling.
Jonathan's heart went out to Miss Pembroke. What
would she have if she married Gregory? Certainly no
babes. A cold, lonely bed. And the knowledge that her
rakish husband found comfort in the beds of other
women. Glee Pembroke deserved better.

"We cannot fill the nursery fast enough," Felicity
Moreland said with a laugh.

Jonathan's glance darted to Mrs. Moreland's tiny
waist, and he found it difficult to believe she was in-

creasing. He envied the woman's fortunate husband. For Felicity Moreland, with her blond fairness and shimmering blue eyes, was an extraordinary beauty. Like her sister.

From the nursery, Miss Pembroke led him to her brother's study, where the viscount was working with his steward.

"How good it is to see you again, Jonathan," George said as he stood up.

Despite Lord Sedgewick's wild ways, Jonathan had always liked him. But the man who stood in front of him bore little resemblance to the irresponsible fellow he had been before his marriage. The viscount he had known would never have bothered meeting with his steward for he would have been too busy drinking and gambling and bedding loose women. That he was obviously content at Hornsby was indeed a surprise.

If only his brother *could* be more like Sedgewick. If Gregory could only do what their father had wanted him to do. But Gregory could no more change his ways than a leopard could change its spots. A more inflexible man than Gregory had never been born.

The three of them left Sedgewick with his steward and went for a walk around the park. 'Twould be difficult to malign his brother while he was present, but Jonathan must lay the foundation. "While I envy you your beautiful betrothed," Jonathan said to his brother, who was holding the hand of his affianced, "I cannot help but pity poor Miss Pembroke." He turned to her. "Though you've known my brother most of your life, I daresay you cannot truly know of his character. Else you wouldn't have him."

Gregory's eyes went cold as he contemptuously studied his brother.

Glee laughed. "I assure you I know all of your brother's vices, but I'm convinced that with maturity—

and marriage—he will change for the better. You'll be proud of him."

They had nearly completed the circle around the park and now faced Hornsby Manor. It was a magnificent house—truly fit for a peer of the realm—with its aged brick and many wings jutting from the regal edifice. How proud their father would have been to align his family with such a noble house. If only Gregory weren't so blasted stubborn! He was no more flexible in his opinions than an iron sword. Jonathan knew with a conviction as strong as truth that even Miss Pembroke's many attributes had failed to capture his brother's prurient heart. "My brother has brought me pride in many ways. His athletic feats are still talked of at Oxford."

"I'm afraid, my love, Jonathan is exactly like our father was," Gregory said to Glee. "He tends to judge me with the eyes of a disappointed father. Papa wanted me to be like him. To tend to the estates at Sutton Hall. To be a faithful husband and sire hordes of children to carry on our respectable family name."

"What you have cited are things Miss Pembroke must also desire," Jonathan said, giving Glee a furtive look.

She lowered her lashes. "If you think to make me change my mind, dear brother, you must think again. I have loved Bl—Gregory all my life. Nothing will make me cry off." Color hiked up her fair cheeks.

Just as he thought. He was, indeed, powerless to prevent the marriage. Jonathan would have to wait until Gregory's poor wife was prostrate from his ill treatment. Then Jonathan would secure the information he needed to challenge his father's will.

Jonathan offered them a smile he was far from feeling. "I shall leave you two lovebirds alone. Daresay I need to clean up properly before supper. It's at six of the clock, is it not?"

"Yes, we keep country hours," Glee said.

"I'm sure you'll want to rest after your tiresome journey, too," Gregory added.

"Mother's resting as we speak," Jonathan answered.

Gregory stiffened as he watched his brother enter the house. Aurora was here though he had not invited her. He had wanted only those who would wish him well—those he loved and those who cared for him—at his wedding. Though it was not to be a conventional marriage, it would be Gregory's only marriage. A most solemn—and sacred—occasion. And he did not want his she-devil of a stepmother here.

"Are you all right, Blanks?" Glee asked, concern in her voice. Her beloved's face had gone white, and it frightened her.

"Never been better," he said, as he turned to her, a grin pinching his tanned cheek.

She colored. 'Twas so embarrassing to face him after she had blathered of her devotion to him. *I have loved Gregory all my life.* Why had she allowed those words to slip from her tongue? Now Blanks would know what a scheming hoyden she was.

But to her complete surprise, Blanks swept her up into his powerful arms and gave her a hearty—though passionless—kiss. Then he set her down.

His handsome face was all smiles, his dark eyes glittering. "You were magnificent! Perhaps it *was* my lucky day the day you forced me into marriage. *I have loved Gregory all my life!* What a clever thing to say! I commend you on your ability to think under pressure.

I can see you'll do well convincing my brother ours is a love match."

Her heart fluttered. *It was a love match. A one-sided love match.* "Trust me, dear Blanks, I can be most convincing. You'll not regret our uncommon alliance."

She placed a gentle hand on his forearm. "Oh, look, Blanks! The leaves on the elm are beginning to blossom. A new beginning. Just like us."

TEN

Before dinner that night Glee felt obliged to introduce herself to Blanks's stepmother for a few private words. Already dressed in the russet gown she would wear to dinner, Glee strode to the east wing and softly knocked on the door to the room given Mrs. Blankenship.

"Yes?" a voice called from within.

"It's Glee Pembroke. Do you have a moment, Mrs. Blankenship?"

"Come in." The woman's voice was harsh.

Perhaps she was not yet dressed, and Glee would be viewed as an intrusion. "If you're not ready . . ."

"I'm ready." She sounded impatient.

Glee slowly turned the knob and entered the sage-green chamber as Mrs. Blankenship's maid exited. Aurora Blankenship stood up to greet Glee. The woman was twice Glee's age and was barely taller than Glee, though her thick body with no waist differed vastly from Glee's. Mrs. Blankenship bore a striking resemblance to Jonathan.

"I wished to meet with you privately before our families assemble for dinner," Glee said.

The woman stared openly at Glee, her green eyes slitted as she moved her head up and down the length of Glee. "I see Gregory has done very well for himself. You're not only pretty, but you also come from a titled family. My husband would have approved."

"You malign your son if you believe he selected me for such insignificant attributes."

Aurora Blankenship tossed back her head, her gray-ish-brown locks skittering, and laughed heartily. "First of all, Gregory is *not* my son," Mrs. Blankenship said with emphasis when she finished laughing. "And secondly, I hardly need malign Gregory when his actions do so thorough a job of it already."

Glee instantly regretted her unwise decision of making herself known to the vicious woman who had been the only mother Blanks had ever known. "If you think to poison my mind against Gregory, I warn you, I'll hear none of it. There's nothing you can say that will make me love him less."

Mrs. Blankenship's eyes narrowed as she continued her lazy perusal of Glee. "You're merely attracted to his tall body and pleasing appearance." Her eyes lowered and her voice softened. "A pity my Jonathan did not inherit his father's height—or his wealth."

Glee's heart melted for her beloved Blanks. Had he always been forced to endure this wicked woman's prejudice? "My only pity is for you, Mrs. Blankenship, for not knowing the wonderful man your stepson has become."

Then, with no further words, Glee turned and left the woman's room.

Only Jonathan separated Glee from Aurora Blankenship at dinner. A most unpleasant dinner, to be sure, for Aurora Blankenship preferred to dominate the conversation.

"Now that you're to be a married man," she said to

Blanks, who sat across the table from her, "you could learn economy from your brother. Jonathan's scorn for frivolousness allows him to channel his money into more worthy endeavors than your set is prone to do."

To Glee's consternation, Blanks made no effort to change the direction of her conversation. Nor did he in any way acknowledge it. He merely listened to her, his ever-present grin sliding across his face, and continued eating his sturgeon. Had he grown inured to Aurora's humiliations? Poor, sweet Blanks.

When the second course was served, Aurora started in on George. "A relief it is to see you nicely settled here at Hornsby and not gallivanting with Gregory's set. I used to tell Mr. Blankenship it was a pity Lord Sedgewick should be caught in Gregory's net, for I believe you must have more in common with my Jonathan. My uncle, you know, was Sir Quimby."

"I did not know," George said absently as he studied his spoon full of peas.

The horrid woman was jealous of Gregory's association with a peer! Nothing on earth would give Glee greater pleasure than hurling her own peas into Aurora Blankenship's mean face.

The woman rambled on about Blanks's many shortcomings, and he never once defended himself. Glee's heart bled for him.

Then Aurora addressed Glee. "I hope you're up to the challenge of being married to Gregory. Time and again his father had to extricate the boy from one scrape after another. Now that my dear husband's gone, I fear you'll be called upon any number of times to bail him out of trouble."

"I will always be there when my husband needs me, but I can't fathom him doing anything of which I would disapprove. You see, Mrs. Blankenship, I've known him almost as long as you, and I find nothing at all objectionable in him." *Nothing but sharing Carlotta Ennis's bed.* And that she had already accounted for.

To Glee's utter surprise, Jonathan clapped his hands together. "Well spoken, Miss Pembroke."

The brothers exchanged amused glances, Blanks's smile ever ready. So Jonathan *was* aware of his mother's cruelty toward his brother. Aware but not unreceptive. Glee decided she detested mother as well as son. When she and Blanks were married, she vowed to have nothing more to do with the pair of them.

A lump lodged in Gregory's throat the next morning as he stood at the front of the little chapel, his brother at his side, watching George escort Glee down the aisle. His wedding day. His bride was undoubtedly the most beautiful woman he had ever beheld. She wore a gown of snowy white silk threaded with silver. A cascaded veil of filmy white silk did little to hide her glorious auburn hair. Upon the satiny skin above her bodice, his mother's emeralds rested. They were a perfect match to Glee's sparkling eyes.

Glee came to stand beside him, and he took her quivering hand, only to realize his own was also shaking. She looked up at him, squeezed his hand, and smiled.

It was such a simple gesture, yet her easy smile calmed him. After all, his bride was just Glee, a woman he had known since childhood. A female he had treated as another male for most of those years. Most of all, she was a friend. Perhaps marriage, to Glee, would not be so repugnant as he had imagined marriage to be.

This would be his only wedding. Ever. And he was glad to share it with those he cared most about. George. Jonathan. Appleton and the twins. And Glee.

For he could not deny he cared for her. He just did not care for her in the same way a man cared for his wife.

He was not nearly as nervous as he had thought he would be when the vicar started the wedding ceremony, but he was completely astonished over his own response when the vicar asked him, "Do your take this woman to be your wife?"

Gregory swallowed hard, and in a voice trembling with emotion, he answered, "Yes." Then his eyes filled with tears. A glance at his bride confirmed that her eyes also had become moist.

After the ceremony, he and Glee served as host and hostess at their wedding breakfast. Here is where he made every effort to convince Jonathan of his love for Glee. Every time she spoke, he looked at her with glowing admiration. Between each course, he took her slim hand within his and pressed soft kisses into her palm until the blush colored her cheeks.

When the servants carried away her unfinished toast, his brows lowered in concern. When she did not touch the comfits, he stroked her face as would a lover, and he inquired if she felt altogether well. With smiling eyes she looked at him and assured him she felt all that was healthy but that her appetite was not as great as the lavish fare that spread over the table and throughout every sideboard in the room and the adjacent butler's pantry.

Once the last of the sweetmeats was consumed, Gregory rose and, with a voice choking with emotion, thanked all of their friends and loved ones for attending their wedding. He looked down at Glee adoringly. "My bride and I must journey now to Bath in order to arrive before dark."

In the event of inclement weather, he had brought

Glee's new carriage to Hornsby for their return to Bath. He saw her into it, and spread a rug over her lap.

"She won't need that with you to warm her!" George said good-naturedly.

Glee turned crimson.

With the carriage door still open, the two of them said goodbye to their well-wishers.

Then, meeting Appleton's gaze, Gregory challenged his friends. "A pony says my matched bays will get us to Bath before your old nags."

"You're on!" Appleton responded, hurriedly moving toward the stable.

Elvin answered for himself and his twin. "We'll hate to take the groom's money," he boasted with a smile before he and his brother started after Appleton.

With the carriage rattling over the long avenue to the manor house, Glee pulled off her headdress and settled back into the squabs with a sigh. Even during their wedding day, she would not be alone with her new husband. They would share the day with his bachelor friends. And she would appear to be enjoying every minute of their company.

She smiled at her husband. "The bays are beautiful, but do you really think they can outdistance a lone rider? George always said Appleton was every bit as talented as you in selecting outstanding horseflesh. And five-and-twenty pounds is a great deal of money to lose."

Blanks shrugged. "It'll be close, but it will make the ride faster—and jollier." He moved across the carriage and sat beside her, taking her hand in his. "Never worry about the money. You are now a very rich woman."

It seemed peculiar that she was now rich. Even more peculiar was the idea that her husband believed her mercenary enough to wed for money. "I daresay the wager's quite a lark. Mr. Appleton and the twins are so very much fun to be around."

"Quite," he uttered, lifting the carriage's privacy curtain in order to catch a glimpse of his challenging friends. "They haven't finished saddling yet, I suppose," he said, dropping the curtain and meeting her gaze.

"You were a wonderful husband! So solicitous you almost fooled me. I am sure you fooled Jonathan."

"Let us hope," Gregory said solemnly.

Now it was time for Glee to begin Phase II of her battle plan.

"Oh, please, Blanks, have the driver slow down so I can make a wager with the fellows. Since I am now a woman of means, I shall wager five quid that we win."

Blanks straightened up and shot her a queer look. "I'll do no such thing. A lady doesn't wager on horses."

"Silly, I'm not a lady anymore. I shall be one of the bloods. We'll have great fun."

"Bloods? That is not a term a lady uses. And I won't have my wife cavorting with bloods."

Though she rather liked that he referred to her as his wife—it sounded so blessedly good—she had failed to achieve her goal. For her Phase II consisted of emulating a fast woman. After all, Blanks had always been enamored of fast women. "Really, Blanks, you sound so terribly prudish. Better that I *cavort* with your friends than take a lover. And I've promised not to do that the first year of our marriage."

The very idea of Glee taking a lover—their first year of marriage or at any time thereafter—fairly singed his hair. Glee was, after all, a lady. A complete innocent. Besides, he could not claim another man's child as his own. Ever. Nor would he countenance the thought of seeing his wife prone on childbed. "Having my wife spoken of in demeaning terms is something I will not tolerate. You *will* behave with propriety."

Her mouth slid into a challenging smile that reached her emerald eyes. "We'll see."

He struggled to control his rising temper.

"What time think you we will arrive in Bath?" she asked.

He shrugged. "The weather's fine. The horses are well rested. I hope to be there by nightfall."

"It does get dark so dreadfully early this time of the year."

He nodded absently.

"Have you seen Thomas's little lame lad?"

At first he did not comprehend. Then he remembered the lad in front of the milliner's where he purchased Carlotta's pretty hats, and he vaguely remembered that Felicity's husband had provided assistance that enabled the little boy to walk.

It brought to mind his own recent preoccupation with the urchin in front of his solicitor's office. He had been unable to shake the pity he felt for the wretched boy. The lad was so small to be so ill-treated. "The milliner's lad prospers, and he walks everywhere now—though he has a pronounced limp."

"He's not the milliner's lad. His mother assists the milliner. Isn't it wonderful what one man's care and ministration can do for helpless creatures? I vow, now that I'm a woman of means, I shall help other prostrate children."

Had she intruded on his thoughts? 'Twas the very same thing he had been thinking. "Then we must start with the wretched lad who hangs about my solicitor's office. When last I saw him, snow was falling on the ground and the lad had no coat, and there were great, gaping holes in his shoes."

Her brows lowered and she murmured her pity. "Surely you offered him assistance?"

"I merely gave the clerk enough money to procure shoes and coat for the lad."

"We'll have to do more, Blanks."

His very thoughts. "Yes, I know, my dear."

"I know what we can do!" she shrieked with excitement. "Since we're to have no children of our own, we'll bring him to live at Har—I mean at Blankenship House."

"I've told you I don't want children."

"But you've admitted you have worried about the lad. That proves you *like* children."

"Of course I like children. They're such helpless creatures."

"And you've agreed to help the most helpless."

"Yes, but having the responsibility of raising one is something altogether different. 'Tis much easier to empty one's pockets."

"Does the boy have a family?"

"Mr. Willowby's clerk said he had no father. His mother cleans the building where Willowby's offices are housed."

He watched her slim little face as she nodded thoughtfully. "You must introduce me to the boy."

"As you like." Gregory lifted the curtain and saw Appleton a distance of half a mile behind on the level country road. He had gained considerably on the twins, who were but two specks on the horizon.

"Did you ask your stepmother to our wedding?" Glee asked.

How had she guessed? He had kept his dislike of Aurora as concealed as a grave. "I did not."

Glee's eyes narrowed. "A more beastly woman I've never met! I declare, I don't know how you tolerated life under that woman's roof."

"Another thing on which you and I agree."

"Why do you allow her to remain mistress at Sutton Hall?"

"Only until you come, my dear."

"It will be my pleasure to usurp the woman, for knowing your amiability, I surmise that she has always been the evil stepmother."

A feeling of warmth and contentment mingled with Glee's rosewater fragrance rushed over him. "You exaggerate my amiability, I'm afraid. Where Aurora is concerned, I've been no saint."

"But you could have been no more than a babe when she had to take the place of your mother. You could hardly have been mean-spirited then."

"I suppose not." He shifted his weight and stretched out his long legs. Glee's questioning made him uncomfortable.

"Did she always show so marked a partiality toward Jonathan?"

"Who can blame her? Jonathan was her very own flesh and blood. Not the progeny of a dead woman whom she envied excessively."

"She was jealous of your mother?"

He smiled as if he had been asked to recall a humorous event. "She had every portrait of my mother— indeed, everything that indicated my mother had ever lived at Sutton Hall—removed when she married my father. I only knew of my mother's loveliness from the servants. Aurora could never bring herself to utter my mother's name. She vengefully referred to her predecessor as *your mother*. I think, more than anything, it was to remind me that she was *not* my mother."

"So she was never affectionate to you," Glee said sorrowfully.

He gave a bitter laugh. "Hardly."

"Yet she was affectionate with Jonathan?"

He continued to smile. "He was unquestionably the light of her life. She was forever lamenting that our father's lands would not go to him, since he was the good son."

"She said that in your presence?" Glee asked incredulously.

"Every day."

"So you determined to show her how truly bad you could be."

He chuckled. "Something like that."

"I vow, I detest the woman excessively!" She turned to him, "I don't see how you could be close to Jonathan."

"I wouldn't call it close. Naturally, I love him. He's my little brother."

"Did he resent that you—and not he—was first-born?"

Gregory shrugged. "I don't think so. At least not until later when he began to fear I would squander away Sutton Hall. Then he rather aligned himself with his mother. Also, being a pinchpenny, he heartily disapproves of the manner in which I spend money, or to quote him, the manner in which I waste money."

"I don't see how he could not be jealous of you. You're far more handsome and personable. You excel in sport. And you control the purse strings. It's only natural he would resent you."

No woman—not even Carlotta, who professed to love him—had ever taken such an interest in his forlorn youth. Nor had anyone else ever guessed the extent of his childhood suffering. Yet, his slim wife, who wasn't much more than a child herself, displayed uncanny understanding of human nature. *"Resent* isn't the right word. There's always been some degree of jealousy, which was only natural. I was bigger and stronger and faster—all things he envied. I daresay there's not a younger brother in the kingdom who hasn't envied his older brother at one time or another."

She smiled wistfully. "Or younger sister. I used to lament that I couldn't be blond and blue-eyed like my beautiful sister. But I've always loved her fiercely."

"As I love Jonathan and he loves me." He gave her a long look. "While I admit your sister is an extraordinarily beautiful woman, I think you are even prettier."

A smile slanted across his face as he watched the color rise in her cheeks.

"Remember to say such flattering things when we are in company. All of Bath will believe you're in love with me," she said with a self-conscious laugh.

"It will take no effort for me to compliment your beauty. It's as evident as the stars in the sky."

"Now you've gone and put me to the blush."

"My blushing bride," he said with a possessiveness he did not feel.

She looked up at him with hopeful eyes. "I cannot believe I've known you all my life and am still learning more about you. I think that's important for a husband and wife. It's important, too, to be friends." She lowered her voice to a soft murmur. "You'll always be my greatest friend, Blanks." Then she squinted her eyes and declared, "And I must warn you I most decidedly hate Aurora."

It seemed rather an odd thing to have a woman for his champion. Only his nurse—who had never been foolish enough to stand up to Aurora—had ever seen Aurora's injustice. Would Glee still care so greatly for him when he left her childless or when he slaked his hunger in the arms of another woman?

ELEVEN

When Appleton flew across Bath's Pulteney Bridge before their carriage, Glee was far more concerned over the hard-worked bays than she was over her husband's lost five-and-twenty pounds. For in his quest to win, Blanks had ordered the coachman to push them to their limit.

But after alighting from the carriage in front of the new town house and examining the horses for herself, Glee realized Blanks knew his horses' limits far better than she did. They were heavily lathered but other than that appeared to be unharmed. She removed her gloves and stroked each of their muzzles, murmuring softly to them.

Once the coachman took them off through the dusk to the mews, she turned to her husband and Appleton with merriment on her face. By this time the twins had ridden up and were dismounting. "You gentlemen must do us the honor of being the first to dine with us at our new home. I'm sure the staff Blanks has procured will be able to assemble a humble meal," she said.

Appleton's puzzled gaze shifted to Blanks. Color rose in Glee's face for she knew Appleton feared he would be intruding on their wedding night.

"Yes, do," Blanks assured his friends.

"Very kind of you, Miss—I mean, Mrs. Blankenship," Appleton said. "We'll return to our lodgings and hope to make ourselves presentable. Should be back in an hour."

"We'll be delighted," she said happily. "And you must call me Glee for I shall now address you by your Christian name."

"Don't see how I could call you that," Appleton said. Though she would far rather have been alone all night with Blanks, surrounding herself with his friends and becoming one of them was part of her battle plan.

Blanks came to stand beside her and draped his arm around her as they watched his friends ride back in the direction of Bath Abbey. Then Blanks turned toward the town house and opened the door for her.

A man Glee assumed was the butler came rushing forth, a worried look on his face until he recognized Blanks. "Good evening, Mr. Blankenship."

Blanks nodded stiffly, then glanced at Glee. "My dear, I should like to present your new butler to you." He shot a glance at the middle-aged man whose skin was very white and whose hair was very black. "Hampton."

Hampton bowed to Glee. "I am pleased to make your acquaintance, Mrs. Blankenship. I shall tell the housekeeper you are here."

But he had no need to do so because a capable-looking woman who appeared to be a decade older than Glee came climbing up from the basement, a smile on her face as she greeted Glee with a curtsy. "I'm your housekeeper. My name's Miss Roberts, and I shall be most happy to show you all I have discovered about your new house, though I daresay you're fatigued from the journey."

"Tomorrow will be soon enough," Glee said, trying

not to sound too authoritarian. "I'm afraid I've got a demanding request for tonight. We will need dinner for five as we've invited a few of Mr. Blankenship's friends over, but we don't expect anything fancy."

"Oh, that will be no problem. Mr. Blankenship told me you'd be returning tonight, so we've a fine meal prepared. Three more will be no inconvenience whatsoever."

"Very good," Glee said. Then, slipping her arm through Blanks's, she added, "If you don't mind, my husband and I will sweep through the house. It's our first home together, and we're very excited."

Miss Roberts smiled and bowed her head. "I hope you find everything in order." Then she disappeared back down the stairs.

"Oh, Blanks, it's such a wonderful house! And it's ours." She looked up at him, and his smile reached his flashing dark eyes.

He patted her hand. "I must admit having a town house—and a wife—is making me feel very old."

They walked along the marble foyer and entered the morning room, which was bathed in pea-green. "You're still just four and twenty, and quite fancy free," she said, walking through a door into Blanks's study.

"This is where we gentlemen will smoke after dinner," he said.

She nodded up at him, unable to conceal her pleasure at being here in their house, with her arm entwined with her husband's. And she gave a silent prayer of thanks that she had been granted the first part of her wish. Accomplishing the second part was now up to her. She had to earn his love.

They strolled from the gentleman's study across the foyer to the gold dining room. A fire had been started, and the table was already covered with a white cloth.

Glee saw that a place was laid at each end of the long table. She made a mental note to move hers next to Blanks. As they were leaving that room, a footman carrying three more place settings entered the dining chamber.

From the dining room, she and Blanks strolled to the saloon. "As much as I like Mrs. Harrison's furniture, I deplore the decoration of this room," Glee said.

He glanced around the vast chamber and with a puzzled expression asked, "What's wrong with it?"

"The pastels will never do. They're so . . . so insipid. I like bold colors, and they are all the rage in decorating."

He patted her hand. "Then you'll have to redecorate it."

"Exactly what I was thinking," Glee said with a laugh.

"Shall we go upstairs?" he asked.

She nodded shyly. Their private chambers were located on the next floor.

Holding hands, they silently climbed the broad stairway. The first room they came to was Glee's study, where a cabriolet-legged escritoire stood in its center. Sky-blue walls were barely distinguishable from the sky-blue silk draperies.

"I daresay the blue has to go," Blanks said, grinning. "Too pale for my wife."

Sweet heaven, but she loved those words! *My wife.* "I shall be forced to redecorate yet another room," she said.

They went through a door in her study to her sleeping chamber, which was also done in sky-blue. Her cheeks hot, Glee avoided looking at the focal point of the room. The bed. Then Blanks disengaged his arm from hers and looked at her seriously.

Her heart began to drum madly. Was he going to

kiss her? Carry her to the satin bed and make love to her? But, of course, he wouldn't. Blanks was completely inflexible. If he said he would not bed her, she could take his words for gospel. Oh dear, what had she done—tying herself to a man who was dead set against taking his conjugal rights. What if she proved unable to change him? Oh dear, she would not like that at all.

She watched him from beneath lowered lashes and was surprised to see him remove money from his purse.

"It's time I give you the funds with which to embark on your redecorating, my dear. Actually, the tradesmen can send all the household bills to me, but you will need your own money. Do you think you can manage on three hundred a quarter? Of course, I'll take responsibility for the staff and household purchases."

She was stunned. Three hundred pounds! 'Twas more than she'd had at her disposal in her entire life. She leaped to her tiptoes and flung her arms about his neck, kissing him on the cheek. "It's most generous."

Seeing the somber look on his face, she fell back to the soles of her feet. "I'm afraid you'll have to get used to my affectionate outbursts. It's my nature. I hope I haven't offended you."

A heartwarming smile leaped to his face even as he stepped back from her. "What man would object to having a beautiful woman kiss him?"

He might not object, but he certainly didn't reciprocate. She would have to console herself with his declaration of her beauty.

"If I remember correctly, your chambers can be entered through that door," she said, pointing to a side wall of her chamber.

He nodded.

"Would you mind if I have a look?" she asked.

He stepped toward the door. "Not at all."

All she could see when she entered his olive-green chamber was the huge bed in the center of the room. Would she ever lie there beside him? The very thought of it caused a liquid rush to center low in her body. She must not think of it or rush her fences. This would take time and behaving the strumpet, while tempting, was beyond her. How did strumpets behave? She would have to ask . . . Blanks? A gentleman never spoke of such to his wife. Maybe one of the twins could be coaxed into giving her pointers. Or better yet, Jefferson.

She must think of something else to comment on. Finally, she blurted out the first thing that entered her head. "I shall very much like having my chamber close to you in a strange new house. It will make me feel quite safe knowing you're so near at hand."

Uncharacteristically, he did not smile. Was he thinking about sharing the bed with her? More likely, he was thinking of *not* sharing the bed with her. "If you ever have nightmares, call me," he said in a reassuring voice.

"I will." She turned toward her own chambers. "I had best clean up from the journey. I believe I'll ring for a bath."

Dinner was a two-hour affair. Glee used the time to get to know her husband's friends. Not that she did not already know them through her brother. But the relationship she was about to embark upon with them put their friendships in an altogether different light. She started with the discovery that the twin who sat to her immediate left was the shy one, Melvin. She made it her mission to bring him out. "Does it not vex you, Melvin, that no one seems to be able to distinguish between you and your twin, though I daresay the two of you are vastly different?"

He carefully chewed his mutton before responding. Then he cleared his throat. "I've always been content to let Elvin draw the attention. It suits my reserved nature. But it has never ceased to amaze me that to the majority of the population, we are one and the same."

How different the brothers talked! Where Melvin was outgoing, personable, and given to slang, his brother thought carefully before uttering a syllable and spoke with the articulation of a prime minister. "I daresay that's because, to those who don't know you, physical appearance, unfortunately, weighs more heavily. It brings to mind a homely girl who may be beautiful on the inside, but because her appearance is unremarkable, she's overlooked."

"A good analogy, I think," he said, then lifted his claret.

She doubted the word *analogy* would even have been understood by his brother. While her husband and Appleton and Elvin spoke of an upcoming auction at Tattersall's, she continued her conversation with Melvin. "Besides your difference in nature, are there other significant differences between you and Elvin? It appears the two of you rather enjoy the same types of activities."

"I'm afraid I'm not very assertive. I tend to let my brother lead the way. He has a keen sense of fun, so I'm rarely disappointed."

"Then you're not as interested in sporting pleasures and merriment as your brother?"

He thought for a moment before answering. "To a certain degree, I am. But I also enjoy reading—a pursuit I never seem to have the time for."

"It's the same with me," she confided. "There's

never enough time for one to read all that one wishes to read." She sipped her wine. It was very smooth. In fact, Miss Roberts had set a very fine table. Which would reflect very well on Glee.

She looked up and saw that her husband was smiling at her. "Please, Melvin, don't allow my wife to bore you with talk of books." Instead of scorn, Blanks's voice rang with pride, a pride that puzzled her.

Elvin answered for his twin. "Daresay me brother craves such a conversation. I'm forever pulling his head out of a book. Don't understand the fascination they hold over him."

"I'm told it's rather the same with my wife," Blanks lamented in a light tone.

"Then you don't have to worry about entertaining Mrs. Blankenship," Appleton said to Blanks. "Just foist Melvin on her. Daresay the two will be as content as two pigs in slop." Then he turned to Glee, a look of embarrassment on his face. "Pardon me, Mrs. Blankenship. Didn't mean to imply that you were a burd—I mean, oh, confound it!"

"And I daresay he regrets likening you to a pig," Elvin interjected.

Glee met her husband's dancing eyes, and both of them broke into heaps of laughter.

When the men removed themselves to the smoking room, Glee invited herself. "Since there are no other women present, I prefer to join you men. Just think of me as one of you, and don't fret over the smoke. I love the smell of cigars. It reminds me of my dear papa."

Silence fell over the group when she sat beside Blanks on the sofa. Her presence was no doubt a hindrance to their easy flow of conversation. So she took it upon herself to introduce a topic of conversation the gentlemen could embrace. She had not lived her nineteen years with her sport-mad brother not to know what interested young bloods. "When does the racing begin here in Bath? I never can remember."

"Next week," Appleton replied. "Stalwart shall race here for the first time."

"I saw him last March at Newmarket," Blanks added. "A magnificent creature."

For the next hour, the gentlemen spoke of nothing but racing while she feigned a hearty, though silent, interest. She was thankful of the opportunity to watch her husband without drawing his attention. That his friends deferred to him on every subject filled her with pride. His easy wit and perpetual grin were two things she would never tire of. She studied his thick, dark hair and the way it nearly matched his shimmering eyes. Her eyes trailed to his well-tailored coat which stretched across his broad shoulders. Then she looked back up into his handsome face and found that he smiled at her with a grin that lifted only one side of his mouth. His customary amused grin. She easily returned the smile.

Though Blanks invited his friends to play loo, they declined in a most self-conscious fashion. It was obvious they did not want to intrude on the Blankenships' wedding night.

After she and Blanks saw the men from the house, Blanks took her hand, and they began to mount the stairs. Her pulse accelerated and for the first time that night, Glee could find no words to say. Then they came to the door of her sleeping chamber.

"You'll make me a fine hostess, Glee," he said. "You possess the facility of putting guests at ease. You've made a conquest of my friends." He paused. Then he bent to kiss her forehead. "Good night, my dear."

She squeezed the hand that still held hers. "Good night, Blanks."

She watched somberly as he walked to his own chamber. Such was the wedding night of their most unusual marriage, she reflected uneasily. Of course, it was just as she had expected. She must be patient. As a young colt must be slowly brought to saddle and bridle, Blanks would eventually seek her bed. First, she had to get him used to their marriage.

TWELVE

For the next few days Glee contented herself with buying up half of Bath. She sent for painters and ordered new draperies and silk damask wall coverings, and she underwent fittings for new ball gowns that would signal her position as a married woman. She grew anxious to wear her daring new gowns and gauge her husband's reaction to them. The new Glee would look nothing like the innocent virgin she had appeared during her last season in Bath.

All these shopping excursions she conducted on her own, completely alone. It was the first time in her life she had shopped without her sister or a friend. She had considered asking her timid friend, Miss Arbuckle, to accompany her but quickly dismissed such a thought. 'Twould not be in keeping with the new Glee, who would cut a dashing—though scandalous—path through the watering city. All part of her plan to snare Blanks's heart, of course.

Miss Arbuckle would serve another purpose. Later.

For her first assembly as a married woman, Glee chose her most daring dress. Her abigail Patty's eyes danced when she beheld the scarlet dress. "I loves red," she commented. "It's like a poppy in my mum's garden. Don't know why it's out of fashion. I daresay your wearing it will make it all the rage again."

But the abigail's tone changed once she had assisted her mistress into it. "Oh, dear," the young maid said. "You will have to return for a better fitting."

Standing up straight and regal before her looking glass, Glee perused the new gown from every possible angle. First, she faced the glass. Yes, it draped off the shoulders, leaving her white shoulders completely bare. Then she turned sideways, secretly pleased at the view of her breasts barely dipping into the skimpy bodice. But the dress did cover her breasts, and in so doing, exaggerated the size of her modest bosom. It pleased her that she looked somewhat like Carlotta Ennis—though her bosom was actually much smaller than her rival's. She turned around and glanced over her shoulder into the glass and observed the way the train commenced near her waist, revealing her ivory back. Completing her turn, her eyes trailed along the length of the clinging silk crepe gown. "It fits exactly as I instructed Madame Herbert."

Patty's eyes widened. "My mama said the ways of the *ton* were different."

Patty's shock was exactly the reaction Glee was hoping for. Blanks did so hunger after loose women. She only hoped she looked loose enough.

There was a soft knock on her chamber door. She glanced at Patty and with a slight nod dismissed her. "My husband will fasten my necklace," she said.

Patty opened the door to Blanks, then excused herself as Blanks came into Glee's dressing chamber.

"Oh, Blanks, do fasten these rubies for me," she said, handing him the jewels. "Then I shall be ready for the assembly." She cast an embarrassed glance at him. She had felt utterly confident before he stepped inside her chamber. Now she felt as if she stood before him completely naked.

To her surprise, he surveyed her under lowered, scowling brows. "Surely you don't intend to wear that dress in public, do you?"

Though crestfallen, she held up her head proudly. "Why not?"

"A maiden does not dress like that."

"Like what?" she challenged.

"Like a doxy."

She took a single white glove from her dressing table and slipped her hand into it, finger by finger, seductively looking up at him as she carefully slid up the sleeve. "First of all, dear Blanks, no one at the assembly tonight will think of me as a maiden. To all the world, I'm a married woman." She lifted her long lashes and spoke throatily. "A woman who has been bedded by a man known for his virility. And second, you cannot tell me you object to women who dress as I am, for I know otherwise. Does not Carlotta Ennis dress in much the same fashion as I am dressing?"

"I did not ask Carlotta Ennis to marry me," he said savagely.

"Then you're saying I don't dress as a wife should?"

"Yes, I *am* saying that."

"But, for all practical purposes, I'm not really your wife," she said with a smile. "If I cannot elicit passion in you, it would please me to elicit it in other men."

Anger flared in his dark eyes. "You will do no such thing!"

She began to casually slip on the other glove. "Don't worry, Blanks, I've given you my word I shall not have an affair. And don't worry about your hard-earned reputation as a lady killer. All of Bath will believe you pleasure me well."

Once again, she handed him the rubies. Shooting

her a menacing glare, he took them and fastened them around her graceful white neck, mumbling curses under his breath.

When he finished, she tucked her arm into his as they left the chamber.

Sitting in the carriage on opposite sides from one another, he spoke not a word. All in all, his reaction was quite satisfying. If she didn't know better, she would swear he was acting possessive.

Gregory could not remember when he had been so angry. Even when his solicitor had told him of his father's strange will, his fury had not been this great. Yet, though Glee was his wife, he was powerless to stop her from conducting herself in so bold a manner. How could he impose his will on her when it was his very same will that was keeping her from bearing the children he knew she wanted?

When they arrived at the Upper Assembly Rooms, he escorted her into the ballroom.

Glee looked up at him and flashed a smile. "I daresay you'd rather be in the card room than dancing attendance upon me. I assure you, I shall get along tolerably without you, dearest."

His anger was boiling over. "But, my dear, I've the rest of my life to play cards. Tonight I will dance with my bride." Better him than someone like Jefferson, who might take Glee's new look as an invitation for an affair. And Glee, in her innocence, might very well succumb—out of curiosity or to test her own powers. In that dress she invited a man to put his hands on her, to kiss the creamy swells of her breasts and when she turned, he saw her back—slim, scandalously bare. He took her shawl and laid it across her shoulders. "Be careful, you'll catch a chill."

"How very kind of you," she said, smiling. "The first set must be ours."

The first dance of the set was a minuet. Every time he gazed upon Glee's bodice he had an overwhelming urge to bring the shawl she had hastened to remove. He shuddered when the dance demanded she dip into a curtsy. From the corner of his eye, he saw that Jefferson, too, was watching Glee. Gregory had a strong urge to blacken the man's eye for the way he watched Glee move so gracefully over the dance floor. Whenever Gregory looked up from showering attentions on his wife, Jefferson was watching Glee with naked desire. Gregory found himself enumerating all the women—virgins and married women alike—who had been seduced by Jefferson, and he grew angrier with each note of the music.

The second number of the set was a waltz. Gregory scooped his diminutive wife to his breast and whispered into her ear as the music started. "Remember, I'm to convince the world ours is a love match." Then he proceeded to demonstrate his devotion. He held her as if she were a treasured object and gazed devotedly into her face.

"There's a dilemma I should like your advice on," Glee said. "What is that, my love?"

"Really, Gregory, you don't have to address me so. No one can hear you over the music and conversation. What I want to know is how do I act when I meet Mrs. Ennis in public? Should I give her the cut direct?"

He began to cough. "You will do as I and cut her," he finally said sternly.

"Oh, dear, I hope our marriage hasn't angered your mistress."

"I no longer have a mistress. Remember, I'm supposed to be in love with my wife."

He'd wager a monkey on her lack of sincerity. As

the waltz continued, Gregory realized the time had come for him to warn his young bride about men like Jefferson. "Now that you're a married woman, I must warn you that there are certain men who thrive on taking their pleasure with other men's wives."

"Or widows," Glee interjected.

Carlotta Ennis was proving to be a dead horse Glee never tired of beating. He wished he had never met the black-haired vixen. "Never concern yourself with what happened when I was a bachelor. It's what happens while we are married that concerns me. And since you're my wife, I grow concerned that other men will find you . . . well, not only beautiful, but also . . . available for certain indiscretions."

She gave him a puzzled look.

He did not want her to lose that look of wide-eyed naivete—at least not with another man. Damn it, this marriage was becoming more complicated than he had bargained for.

"Tell me, Blanks, did you ever have a married woman for a lover?"

He cursed under his breath. "Confound it, Glee, we're not talking about me. I've told you what's in my past is now buried. What I'm trying to do is prepare you for the onslaught by unscrupulous men. Men like William Jefferson, who is not received in London."

She smiled up at him, then saw Appleton and the twins standing on the fringes of the ballroom scowling at Blanks. "Surely you're not suggesting Appleton or the twins would want to take advantage of me?"

"Of course not! I trust those three completely. But there are men in this very room who derive a great deal of pleasure in the beds of married women."

"Goodness, Blanks, you will put me to the blush. Surely you don't think I would even contemplate such an alliance?"

How odd it seemed to be having this conversation with the virgin Glee. She was but a babe in the woods. "Of course not. You're a lady. But I felt it my duty—my husbandly duty—to warn you."

"I'm happy to see you're taking your husbandly role so seriously," she said.

The set came to an end, and as he walked his wife to the side of the room, he noticed his friends moving across the ballroom to them.

What he did not notice was that Jefferson also advanced from the opposite side. Jefferson drew Glee's hand into his and settled his lips on it. "I beg the next set with you, Miss—Mrs. Blankenship," he said.

The fiend had wasted no time! Gregory's hands itched to grab the man's stiffly starched cravat, then give him a facer.

"Very well," Glee said sweetly. "How colorful your waistcoat is, Mr. Jefferson." Her eyes skimmed the fuschia that stretched across his slender waist.

Surely Glee could not admire the fop's loud clothing! Then Gregory glanced at her own bright red dress. Why had he never before noticed his wife's taste tended to the gaudy?

From beneath lowered lids, Gregory watched as Jefferson lingered with Glee's hand in his. "Then I'll collect you for the next set." He swept into a gallant bow and left.

Gregory had a mind to forbid his wife to dance with the man, but he could hardly do so in front of his friends. He turned and greeted them. At least *they* had the decency to divert their gazes from his wife's practically uncovered bosom!

Glee greeted each of them with their Christian name and an offer of her hand before Jefferson claimed her.

"Knew we'd have to rescue you," Elvin uttered to

Gregory. "Looks like Mrs. Blankenship will not lack for partners while we try our luck in the card room."

But Gregory could not remove his eyes from Jefferson and Glee. The man's sensual gaze would not drop from her for an instant. From this distance, Gregory had to admit she was devilishly fetching. Any man would . . . Bloody hell! He didn't want any man to look at *his* wife like that. He finally tore his eyes away from Glee and looked up at Melvin. "You fellows go on along. Cards have no allure for me tonight."

"Not when your wife is so deuced lovely!" Appleton said, his glance sweeping to the dance floor.

Glee was utterly vexed with Mr. Jefferson, but she wouldn't give her husband the pleasure of admitting the man's scandalous behavior. Besides, she rather liked it when Blanks acted jealous. She also liked to dress like a doxy for Blanks, but dressing so skimpily for another man was something altogether different. Mr. Jefferson would not remove his gaze from her body. Really! She could not have felt more naked had he removed her gown. Which was something no man—save Blanks—would ever do. She fought the urge to jerk up her bodice, contenting herself with wrapping her shawl around her.

Then, when they waltzed, she had a mind to stomp on Mr. Jefferson's toes.

"Marriage agrees with you," Jefferson said hungrily. "But I must warn you, no matter how thoroughly you give yourself to your husband, he will need other women—if you understand what I mean."

"You no doubt refer to a mistress," she said in an icy voice.

"Just so."

"And in such an event, you no doubt would welcome me to your arms."

"You are a fast learner. To think, a week ago you were the prudish Miss Pembroke. And now you are the sated Mrs. Blankenship."

"Sated by a man who offered me his name as well as his bed."

Jefferson looked solemn. "I would have offered my name if Blankenship hadn't rushed to Warwickshire and claimed you."

The waltz came to an end, and she was happy to get away from William Jefferson.

She was happier still that her husband did not once go to the card room that night, nor did he allow her out of his line of vision.

THIRTEEN

When Blanks joined her in the morning room for breakfast the following morning, Glee's heartbeat accelerated, and her fingers flew to her hair to fluff it. Would his presence always send her heart fluttering while at the same time sinking her own self-worth? Her husband was freshly shaven with carefully pressed clothes, his shirt points white against his bronzed cheeks. When he grinned at her as he strolled into the room, she could have swooned at his booted feet.

"I can see that marriage must agree with you," she said, trying to sound casual, "for George tells me you never rose before noon when you were a bachelor."

He looked up at the clock upon the mantel. "I must meet with my solicitor this morning."

So he hadn't risen for her, she thought dejectedly. She poured him tea and sweetened it for him. "Three spoons of sugar, if I remember correctly," she said.

He sat beside her, a look of admiration on his face. "You have a facility for remembering unimportant things."

Not meeting his gaze, she stirred the tea and handed it to him. "What one's husband desires is nothing trivial. I mean to make you a good wife."

She could see that her response had made him uncomfortable. "What would you like Cook to prepare for dinner tonight?"

He slathered additional butter on his toast. "Whatever suits you."

"You thwart me," she said with a pout. "How can I be a good wife if you will not tell me what it is that suits you? I know you do not like tongue and are partial to lobster. Should you like buttered lobster tonight?"

He grinned at her. "I should like it very much."

"With plum pudding?"

"How did you know of my partiality for plum pudding?" he asked wondrously.

"It's my business, as your wife, to learn what it is that pleases you, dear Blanks." How she loved referring to herself as his wife!

He seemed uncomfortable again when he said, "You mustn't take your role so seriously, for I don't mean to."

Why must he remind her of how acutely he did *not* want a wife? "It pleases me. I told you I very much desired to be a married lady."

"And I have obliged you," he said ruefully.

Over the edge of her cup, she watched his face and the hopelessness that shone in his eyes. Like a trapped animal. And it was all her fault. Would she have to carry this guilt throughout her life? Would he never be content with his fate?

Her husband ate quickly, then excused himself. Her first pangs of disappointment gave way to relief that she would be on her own today. For she planned a frivolous purchase of which he would no doubt disapprove.

Moments after Blanks's departure, she heard Appleton speaking with the butler, and she raced to meet him before Hampton closed the door upon him.

"Please come in, Timothy," she said breathlessly as she swept into the foyer. "There's a matter upon which I need your advice."

He entered the house and followed her to the library where they sat on facing brocade sofas before the fire.

"Really, Mrs. Blankenship, you shouldn't address me by my Christian name in front of others."

"Pooh! Hampton's merely the butler."

"But if the practice becomes too familiar, I fear your reputation will be tarnished, and Blanks wouldn't like that above half."

"Fiddle! You, of all people, must know that my husband is enamored of fast women."

Appleton coughed. "Not for a wife, I daresay."

"I fear you are judging Blanks by your own standards, Timothy. And . . ." she added, "I much prefer that you address me as Glee."

"But . . ." he faltered, his lips a grim line across his face. "Can't do it. Too personal."

"Then perhaps you could give me a nickname."

He studied her for a moment. "Like Pixie?"

"If you think that suits me," she said primly.

"Pixie," he said, as if he were thinking aloud. "Yes, that's much better than . . . that Christian name of yours. Daresay others won't have a clue when I speak of Pixie."

She tucked her feet together and crossed them at the ankles. "You are probably wondering why I wanted to speak to you."

Not removing his gaze from hers, he nodded.

"Since my husband will be tied up with his solicitor for most of the day, there is a matter I must consult you on."

"Can't it wait 'til Blanks returns?"

"No, it can't. I wish to . . . to surprise him." She leaned toward him and spoke with enthusiasm.

"Blanks wishes for me to cut a dashing figure in Bath, and I have decided I will need a high-perch phaeton of my own."

"But you're a . . ."

"I know very well that I'm a woman, and women don't usually possess phaetons, but I think it will suit my new station. And I can purchase it with my own money." Money she had received from her husband, that is.

"Are you certain Blanks won't mind?"

"Quite."

At the coachmaker's Appleton, with his discerning eye, was quickly able to dismiss several inferior vehicles until one was offered that closely resembled Blanks's own phaeton. Appleton nodded his approval, and a price was settled upon.

Glee had not realized a simple little phaeton would cost so much. Two hundred and seventy-five pounds! Which would give her but twenty-five more to last the next three months. She would have to economize enormously.

Glee gazed from the shiny black phaeton back to Appleton. "You've done an excellent job, Timothy. It's exactly what I should like." She turned to the lean coachmaker. "I'll take it today. Send the bill to Mrs. Blankenship at Queen Square. My groom will return soon with a horse," she told him.

As she and Appleton walked back up toward Queen Square, her arm tucked into his, he asked, "Do you know how to drive a phaeton?"

"Oh, yes. I've driven my brother's around Hornsby for years."

"And he didn't object?"

"Not at all." Which wasn't exactly the truth. George had made it clear she could drive his phaeton at Hornsby Manor and its environs, but *not* in a city like Bath. So she had not precisely lied.

She slid an undetected glance at her companion. Timothy Appleton, though he possessed an enormous capacity for levity, was not a man who appealed to women. In company of the fairer sex he was far more reserved than he was with bloods. To make matters even worse, he was quite plain-looking with his fair coloring and slim build. Because he was a man of means, he dressed with quiet good taste, but his lack of height—and lack of a full head of hair—rendered him as unnoticeable as the wallpaper in her bedchamber. No wonder his amusements centered around other bloods!

"Will we see you at the Assembly Room on Thursday?" she asked him.

"Deadly dull affairs, if you ask me," he said.

"That's why your presence—and that of the twins— is so sought after by Blanks. I'm sure the three of you can think of something to liven things up a bit."

"Are you now?" he asked with a chuckle.

He dropped her off at the door to Blankenship House. "I shall see you Thursday night, Pixie," he said with a broad smile.

"We'll have great fun," she answered.

As Glee read through the day's post, her brows lowered. The bills for her dresses far exceeded the twenty-five pounds that remained from the generous allowance Blanks had given her. And she absolutely would *not* ask her husband for more money. Demanding more than her husband had generously offered was not the right way to begin their marriage. Would the dressmakers be content to wait until the next quarter for payment? Oh, dear, what was she to do?

* * *

During the hours he had sat poring over accounts with Willowby, Gregory's thoughts continually flitted to Glee. Though she had tried to hide it, she had become deeply wounded by his insensitive remarks this morning at breakfast. He would have to make it up to her.

When he left the solicitor's office, looking far and wide for signs of the pitiful urchin but not finding him, he went straightaway to the jewelers. A nice little pair of diamond earrings should make up to Glee for his cruelty.

Acquainted with Gregory from the purchases he had made for Carlotta, the jeweler showed him pearls first.

"I think I should like diamonds," Gregory said.

The jeweler's eyes sparkled. He unlocked the case and pulled out a tray of modest baubles.

"Something more substantial, I should think," Gregory said. "It's for my new wife."

"Ah!" the middle-aged jeweler said. "You want *forever* jewels."

Forever. Blast the word! He supposed he *was* now bound to Glee forever. The concept was not only daunting, it was frightening.

Next, the jeweler showed him a tray of dazzling earrings. At first Gregory thought to purchase the most expensive. After all, the girl *was* his wife. Then he decided they were far too big for Glee's delicate face. The next largest pair would look most becoming on Glee.

He fleetingly pictured her upturned face all smiles when he presented the earrings to her. Would she throw her arms around him again as she had when he gave her his mother's necklace? 'Twas bloody difficult to feel her breasts crushed into his chest and not want . . .

Bloody hell! He must squelch such demonstrations on her part.

When he stopped at the Pump Room and met Appleton there, Gregory learned enough to make him regret the purchase of the earrings.

"So you've finally finished with your solicitor," Appleton said.

"How do you know where I've been?" Gregory asked.

"Pixie told me."

"Who?" Gregory asked.

"Your wife. Said for me to give her a nickname, and I think Pixie suits her, don't you?"

The adjective might very well suit her, but he did not at all like to think of other men giving his wife nicknames. "What's wrong with Mrs. Blankenship?"

Appleton handed the attendant his glass. "She don't like it. Wants to be my friend—like you. I sure as Jove don't call you Mr. Blankenship."

Gregory peered at Appleton through narrowed eyes. "How long did you spend with my wife?"

Appleton thought for a moment. "Two or three hours, I'd say."

"At Blankenship House?"

Appleton shook his head. "Oh, no. I only entered when Pixie asked me to come in. Said she needed my advice."

"On what?"

"On purchasing her phaeton."

Gregory's temper began to flare. "Her what?"

"Phaeton. Just told you." Appleton's quizzing gaze swept Gregory's face. "You do not approve."

"Of course I don't approve. A lady doesn't—"

"But she told me you wouldn't object. Said you

wanted her to cut a dashing figure in Bath. I never questioned her because I've known you to be attracted to women who cut a dashing figure. Like raven-haired women who always wear purple."

Was this why Glee persisted in vexing him? He could not allow his wife to ride through Bath unescorted in a phaeton—no doubt wearing her scandalous red dress!

"I believe I'll go see my wife," Gregory said, bowing to his friend.

A trip to the mews confirmed Gregory's fears. Glee had, indeed, purchased a shiny new phaeton. He did not like it above half. But he could not very well forbid her to ride it. After all, he was not truly her master. And, Lord knows, the girl would have enough to endure being married to him.

As she dressed in a daring black silk gown for Thursday's assembly, Glee nodded to Patty to open her dressing room door after hearing Blanks's knock. Patty did so, then silently retreated.

Glee stood up to greet him, dipping him a curtsy. "We shall match!" she exclaimed, running her eyes over his black clothing.

He watched her with smoldering eyes. "But I don't have red hair, my dear. And I must say your hair is most striking with black—as is your fair skin."

Thank heaven he did not disapprove of her dress! She rushed to him and grabbed both his hands. "I'm happy I please you."

He kissed each of her hands, then detached his entwined fingers from hers. "I've bought you something." He reached into his pocket and withdrew sparkling diamond earrings that would dangle from her ears. "Can't have my wife's ears naked."

His thoughtfulness and kindly words nearly brought tears to her eyes. But she couldn't become a watering pot. 'Twould not at all be the action of the fast women he so admired. "You shouldn't have. I don't deserve such consideration, but I must say they're beautiful. You'll have to fasten them on for me."

She trembled under his gentle touch as his hand brushed her ear. "Oh, Blanks, I truly don't deserve such a kindly husband. And to think you are even gracing the dull Assembly Rooms for my benefit!"

"It's all part of the plan, my dear. Everyone in Bath is to be convinced of our devotion to one another."

Why must he be so adamant about keeping to his blasted *plan?* If only he could spontaneously perform his husbandly acts, she thought morosely. She slipped her arm into his, and they began to leave the chamber. "You will be most pleased I have persuaded Appleton and the twins to join us tonight so you won't be so terribly bored. Timothy has promised to liven tonight's action."

Blanks frowned. "I don't think you should refer to my friends by their Christian names."

"Oh, la!" she exclaimed. "How many times have I told you that you mustn't think of me as a wife but as one of the bloods?"

His brows knitted together and a frown tugged at his mouth as they descended the stairs.

His wife had been right, Gregory reflected. Appleton and the twins had yet another prank to offer at the Assembly Rooms that night. Since Glee had insisted on a proper dinner before traveling to the Assembly Rooms, they did not arrive until the dancers repaired to the tea room at nine. And there, serving tea in costumed livery, were his trio of friends. For all the world, they appeared to be taking their jobs most seriously. He looked at them, exchanged an amused glance with his wife, and they both burst out laughing.

Still laughing, Glee took his hand and walked toward the table where Appleton was serving. "We must let Timothy wait upon us," she said happily.

She and Gregory sat at a small table covered with a white cloth, and he made eye contact with Appleton. "What other manner of entertainment do you provide tonight?" Gregory asked his friend in a voice barely louder than a whisper.

"Drink your tea, and you'll know," Appleton said with a wink.

Good heavens, did his friends think to render the assembly more jovial by adding spirits to the tea? Gregory picked up his cup and sipped. Very definitely strong arrack. Then, despite himself, Gregory smiled and drank up. "Perhaps you're not so thirsty," he said to his wife. It wouldn't do at all for Glee to get foxed. After all, she *was* George's little sister. And Gregory's wife.

Her eyes widened as she looked at him. "You think they've spiked the tea?" she whispered.

He nodded.

She smiled sheepishly. "What a devilishly clever thing to do!" She lifted her cup and drank. "I agree with your friends. These affairs are far too sober. What's needed is more gaiety."

To his consternation, Glee finished her cup and asked Melvin, when he visited their table, for another. Since Gregory had no doubt he could hold his liquor far better than his wife, he also allowed Melvin to pour him another cup.

Then Melvin rushed off to another table to serve more demanding patrons.

"You know, Blanks," Glee said, "you could never go undetected as your friends have."

"Why?"

"Because you're far too handsome. Your friends are, all of them, rather ordinary looking. But not you. All the women would be sure to remember you no matter how you dressed."

He did not know how to take his wife's words. He'd been told since Oxford how agreeable women found his appearance, but Glee did not say *she* personally found his appearance agreeable. Fact was, she didn't think of him that way at all. He supposed she thought of him rather as she thought of George. Why, she hadn't even expressed one bit of outrage at the fact he had a mistress. She talked of Carlotta as one would speak of the village vicar. Which wasn't at all the thing.

Also, he did not like to hear praises for the appearance over which he had no control. "Beauty, as they say, is in the eye of the beholder. I'm certain any number of women here would find my countenance quite ordinary." Which he knew from repeated experience was not at all truthful. "Besides, any number of people here have recognized the twins. They may not know their names, but it's hard to go unnoticed when one stands next to one's exact likeness."

She swiftly finished her second cup of arrack tea. "If that's what you prefer to think, Blanksie."

Good heavens! His wife was getting foxed. He shouldn't have let her drink the wretched stuff. After all, she was far younger than he and not at all accustomed to drinking strong spirits. And knowing his friends, the arrack was the most potent available. He frowned at Elvin as he passed by with a tray of tea. The fellow was getting all too confident, balancing the tray on one hand.

Gregory had no sooner thought of Elvin's lack of

skill when the fellow's tray went crashing down on the Dowager Countess Richdale, who leaped to her feet and began to scream.

Gregory turned his head to keep from laughing at the foul-mouthed dowager as she went chasing after the fleet-footed Elvin.

Glee was not so polite. She laughed out loud, then turned to him. "How I wish I'd thought to dress as a servant tonight! How fun it must be."

"You, my dear wife, could hardly conceal your beauty."

She shot him a puzzled look, then smiled and cupped her hand against his cheek. "What a very sweet thing to say, Blanksie."

Good lord, but she really was foxed. It wouldn't do for her to dance, unless it were a waltz with her husband.

But after the refreshments, Glee expressed no interest in dancing but in playing cards instead—which was all very good with him.

He settled her at a whist table and went off to see if Elvin had come to harm at the hands of the irate dowager.

Since she was said to be skillful at cards, Glee had decided wagering on whist would be the method by which she would earn money to pay for her new gowns and see her clear until the next quarter.

She and her partner, a somewhat elderly man unknown to her, won the first hand, which apparently broke one of the gentlemen playing against her. He rose from the table and excused himself, saying it was growing late. It made her feel wretched to have taken the man's last sovereign.

The man was replaced by William Jefferson. Since

her first assembly as a married lady, Blanks had warned Glee against fostering a friendship with the handsome bachelor. Blanks had even told her William Jefferson was not received in London. What could the man have possibly done to be cut in society? Color hiked up her cheeks. Of course, she knew what he had done! He had told her himself he had a thirst for married women. Mr. Jefferson must have dallied with the wife of a powerful man.

Well, he'll not use me in such a manner, she vowed. She would use him only to ignite Blanks's jealousy. For she knew where William Jefferson was concerned, Blanks must be jealous.

Their play continued for several hands. Blanks popped into the room to check on her several times, and each time he frowned at Jefferson.

As the play progressed, Glee's confidence in her skill diminished. She had lost twenty-five pounds. Any more losses, and she did not know what she would do.

The hour was growing late. Only half an hour until the Assembly Rooms closed at eleven. Perhaps Lady Luck would smile on her, and she could win back her twenty-five pounds. Such failure was totally alien to her.

When the next hand was dealt and she picked up her cards, her heart fell. Her whole body tensed. She was not strong in any suit and would never be able to win this hand.

With trembling hands and sinking stomach, she played out the hand. Jefferson won and, with a sly smile on his face, he scooped up his winnings.

"I shall have to owe you the remainder, Mr. Jefferson," she said timidly after the other two players had retreated from the cloth-covered table.

His eyes swept over her and settled on her face.

"Then I'll just take your earrings to secure payment," he said blandly.

She thought she had never seen a colder man. "But . . ." How could she give him the earrings her beloved Blanks had just bestowed on her that night?

"You'll get them back," he assured. "I'll receive my payment. All that I desire is a kiss from you, and I mean to have it."

He made it sound so simple. Merely kiss him, and she would have her earrings back. But she didn't want to kiss him. She didn't ever want to kiss anyone except Blanks. Surely she could think of a chaste manner in which to comply with Mr. Jefferson's demand.

"I would rather wait until the next quarter and pay you back real money—with interest," she whispered.

"Since I'm the one owed, I'm the one to dictate terms," he said harshly, then gave her a sinister smile.

"It appears I'm at your mercy, Mr. Jefferson." She stood up, removed her earrings and tossed them on the table, then swept from the room.

FOURTEEN

Why had he let that red-headed pixie talk him into marriage? Gregory lamented as he sat waiting for Glee to come down to breakfast. He picked up the spoon and began to stir—for the twelfth time—his now-cold tea. He had already been there half an hour, angrily drumming his fingers into the linen tablecloth.

He'd had nothing but aggravation since his marriage, a marriage Glee had once made sound so wretchedly simple. And it was anything but. In fact, he could not remember ever being more vexed in his entire life. Not even with Aurora.

The trouble with having a wife meant you were completely responsible for her. He had never been responsible for anything in his four and twenty years, not even his errant self. And now he was being charged with the impossible task of reining in his hopelessly irresponsible and irrepressible wife.

Vexing him at every turn, the chit needed a sound spanking like a child. But he was not the one to administer it. He still felt too guilty over robbing Glee of the normal marriage he knew she truly wanted.

But, sweet heaven, she could try his patience! First, his vexatious wife had caused his blood to boil with that scandalous red dress. One as lovely as Glee need hardly resort to outrageousness to draw attention. As her husband, he then had to keep a careful watch over her to prevent scoundrels from taking advantage of her when she wore that deuced red dress.

Then there was her propensity to address his friends by their Christian names. Anyone would think they were on very familiar terms indeed, he thought, his temper scorching.

And he didn't above half like his wife dancing or playing cards with the devil incarnate, William Jefferson.

Then, of course, there was the maddening business about that damned conveyance. Gregory fumed over his wife's purchase of the phaeton. The purchase itself was innocent enough. He would never begrudge her anything because of mere money. But the idea of her flying through Bath flicking the ribbons and driving like a man fairly irked him. Especially when he pictured her doing so in the scarlet dress! Yesterday, he had been too angry to even bring up the matter of the phaeton with Glee, but he would have to broach the subject today.

Summoning the most fury in him, however, was the absence of the diamond earrings he had presented her with the night before. He knew without a doubt she had worn them to the previous night's assembly, and he was certain she had not worn them home. How could one lose *two* earrings? He was rather convinced one couldn't.

Then what *did* happen to them? Had she found them so unacceptable that she had removed them rather than be seen in them? Or had she given them away out of displeasure? Surely she hadn't lost them at whist. Whatever the reason they had gone missing, he was deuced low over their loss. By Jove, he had put himself out on her account. He had made a not insignificant purchase and had been rather pleased with himself over his thoughtful action.

Nothing would please him more than demanding an explanation from Glee. But he hated the man he was becoming and vowed to be patient. 'Twas better than confirming Glee's charges that he was an ogre. Perhaps she would wear the earrings again. He would give it a fortnight before he would demand an accounting.

He stretched his arms over his head and yawned. A pity he had awakened so deuced early. Were he still a bachelor, he would be comfortably snoring away in his chamber right now. But since marrying the exasperating Glee, he had not been able to sleep until afternoon on a single occasion.

As Glee jauntily sauntered into the morning room, where their breakfast table was set up, Gregory glared at his wife.

"A lovely day, is it not?" she asked cheerfully. She went first to the windows and drew open the green silk draperies, flooding the room with light. Then she stopped and closed a hand over his shoulder, her brows lowered in concern. "Are you quite well this morning, Blanks?"

His brows pinched together, Gregory scowled up at her. "Is there some reason why I shouldn't be?" he demanded.

She drew tea from a sterling urn and sat down next to Gregory. "Of course not."

"Correct me if I'm wrong," he said in a level voice, "but it was my understanding that husbands and wives communicated with one another."

She smiled at him. "Oh, they do, Blanks! I'm so grateful you understand that. Is there something you want to communicate with me about?"

He must repress his urge to strangle her. "There is." He glared at her. How sweet she looked this morning in her muted turquoise morning dress of soft muslin. Like a girl, really. Why couldn't she dress so sweetly all the time? What was this penchant she seemed to have developed for wearing scarlet? And black?

She smiled up at him innocently and set down the knife she was using to slather her toast with jelly.

"*You* haven't mentioned to me a rather significant purchase you made yesterday," he began.

Her brows plunged while she thought. "Oh! The phaeton! Should you like to see it?"

"I have."

Her eyes rounded, and her uplifted lips fell. "You're not happy with it? Timothy assured me it was of very fine quality."

He continued to glare at her. "Why didn't you discuss the purchase with me first?"

"You're jealous of Timothy?" she said with a pout.

He scowled. "Oh course I'm not jealous of Timothy, er, Appleton."

"Then why do you act so angry?" she asked.

"I'm angry that you bought a phaeton without discussing it first with your husband."

"But you said you weren't to really be a husband, so I thought not to bother you with such unimportant matters."

He pounded the table. "It was *not* an unimportant purchase. In fact, it wasn't at all the type of purchase a woman should make. Especially without her husband."

"But I did seek Timothy's advice."

"Did George completely fail to instill propriety in you?" he asked angrily.

She jerked up her head, a haughty expression on her face. "You don't have to bring my brother into this."

They faced each other, flaring eyes locked. It was as if neither of them would flinch first, so intense were their unwavering gazes. Then all of a sudden, Glee's face softened. "Forgive me, Blanks," she said contritely. "You're absolutely correct. You're my husband, and I should always defer to your opinions. Would it please you if I returned the phaeton?"

He thought about the poor coachmaker who had likely tipped a few bumpers last night to celebrate having made a sale. "It's not the phaeton, nor the money. It's the idea that my opinions weren't solicited by you."

She lifted her thick, dark lashes. "I've been most insensitive. I'm sorry."

Now what was he supposed to say? *All I really want is for you never to make a public display of yourself on the phaeton's high perch.* When, truth be told, what really bothered him were the missing earrings. And he begrudgingly refused to speak of them.

Now she made him feel the oppressor when he was being the oppressed. She did display extraordinary understanding.

"I thought perhaps the two of us could take a turn about Bath in your new rig," he said.

Her lips lifted into a smile. "Could we see the lad who hangs about your solicitor's?" she asked hopefully.

He frowned. Why did she have such a knack for reading his mind? Were there other matters she read with equal accuracy? The thought frightened him. He hadn't ever wanted to be that close to a woman. He hadn't ever wanted to be saddled with a wife. "I looked for him yesterday while I was at Willowby's but saw no sign of him."

She shrugged. "We'll just have to make inquiries."

"And when we find him?"

She shrugged again. "I'm not really sure . . ."

"Together, we'll be able to think of something," he assured.

After the groom brought around Glee's new phaeton, Gregory assisted Glee in climbing up on the box, then joined her and took the reins.

They went north first and circled along the Royal Crescent, then came back down Milsom Street past Bath Abbey and stopped near the quay and the three-story edifice where Gregory's solicitor had offices.

The lad was in front of the building, Gregory noted with satisfaction. Giving Gregory even greater pleasure was the fact that the boy sported a new woolen coat and sturdy new shoes.

"Is that him?" Glee asked.

Pulling the phaeton parallel to the building, Gregory nodded.

The lad, a huge smile on his thin face, came running toward the phaeton. "Need an experienced ostler?" the boy asked excitedly.

Gregory's eyes narrowed, a grin pinching his cheek. "Do you remember me, lad?"

The boy nodded. "You're the gent what gave me a crown."

"There'll be another crown for you today if you watch the horse while my wife and I take a short walk to unstiffen my wife's legs."

"Ye can count on me," the lad said confidently.

Gregory disembarked and offered a hand to Glee.

"And what might your name be?" Glee asked the boy.

"Me name's Archibald, but those what know me calls me Archie."

Smoothing her skirts as she got to the pavement, Glee asked, "And how old are you, Archie?"

"Eight," he boasted.

"You seem rather young to be wandering the streets with no adult," Glee said.

Gregory scowled at his wife. She would have to be

blind not to have seen hundreds of the boy's class similarly unchaperoned. Gregory's chest tightened. A pity he couldn't help them all.

"Oh, me mum's just inside the building if I should need her."

Gregory laid a hand on the boy's bony shoulder. "I had need of you yesterday but couldn't find you."

The boy's cork-colored lashes downcast, he shrugged. "I had to help me mum yesterday, but I'm here most days."

"You help your mama clean?" Glee asked.

The boy shook his head. "She don't ever let me clean. The nobs don't like having a child underfoot."

Archie did not divulge in what manner he had helped his mother on the previous day, Gregory mused.

"Did your mother work yesterday?" Gregory asked.

"She did her work later. So long as she gets her work done, it don't really matter when she begins," the boy said defensively.

Glee mussed his light brown hair. "I'm sure she is a very good worker. As are you."

The boy looked up at Glee, shading his blue eyes from the sun. "How'd ye know?"

"Oh, I can tell by looking at you what a very fine helper you must be. And my husband has bragged of your service to him any number of times."

Archie tossed a satisfied smile at Gregory.

As Gregory and Glee strolled through lower Bath, they had the good fortune to run into Appleton and the twins, the three of whom promptly addressed Glee as Pixie, much to her husband's consternation. Gregory glared at his friends but said nothing.

The five of them fell into step in two rows along the pavement. "We were turned out," Elvin announced dejectedly.

"Turned out of what?" Gregory asked.

"I expect they were given their walking papers from the serving staff at the Upper Assembly Rooms," Glee said.

The three bachelors nodded.

"Elvin was caught in the act of . . . enhancing the flavor of the tea," Appleton said.

Melvin and Elvin laughed. "Then they realized we weren't the regular staff and made a big scene," Elvin added.

"And I thought you did such a very good job," Glee said with mock outrage.

Appleton turned around to address Gregory, speaking with naked admiration. "A deuced fine wife you've got for yourself."

"If one has a penchant for extricating one's spouse from scrapes," Gregory mumbled under his breath.

Appleton offered Glee his arm, and they walked together a few feet ahead of Gregory. "I say, Pix, I've had another deuced good idea on how to enliven the Assembly Rooms next Tuesday."

Gregory—quite oddly—fumed as his wife expressed an interest in Appleton's schemes. The both of them were far too old to behave so childishly.

"Elvin and I plan to pen a note to Miss Holworth that purports to be from a secret admirer. The note will request that she meet her admirer at the Bennett Street entrance to the Assembly Rooms at nine."

Elvin came up on Glee's other side. "Then we'll also send a note to old Mr. Goodfellow, begging him to meet Miss Holworth at nine at the Bennett Street entrance."

Glee was silent a moment before reacting to the trio's scheme. Then she spoke cautiously. "I daresay your lark will cause much merriment, but let's hope it's not at the expense of either participant. For I know of nothing against Miss Holworth, save a profound shyness. Now, if Miss Eggremont were to be the pawn . . ."

Elvin coughed. "But Miss Eggremont's a paragon!"

Glee frowned. "And well she knows it."

"If Pix says Miss Eggremont needs taking down a notch, Miss Eggremont it will be," Appleton said.

Gregory unaccountably swelled with pride. Glee wanted no part of a scheme that would entrap innocent persons. And Jane Eggremont, he had to admit, was far from innocent. In fact, she was a worthy target for such a prank. A more self-centered woman he had never met.

"What of old Mr. Goodfellow?" Elvin asked.

Glee thought for a moment. "The poor man has only just come out of black, and I hear he still mourns his deceased wife dreadfully."

"She's got a point there," Appleton said.

Despite their childishness, Gregory was getting into this. "What about Jefferson?" he asked.

"He's far too handsome," Glee said. "What's needed is a man who thinks he is much more worthy than he actually is."

"Sounds like Jefferson to me," Gregory mumbled as he watched his wife's back. And the backs of the two men at either side of her. Anger swelled within him. So his wife found Jefferson handsome. Gregory's hands coiled into fists.

"What about Thornton?" Melvin asked.

Gregory's vision shifted to Melvin, who walked beside him. A very good idea. Thornton was a pompous, arrogant ass.

"He'd be perfect!" Appleton exclaimed.

So it was settled. Next Tuesday, Miss Eggremont would receive a note supposedly from Mr. Thornton, who begged a private meeting with her. The two of them, Gregory thought, heartily deserved to be made a laughingstock.

"Where are we going?" Melvin asked.

"I want you to see my new phaeton," Glee said. "Timothy helped me select it."

"Blanks didn't object?" Elvin asked.

Blanks spoke in an even voice devoid of emotion. "I wasn't overjoyed."

"But in the future I will consult my husband before making any out-of-the-ordinary purchases," she said.

Gregory's insides collapsed. She hadn't really got the point of his anger.

She turned her head around and smiled at him. "Blanks, dear, would you object if I have my phaeton painted bright red?"

A red phaeton! What would the minx think of next? He shuddered to think. "So long as you don't wear the red dress when you ride in it," he answered with a calm he was far from feeling.

"I cannot understand why you dislike that dress so much. I've received any number of compliments on it."

Gregory mumbled an unintelligible retort.

When they reached the phaeton, Gregory tossed Archie two crowns and happily watched the boy's face brighten. "I've a mind to hire you to come work in my stable," Gregory said to the boy.

A wistful look crossed the lad's face. "I can't leave me mum."

"But your mother could enter into service at our house, too, and the both of you would have your own room and board furnished," Glee said.

The boy shook his head. "Me mum's happy where she is."

Not only during the drive back to Queen Square but throughout the rest of the day, Gregory pictured the wistful expression that had come over Archie's face when he offered the lad a groom's job. What compelled the lad to refuse an offer that would improve his—and his mother's—life?

FIFTEEN

The trio came to dinner that night, and silliness prevailed. But Gregory's low spirits prevented him from joining his wife and friends in their levity. He did not at all approve of his wife's familiarity with his friends. Nor did he approve of the encouragement she gave their schemes. She was far too enamored of pranks for a married woman. The whole lot of them had no more maturity than young Archibald.

But it was Archie himself who caused Gregory the most consternation. The lad had fairly shot down Gregory's hopes by refusing to come into Blankenship service. Why had the blasted lad refused? Gregory had been smugly content the boy would come under his protection, and he would never again have to put himself out for or worry about the lad. The boy himself obviously had no desire for security. Damn him.

Archie, unfortunately, had other allegiances. And Gregory meant to uncover the wherefore of them.

The following morning he went to Willowby's office on the pretext of having the solicitor look over some leases. Once again, there was no sign of the lad.

To Willowby's clerk, Gregory asked, "You procured the shoes and coat for the wretched lad, I see."

The clerk looked up at him, grinning broadly. "His mum was very grateful."

"Did you tell them . . ."

"I said the benefactor was one of Mr. Willowby's wealthy clients."

Gregory nodded. "I got the impression they—mother and son—were extremely poor. Do you know if they've got permanent lodgings?"

"Couldn't say, sir," the clerk responded as he shuffled papers around his desk. "Though it grieves me to say it, the pair of them look to emerge from the gutter half the time."

Gregory winced. "I'm particularly interested in facts about the boy—if you should learn anything."

The clerk looked up from his papers. "Yes, of course, Mr. Blankenship."

Gregory then went to another tenant of the building and asked the clerk there if he knew where Archie and his mother lived. The man shook his head, unable to reveal any more information. Gregory went to leave the office.

"Wait," the clerk said, "I don't think they have permanent lodgings. It seems to me that Mrs. A. carries all her worldly possessions about in a cloth bag that goes everywhere with her."

Gregory looked puzzled. "Mrs. A.?"

"The lad's mother. She says her foreign last name's too difficult to pronounce."

"The woman speaks with an accent?" Gregory asked.

"Oh, no, she's most likely a British native. I believe her former husband was the foreigner."

"The lad's father, that would be," Gregory said.

"I suppose, though I daresay he looks as British as me."

Gregory noted how fair the clerk was. "Is Mrs. A. working today?"

The clerk withdrew his watch from his waistcoat pocket. "She often comes in late, but she works late and works hard."

Gregory nodded and left. Why would the boy not delight in the chance to procure a comfortable home for himself and his mother? And to get paid to care for the horses he was so enamored of?

That afternoon, the trio assembled at Blankenship House where they had previously decided to meet before departing for the prizefight which was to take place a few miles from Bath.

Gregory was most vexed. He had looked high and low for Glee but had been unable to find her. Something about leaving her for several hours made him nervous. There was no telling how much mischief she could do. She could cavort with Jefferson. Or race her phaeton through town. Or order more scandalous dresses. Or give away his mother's emeralds. Or, perish the thought, bring home urchins to lavish her attentions upon.

Where had that wife of his gone? His lips a grim line, he thought about not going with his friends. Leaving Glee to her own devices could prove regrettable.

"You quite the thing?" Appleton asked Gregory with concern.

"I'm fine. It's just that I hate to leave without telling my wife." What a henpecked fellow he must seem!

Smiling, Appleton clapped him on the back. "Never thought I'd see the day when you'd be deferring to a chit half your size."

"Don't call my wife a chit!" Gregory remonstrated.

Appleton and the twins exchanged amused glances,

then Elvin set a hand to Gregory's back. "Shall we go?"

His tiger brought around Gregory's phaeton and, with reluctance, Gregory hopped on the box. "Care to ride with me, Melvin?" Gregory asked.

Appleton had lined up his phaeton next to the twins', and Blanks's phaeton made a third, resembling a Roman chariot race.

Melvin smiled and shook his head sheepishly. "I mustn't hoard your other seat. You never know when you might need it to transport an important person."

The lot of them were dicked in their nobs, Gregory was convinced, though he had never thought to throw Melvin's name into such company. Melvin, who used to be the level-headed one.

After they crossed the River Avon, they were soon in the countryside, greatcoats flapping in the wind as they put more distance between them and the city. Soon, a knot of carriages, gigs, horses, and shabbily dressed pedestrians signaled the location of the fight. One after another, with Gregory leading the way, they turned off onto a lane thick with merrymakers and drove past throngs of happily shouting fight attendees. Gregory flicked a glance to Melvin, who was closest to him. Why was the fellow smirking? Gregory's gaze shifted to the others, all of whom were smiling.

A smile curled on Gregory's own lips. Nothing like a prizefight to equalize all men—from swells to servants—united in their love of manly sport.

And there was no sport more manly than pugilism. What courage these men had! Who could not admire these marvelous beasts whose fancy footwork and skill with their bare hands put them in dire danger every minute they were in the ring?

Gregory led the others past those who had gathered leisurely to celebrate and make the odd bet. He pulled to a stop when he found a space on a knoll where the three phaetons could line up next to each other and still be able to see the fight some forty feet away.

His friends parked their vehicles next to his, then all of them disembarked to go make wagers. Gregory meant to wager on The African, a magnificent creature. As quick on his feet as any fighter he had ever seen. Gregory had seen him fight in London last spring. Not even Gentleman Jackson was as fleet of foot.

While they walked to betting cages, Gregory nodded any number of times at acquaintances of his who had gathered here this day, perched above the teeming crowds on the seats of their conveyances.

Gregory put a hundred quid on The African.

"I've got fifty quid that says the Englishman will get the best of your black," Appleton said to Gregory after he placed his wager.

"I do hate to take your money," Gregory said by way of an agreement.

The four of them chuckled on the way back to their rigs. As Gregory neared his, he saw that his blasted tiger had helped himself to the master's seat. The gall! Gregory strode over to his phaeton, a frown on his face.

As he drew closer, he saw that his slip of a tiger—dressed in green-and-gold livery with powdered hair—was not his tiger at all, but his perplexing wife dressed as a lad! Drawing his brows together, Gregory openly scowled up at Glee, his fisted hands on his hips. "What do you think you're doing here?" His eyes trailed over her smooth breasts which the tiger's shirt did little to conceal. How could he not have noticed it was his lovely—maddening—wife in the child-sized Blankenship livery?

His glance flicked to his friends, who burst into laughter. "You knew all along, didn't you?"

"Of course," Elvin said. "It was Appleton's idea. And a capital one at that!"

Glee's eyes grew wide as she watched him. "I did so want to see a mill firsthand, and I dared not ask you for I knew you'd become angry. Really, Blanks, there's no end to your old-fashioned views of what a wife is to do and not to do!"

Appleton, his eyes glittering with amusement, was quick to champion Glee's cause. "Marriage really has made you old-fashioned."

Gregory glared at his friend. " 'Tis not my old-fashioned notions." Then he met his wife's frightened gaze. "Take a look about you, Mrs. Blankenship. Do you see any other women here?" His shimmering brown eyes flared in anger.

She gave tit for tat, mimicking him by thrusting hands to hips. "How do you know other women are not also dressed as tigers?"

Her husband did not deem to answer her, but hitched up his leg and hoisted himself to sit beside her, refusing to make eye contact with her. Barely able to control the angry tremble in his voice, he said, "You vex me to death, woman. I can see I shall be forced to hire a companion to shadow you everywhere and keep you out of trouble."

"I won't stand for it. *You* can go wherever you want and do whatever you want, and I mean to as well."

Curiously, it bothered him that she did not care what he did. "Perhaps I'll just lock you in your chamber," he idly threatened.

She sighed. "Very well. I promise not to dress like your tiger any more. Though you must admit you never even suspected—"

"Of course I didn't expect my wife to be dressed as a boy! As my wife, you're expected to be one of the most respected matrons in Bath." He slipped a sideways glance at her.

Her lashes sweeping low, she swallowed and softly said, "I wouldn't have done it had I known you'd be this angry. I fear I've been a very disappointing wife, but I promise to behave better in the future."

Damn, but the chit looked as if she were going to cry! He couldn't allow that. The sight of a woman crying completely undid him. He patted her tiny hand. "I have your word?" he asked softly.

She nodded with contrition.

Perhaps he wouldn't have to be so stern in the future. A future with a well-behaved wife. He leaned into the back of his seat, rather fancying the idea of Glee conducting herself with deportment.

His contentment was short-lived.

"Blanks, will you place a wager for me?" she asked.

He tried to gain control of his emotions before responding. "Women do not wager on prizefights."

She stuck out her bottom lip and frowned. "It's just as I said. You're being an old stick."

He whipped around to face her. "I am not! I'm merely trying to hold rein on my very vexing wife so she does not do irreparable harm to her reputation."

"You weren't at all like this . . . before we were wed. You used to live for a lark."

"Yes, Blanks, she's right," Elvin said. "You've let marriage greatly alter your personality. Just like Sedgewick."

From the corner of his eye, Gregory saw that Melvin silently nodded his agreement with his twin.

They were, of course, right. He had never imagined this marriage would change him so thoroughly. But, bloody heaven, it had! Why could he not be his old devil-may-care self? He looked down at his petite wife. She was the reason. Damn! He had never cared a fig for his reputation before now. A man was expected to indulge in the occasional lark. But a woman . . . He could not bear to see Glee receive the cut direct. To be shunned by the *ton*. No, by God, he'd protect her even if he did have to lock her in her room.

Glee turned to Melvin. "Could I persuade you to wager for me?"

Melvin's eyes flicked to Gregory's.

"He will not!" Gregory said sternly.

Staring at the canvas surface where the fighters were to face off, she spoke with controlled anger. "You're being a positive ogre, Blanks."

"Me? What about my wife who's forever thinking of new ways to put me out of charity with her?"

"Well, well," a man to the side of them said.

Gregory spun around to face William Jefferson as he walked up beside Glee.

"Fancy that!" Jefferson said. "Mrs. Blankenship at a mill! And dressed as a male." His eyes met and held Glee's.

Gregory would love to get him in the ring right now. "My wife goes wherever I go," Gregory defended.

"How cozy," Jefferson said, not removing his gaze from Glee.

"I suggest you take your seat, for the fight's about to begin," Gregory told Jefferson.

He doffed his cap at Glee, then left.

Once he was gone, Gregory spoke sternly to his wife. "I don't cherish the idea of my wife being the most shocking woman in Bath, and I don't like Jefferson getting the wrong idea about you."

"I have been most vexing to you, Blanks. I *will* try to be better."

He instantly softened toward her, repressing the desire to take hold of her hand—which wouldn't do at all. One could not hold hands with one's tiger. And he was not about to let it out that his wife had demeaned herself by travelling to a mill. Dressed as a male, no less.

Soon the two magnificent specimens they had come to see joined one another on the center of the canvas, and the crowd hushed.

"I've never seen such huge men!" Glee exclaimed.

Unable to remove his own approving gaze from the fighters, Blanks nodded.

When the two principal participants moved away from each other, the crowd turned so silent, a single sneeze would have been an intrusion.

As soon as the bell struck, the crowd began cheering and shouting, their favor evenly divided between the two fighters. Gregory and his friends, too, yelled out instructions. Gregory leaped to his feet, shouting encouragement to The African.

Sweet heavens! but the man was quick on his feet, dancing away from every jab thrust by Steady Eddie. Soon, though, he lunged toward Steady Eddie, his fist colliding with Eddie's cheek. The crowd—at the sight of blood spewing from Steady Eddie's nose—began to cheer wildly.

Glee shrieked and Gregory spun around to see what was the matter with her. She buried her eyes in her hands but did not appear to have sustained an injury. *Feminine vapors, no doubt.* His gaze shot back to the fight.

Another jab from The African caused Steady Eddie's eyes to well shut, but he would not give in, despite that blood flowed from his mouth now. Another punch sent Steady Eddie to his knees, but still he managed to pull himself up.

Glee shrieked.

Why had the maddening woman interrupted Gregory's long-waited-for amusement? "What's the matter?" he asked impatiently.

Her head still buried, she shook her head, her shoulders shaking as if she were crying. His heart tripped.

"I can't watch," she finally managed between sobs. "It's so horridly brutal! Can't you stop it?"

He scowled. "I cannot. I told you this was no place for women."

"But I hadn't thought they would throw punches into one another's faces!"

"What *did* you expect?" he demanded.

She continued to babble into her wet palms. "I thought they would punch one another on the arms or the chest or the stomach."

"Wouldn't be bloody likely to knock out their opponents that way," Gregory said.

"You mean . . . that's how the winner is determined? The one who's left standing?"

"Of course," he answered impatiently. "He's got to leave his opponent senseless."

"How dreadful," she shrieked. "How can you bear to watch?"

He mumbled under his breath. He could not bloody well watch it now, with her distracting him like she was doing. His eyes darting from the match to his huddled wife, Gregory sat back down. Glee looked a most pitiful sight, indeed. He spoke softly. "It's not so bad as you think, Glee. I've never seen anyone killed. These chaps have uncommonly hard heads."

Her little shoulders shook with the effort of her sobs. "It's so brutal."

"Why do you think women don't attend these affairs? They're for men's eyes only."

"They're barbaric!"

"Come on, I'll take you home," he said gently.

SIXTEEN

Men did not like crying women. With that thought in mind, Glee dried her tears and faced the angry man who was her husband. He flicked the ribbons in his haste to return her to Bath. She supposed he would wish to return to the mill. Her desire to become one with his friends had sadly misfired on her. Instead of capturing his admiration, she had drawn his wrath, thoroughly succeeding in ruining Blanks's excursion. What had happened to her plan to swaddle him in her love?

She felt remorseful indeed. "Oh, Blanks, I'm truly sorry for ruining your fun—though I fail to see how such a barbaric sport could bring you pleasure."

He slid a frown at her.

"You're sure to regret marrying me," she said, whimpering. "Especially when I promised you we'd have a good time together, that we'd be the best of friends. I've only been trying to share things with you—to be a true friend."

He loosened his white-fisted hold on the reins, relaxed against the back of his seat, and spoke gently to her. "You aren't expected to share everything with me—though I appreciate your intentions."

"You do?" she asked hopefully.

He nodded.

A moment later, a smile on her face, she asked, "Do you know what day it is today, Blanks?"

He thought for a moment. "It's the nine-and-twentieth day of March."

"No, silly. That's not what I meant. It's our two-week anniversary."

"Good God, has it only been two weeks?" he asked incredulously.

"It does seem longer, does it not?" she said wistfully.

They went some distance further when she shrieked. "Oh, Blanks, do put me down right here."

He reined in. "Why?"

"Because it's not fair for me to spoil your time. You have so been looking forward to the fight. I can easily walk the short distance back to Bath."

"I won't do any such thing. Besides, you can't walk that far alone!" He scowled. "I won't have it."

"But no one will know I'm not a lad," she protested.

"I'll know, and I won't tolerate it."

"Oh, dear," she whispered. "Whatever you say, Blanks. I'll try to be a humble wife."

"And the queen will wear rags," he mumbled angrily.

"I really don't mind if you wish to return to the fight. I don't mean to interfere with anything that brings you pleasure."

Her husband, she knew, possessed an especially keen appreciation for merrymaking. And no wonder! That horrid stepmother of his had likely thwarted his every grasp for happiness. No wonder he had preferred to spend his school holidays at Hornsby, and no wonder that—when he obtained his majority—he tended to excessive indulgences. Now that Glee had met Aurora, she understood why Blanks had gone overboard in his quest of pleasure. He'd had precious little of it during his entire childhood.

Glee cast a sideways glance at his alluring profile. His face was uncharacteristically somber, his dark eyes inscrutable. Her glance trailed to his powerful hands that grasped the reins. She fought an overwhelming urge to throw her arms around him and kiss him senseless.

If only she could do something to make him happy. Besides pugilism, what was there? She had not lived nineteen years with her brother not to learn a thing or two about what made men tick. "I shouldn't be offended, Blanks, if you should choose to see Mrs. Ennis." Thank heavens a bolt of lightning had not struck her down for telling so outrageous a lie! The very idea of Carlotta Ennis within Blanks's embrace had the power to rob Glee of her breath—and of all hopes for happiness. But she did love Blanks so. And his happiness is what mattered most to her. Even if that happiness included the purple-hued doxy!

He pulled the reins until his bay came to a screeching halt, then Gregory sat glaring at her. "You might not object, dear wife, but I do. I should not like for my brother to get wind of so . . . so awkward an alliance."

Oh, dear. Glee couldn't seem to do anything right where Blanks was concerned. She could not bring herself to look at him. Instead she sat staring at the soft hills west of Bath, her face contrite. "Of course, you're right. You have an impeccable sense of propriety. A pity I'm such an albatross to you." A mock laugh broke from her lips. "And to think, all I ever wanted was to bring you happiness."

He cupped his hand under her chin and turned her face to his. His eyes suddenly went all mellow and soft. "You're not an albatross."

Now, *she* went all mellow. She was powerless to stop herself from stroking the strong planes of his cheeks, from being compelled to peer into the depths of his deep amber eyes.

He seemed to be moving closer to her. And she ever so slightly moved toward him. She saw the stubble of this morning's shave, and she drew in his subtle musk scent. His lips then settled over hers. Soft, pliable lips. Lips that pierced to her very soul.

'Twas sheer delight, this taste of her lover. Magical. Soul-numbing. Blending. And she never wanted it to end.

Her arms closed around him, and she melted into his powerful chest, his arms closing around her. Their mouths were open, and their breathing was ragged and labored.

To her great distress, he pulled away, then took each of her hands and kissed them. "Forgive me," he said throatily.

Feeling bereft beyond words, she caught her breath and murmured, "You've nothing to be sorry for. You are, after all, my husband. My purpose in life is to make you happy."

He laughed a bitter laugh and picked up the reins, flicking his bay toward Bath.

What had she done which caused the kiss to terminate? Everything had been so utterly wonderful.

Her face crimson, she thought on it during the short ride back to Blankenship House. Obviously, she had not satisfied him. She supposed kissing was something for which a great deal of expertise could be accumulated. And, heaven knows, she had precious little experience. She had never kissed the man she had thought to run off with when she was seventeen. She had only been kissed twice, both times by Blanks. Though their first kiss wrenched her with unexpected, all-encompassing tenderness and a hunger for something deeper, this second kiss consumed her with a near-debilitating passion. A passion as terrifying as her unwavering love for Blanks.

She had not thought she would enjoy that open-mouthed kissing, but with Blanks, it seemed to draw them closer. Closer than she had known two people could be. Was this how it was with Dianna and George? And Felicity and Thomas? Could they claim such boundless pleasure every day of their lives? Her heart thumped. Had it been thus for Blanks and Carlotta?

All that Glee knew was that she had never truly lived before she had come alive in Blanks's arms.

"I think I'm getting a knack for kissing, Blanks," she said in a husky voice. "Perhaps I'll be so improved next time, you'll not hasten to put me at a distance."

He burst out laughing.

What had she said to generate such mirth?

"I would say you're doing extremely well."

She tossed a glance at him and saw he was winking at her! "You're making fun of me!"

"I am not," he protested. Then he grew serious. "It's just that . . . I feel such an utter cad, taking advantage of you."

"You could never do that," she said softly.

How could that wife of his be so maddening? On the one hand, she was a constant thorn in his side. On the other, she enticed him as no other woman ever had. How could one as innocent as Glee elicit such hunger in him? What a brute he was to force himself on her innocence!

He drew up in front of Blankenship House and assisted her in disembarking. He looked down at her in the kelly-green livery. How could he ever have taken her for a lad? She set his palms to sweating and his heart to pounding. He fought the urge to settle his lips over hers once again. In broad daylight in front of Blankenship House! Good God, but he wanted to.

"Please go back to the fight," she pleaded. "I feel dreadful for causing you to miss it."

"If I know The African, the match is already over."

"Then I sincerely hope no one was injured."

"Don't worry so. I'm sorry the brutality upsets you."

"I had no business going. 'Tis not a sport that beckons women, and now I realize why."

He smiled down at her and patted her head. "Go change your clothing, and I'll give you some pointers on driving your new phaeton."

"But it's being painted," she said with fallen face.

"Red?"

She nodded solemnly.

"I can show you in mine," he offered. "They're much the same."

"That's what Timothy said."

"I don't above half like you calling him Timothy."

"But you never objected when I called my brother George."

"That's different. George is your brother."

"As is Timothy. And the twins. At least, that's how I feel toward them."

He gazed hungrily at her, his voice lacking confidence when he asked, "Am I just another brother?"

"Silly, you're far better than a brother. Haven't I always told you that?"

He nodded solemnly.

The best part about giving Glee pointers on driving a phaeton was putting his arms around her in order to show her how to hold the ribbons correctly. His wife proved a most apt pupil. Too good, actually. The next thing he knew, she'd be flying through Bath. *The woman in red.* His wife. He shuddered.

The thing of it was, he couldn't see any way he could prevent her from behaving in such a manner. Theirs wasn't, after all, a conventional marriage. Even if she had said he could be her master. No matter what she said, he could not bring himself to take advantage of her. It was—clearly—not part of their unusual bargain.

It was during one such maneuver when his arms caught around Glee's shoulders that she looked into his face and smiled. "Oh, Blanks, I wish you didn't have to spend so much time with that cursed solicitor of yours."

"Why?"

"Because I much prefer having you all to myself."

Good God, why must she provoke his . . . his physical arousal? Had she no idea what a profound effect she was having on him? He quickly removed his arms from her. Then he sputtered out a cough. "There must be any number of things far more enjoyable than spending time with me. After all, you told me yourself I was an ogre."

Her lashes dropped. They were so long, they rested on her pale cheeks. " 'Twas most uncharitable of me, and you must know I didn't mean it."

"Whether you meant it or not, the words rang true. I've been a beast of a husband."

She shook her head. "Not at all! I've been the beast. You have only been trying to set me straight. George would be proud of you."

Ah, George! Yes indeed, the man George had become would heartily approve of the new, conscience-burdened husband of his little sister. In fact, Gregory was becoming exactly like George.

And that wasn't at all what he wanted.

What, then, did he want? He sat pensively while he allowed Glee to take the reins for a placid ride through Bath. He did not want to be married. He never had. He did not want a wife who thought of herself as one of the bloods. He did not want for Glee ever to become heavy with child. He wanted his freedom. Freedom from all the responsibilities that had crashed in on him ever since he exchanged wedding vows with Glee. The maddening wench!

What, then, were the merits of being free? he asked himself. He could sleep as late as he wanted. He could find his pleasure in the beds of other ladies. He would not have to curb his drinking. He could even once again join Appleton and the twins in their irrepressible pranks.

Enumerating these things that had brought him no end of pleasure in the past made him realize how truly empty his life had been. Always. He would soon be five and twenty. It was time he began to act like a man—not a fun-loving schoolboy down from Oxford.

Marriage was a step in the right direction. But his marriage, of course, was no real marriage. And Glee, of course, was not a *real* wife. Then why did he feel so blasted responsible for her? Why did she elicit such protectiveness in him?

At nineteen, she was much younger. She could profit from his vast experience. The thing of it was that he could not be too demanding of her. It wouldn't do to upset her rather fragile sensibilities. He had been too heavy-handed in his dealings with her up to this point. Subtle persuasion was what was called for.

"I regret that I'm to meet with Willowby again to-morrow," he said.

He didn't think he would ever forget the way she looked at him with such stark pain on her face. Did the chit truly care about him? Good God, but that wouldn't do at all!

SEVENTEEN

"A pity Blanks has to spend so much time with that blasted solicitor of his," Appleton lamented as he offered Glee a cup of water.

Glee took a sip of the water and grimaced. "Do you realize Blanks hasn't accompanied me here to the Pump Room one single time since we married?" She decidedly missed him. She had worn a new dress that shone like polished copper, and she had collected enough compliments to confirm its success. A pity Blanks could not witness her success.

"An estate as large as the late Mr. Blankenship's must be devilishly difficult to administer," Melvin said in a reassuring voice.

"But I daresay Blanks would rather be anywhere than at the Pump Room this morning," Appleton added. "He neither partakes of the water nor tolerates the genteel females who congregate at these affairs."

"Now that he's married, he don't have to worry about the females trying to get their clutches into him," Elvin said. He tossed a glance at Glee. "Beg your pardon for digging up dead bones and all that."

"I cannot agree with you, Timothy, about Blanks not wishing to be here," Glee countered. "Blanks enjoys meeting his friends and keeping abreast of the happenings in the city. I feel quite guilty for sounding so vexed with him. My poor Blanks is missing out on all the fun." Her glance skimmed over the faces of the trio. "Thanks to you three, I don't have to be divorced from society." While watching them, she noticed Miss Eggremont and a bespectacled companion enter the Pump Room.

"Oh, look," Glee whispered. "There's Miss Eggremont with Miss Arbuckle. Allow me to prove to you Miss Eggremont is a most worthy target for Tuesday night's assembly."

Glee made eye contact with the young lady who thought she was an Incomparable. "Oh, Miss Eggremont!"

The woman being addressed cast a glance at Glee, then a briefer glance at the three undistinguished men and, with her mousy female friend, walked the short distance to Glee.

Miss Eggremont was several inches taller than Glee with a pleasantly rounded body, blond hair and a face, that while flawless, missed the mark of being beautiful. Perhaps her best feature was her unerring sense of style. She dressed with excellent taste in a steel-blue gown and matching pelisse trimmed with white fur.

Turning to the unremarkable young brunette woman who accompanied her, Miss Eggremont said, "Miss Arbuckle, you are acquainted with my dear friend Miss Pembroke, are you not? Her brother, you must know, is Lord Sedgewick."

"Actually, I'm no longer Miss Pembroke," Glee said to Miss Arbuckle, of whom Glee was genuinely fond. The two had met at the lending library and had a great many common interests. It was just like Miss Eggremont, Glee thought, to surround herself with plain companions. Giving Miss Arbuckle a sincere smile, Glee added, "I've recently married Mr. Blankenship."

"Oh, I had quite forgotten," Miss Eggremont re-marked, still making no acknowledgement of the twins or Appleton.

"You do know Mr. Appleton and the Misters Steffington, do you not?" Glee asked the ladies.

Miss Eggremont haughtily looked down the bridge of her nose at the gentlemen. "I don't recall." Then she did not give them another second's notice.

Seething over Miss Eggremont's unfriendliness, Glee performed the introductions. Of course, Glee thought, Miss Eggremont wouldn't put herself out over mere *misters,* none of whom was regarded as particularly handsome. Now, if one of them were possessed of a title, a brightly smiling Miss Eggremont would have tripped all over herself hastening to greet them.

This time, Miss Eggremont met them with an in-credibly bored demeanor and quickly made an excuse to leave the little gathering to seek more important personages.

Melvin smiled after she left. "I daresay the woman was singularly unimpressed over the three of us! Now, if one of us were possessed of a title, such as *Lord* Sedgewick, she'd no doubt still be here excessively en-joying our company."

No wonder Melvin was Glee's favorite. His thoughts did so mirror her own, she thought.

"How can you malign Miss Eggremont so?" Apple-ton asked. "Did you not see how lovely were her blue eyes?"

Glee and the twins exchanged amused smiles.

"Daresay, she's above our touch," Elvin muttered.

"You grossly discredit yourself," Glee chided. "It is Miss Eggremont who's not worthy of any of you." It truly was Miss Eggremont's loss that she failed to re-alize the worth of Glee's dear male friends, each of whom was as solid as Gibraltar. Just because they were reticent with women—other than Glee—and dressed with unremarkable, quiet good taste, women like Sally Eggremont slighted them.

Glee silently perused their clothing. The twins dressed the same in fawn breeches tucked into shiny black Hessians, with shirts made of very fine linen, and well-cut tailcoats. Only the color of the tailcoat distinguished them. Elvin wore navy, his brother brown. Each tied his cravat very simply in the hunting style. Timothy Appleton, like the twins, wore fawn breeches and Hessians and a navy tailcoat.

So busy was she building up the men's confidence, Glee did not notice when Mr. Jefferson strolled across the Pump Room to seek her out.

"How very good it is to see you without your husband," he said, bowing. "For taking a turn about the room with you would make me the happiest of men."

He proffered his arm.

She gave him a long look. How unfortunate that he was such an ungallant when the man was so very good-looking with his stylishly cropped dark-brown hair, handsome face, and quality clothing—except for to-day's waistcoat, which was of bright orange satin. She gazed into his sparkling eyes. Really! The man felt absolutely no guilt over taking a lady's earrings because of a mere twenty-five-pound debt.

Tossing a baleful glance at Appleton, Glee took Mr. Jefferson's arm.

Though her demeanor indicated she was not over-joyed at the prospect of walking with Mr. Jefferson, Glee actually was thankful of the opportunity to discuss her missing earrings with him. With only that thought in mind, she wasted no time on pleasantries. "May I hope you have come here to return my earrings?"

"My lovely Mrs. Blankenship, you may hope for

anything you like, but you'll only get the earrings when I get the kiss."

She scowled at him. "You are behaving in a most ungallant fashion. I've a mind to tell my husband of your wicked proposal. I assure you he would hasten to pay the twenty-five pounds."

If only she had the confidence that Blanks *would* make everything right while at the same time forgiving her. The thing of it was that his gift of the earrings showed uncommon thoughtfulness, and he would likely be so offended of her careless disregard for the gift he would never speak to her again. Oh dear.

If only she hadn't purchased the phaeton, she'd easily have had the twenty-five pounds with which to repay Mr. Jefferson. After all, Blanks's allotment to her had been more than generous.

She had foolishly and utterly wasted the money. And she had so wanted to impress Blanks with her capable management of the household and her own affairs.

"I doubt you will allow your husband to know that—in just your first two weeks of marriage—you have run through the money he generously gave you to last the entire quarter." Jefferson lowered his voice and gave her a sly smile. "No matter how well you may pleasure your husband, my dear Mrs. Blankenship, I am persuaded he would be excessively displeased over the loss of your earrings. Such a pity to start off your marriage in so negative a fashion."

Glee gave a cold stare to the man who walked beside her. "How do you know about the *generous* allowance my husband settled on me?"

Jefferson smiled. "Because you have just confirmed it, my dear."

Her eyes narrowed. "You are altogether quite odious, Mr. Jefferson, and whatever gives you the idea I've spent all my money?"

"Because you purchased a phaeton that cost two hundred and seventy-five pounds," he said smugly.

She came to an abrupt halt and spun around to face him. "How do you know what my phaeton cost?"

He shrugged. "Bath is a small town in which information is easily broadcast."

"If you would only be kind enough to wait until the next quarter," she said, tucking her arm into his and continuing the promenade, "I'll pay you double the amount of money owed," she pleaded.

"I have more money than I need."

"Yet you need the kisses of a happily married woman?"

He was spared from having to answer, for he looked up as they came abreast of the Misses Eggremont and Arbuckle, who circled the room in the counter direction. Miss Eggremont smiled happily at him.

He and Glee nodded as they passed the women.

Once they were well past the ladies, Jefferson bent to speak softly. "I believe Miss Eggremont is out of charity with you, Mrs. Blankenship. First, you snared the juiciest plum on the Marriage Mart, and now you appear to have captured me. With your husband's departure from the Mart, I daresay I'm the juiciest morsel left."

"A pity we cannot add modesty to those attributes that make you so highly sought after," she said dryly.

He slanted a glance at her. "If the rest of your body is as saucy as your tongue, I envy your husband."

She held her head high and emanated a confidence she lacked. "He has no complaints."

"Then you won't want to test him. It being so early in your marriage."

That wretched man could read her like the pages of a book! "What is it you want from me?" she demanded.

"I told you. I want a kiss."

"I don't see how I can oblige you. I cannot kiss you in public, and to meet you in a clandestine fashion could bring down on me irreparable harm."

"If you were to be seen. The trick, my dear, is to escape detection."

With lowered brows, she asked, "What are you proposing, Mr. Jefferson?"

"Veiled, you could slip into my house."

"Your house?" she shrieked in outrage.

"My servants are very discreet."

She seethed. Everything Blanks had said about the man was correct. The wicked Mr. Jefferson was, indeed, a conscienceless womanizer. The gall! Trying to lure her into his house. Though she was young and ignorant of sexual matters, Glee knew no woman—married or single—would go unescorted to the house of a bachelor. Not even a woman who wished to appear "fast" to earn Blanks's affection.

To do so would be to sink so low as to never rise back to respectability. Though Blanks no doubt had dallied with women who had been that careless with their virtue, Glee knew he would never countenance such actions in his wife. "And my husband is very jealous," she said. "I will never set foot in your house."

They had completely circled the room, and the orchestra music trailed off as they came back to where Appleton and the twins stood.

"We will see," Jefferson said to her as he smiled broadly at the trio.

None of them returned the smile.

Glee detached herself from Jefferson to join the others as Jefferson bowed his farewells and took his leave of the Pump Room.

"I say, Pix," Appleton mumbled, "forgot to warn

you about Jefferson. The man's a nasty piece of work. You'd best not encourage a friendship with him."

"Blanks won't like it above half if you was to be anything but barely civil with the scoundrel," Elvin said.

"I daresay if Pixie were to give the fellow the cut direct, Blanks would be overjoyed," Melvin added.

"As a married lady, I can hardly cut a man without giving rise to speculative gossip."

"She's got a point there," Melvin said.

"The main thing's that she now knows how dangerous a man Jefferson can be," Appleton said.

Elvin shook his head and began to whisper. "He's very bad form."

Glee peered from Elvin to the other two. "The man's actions and conversations persuade me that you good gentlemen are correct about Mr. Jefferson."

Anger flashing in his eyes, Appleton stepped toward Glee. "What has the beastly man done to you?"

She smiled confidently. "Nothing that I cannot handle."

Elvin, his hands balled into fists, drew closer to Glee. "Are you sure? Nothing would give me greater pleasure than breaking that bounder's pretty nose."

Glee looked at Elvin's nose, then at his twin's identical nose. Unfortunately, their noses were excessively long. A pity. With less obtrusive noses and more hair on their heads, the twins could have been rather handsome. In a bland sort of way.

Melvin's brows lowered and his voice trembled with anger. "It's my belief that vile Jefferson is planning revenge against Blanks for that business with Miss Douglas."

"By Jove! That's it!" Appleton exclaimed.

"What business with Miss Douglas? And who *is*

Miss Douglas?" Glee asked, her anxious eyes darting from one man to another.

"It's not a matter we are at liberty to discuss," Melvin said.

They did not need to discuss it. Glee had a fairly good notion that Miss Douglas had most likely angered Mr. Jefferson by preferring Blanks over him. Really! What woman wouldn't? And knowing Blanks's propensity for fast women, Miss Douglas, no doubt, had a very light skirt indeed. Still, Glee wished she knew more about the mysterious Miss Douglas. What had she looked like? What had happened between her and Blanks? Had he loved her? With a thud in her heart, Glee wondered if Miss Douglas and Blanks still saw each other. Oh, dear.

Her gaze skimming to the other two, Glee smiled and said, "I'm greatly obliged for your concern. Consider me warned about the singularly unacceptable Mr. Jefferson."

"I say," Appleton said, his vision directed some distance behind Glee's shoulder, "is that not your sister and the nabob she's married to?"

"Thomas Moreland," Melvin said.

Appleton nodded. "Just so."

A smile on her face, Glee spun around and saw Felicity and Thomas walking toward her.

Wearing wrinkled merino traveling clothes, Felicity fairly shot toward her sister and secured both her hands. "I knew I should find you here, my pet!" Then her glance scanned the crowd. "Where is that dear husband of yours?"

Glee shrugged. "Poor lamb. He's having to pore over his father's books with that dreadful lawyer."

Still holding Glee's hands, Felicity stood back and studied her sister. The bodice of Glee's copper-colored gown was much lower than anything Glee had ever before worn in front of her sister. "I declare I shall cry," Felicity said, "for my baby sister is now a full-fledged woman."

Exactly what Glee wanted Blanks to think.

Felicity kissed Glee's cheek. "A very beautiful woman, to be sure."

Thomas Moreland moved to Glee and pressed the obligatory kiss upon the back of his sister-in-law's hand, then he and his wife greeted the trio.

"Why did you not tell me you were coming to Bath?" Glee asked.

"We just decided," Felicity said. "I couldn't bear being so far away from you when—as a new wife—you might need me."

"I'm happy indeed that you've come!" Glee said. "You will stay at Winston Hall?"

Thomas nodded. "In fact, George and Dianna will follow shortly."

"How wonderful!" Glee exclaimed. She *had* missed her sisters dreadfully. Unfortunately, their mates' adoration would only make Glee hunger for similar devotion from Blanks. And underscore the perfidy of her own marriage, she thought gloomily.

EIGHTEEN

Despite the chill in the air, Archie was waiting on the pavement when Gregory arrived at Willowby's office that morning. The lad tipped his battered cap. "Mornin', guvnah. Need yer 'orse watched?" he asked hopefully.

Gregory dismounted. "I do, indeed."

Archie smiled up at Gregory. "Will I get to earn another crown?" the lad asked.

"Most likely more. My business today will take several hours, so I'll need you longer."

"Fancy that," Archie exclaimed. "I'm only eight years old and makes more in a day than me mum makes in a month."

Instead of pleasing Gregory, such knowledge only made him feel guilty for being party to a society which did little to compensate its hardest workers. The lad confirmed that cleaning women made a pittance of little more than a penny a day. No wonder the boy was so wretchedly thin. He was unlikely to get one square meal a day. And what of toy soldiers and riding ponies? Gregory thought with disgust. Of course, such privileges of the privileged were denied those of Archie's class.

Patting the boy on his fair head, Gregory moved into

the building. 'Twas bad enough that he was having to dredge through his dead father's most personal affairs, but now Archie's misery also weighed on him. This would not be a pleasant day.

On the cold stone stairway, Gregory passed a person who must be Mrs. A. because she carried a bucket of water and rags and brushes to clean with. Gregory was startled by her youth. She was no older than he, which meant she must have given birth to Archie when she was no more than fifteen. And if he had found her son thin, Gregory must consider the mother emaciated. In fact, she was not much bigger than the little boy who was her son. Gregory had to fight the urge to carry the woman's heavy bucket of wash water for her. Poor, wretched woman!

Her blond hair was the same shade as her son's. She wore one patched muslin dress over another, both of which hung on her bones. Her tiny feet were shod in heavy leather boots that lacked laces and were much too big for her.

"Good morning," Gregory said, tipping his hat to her as they passed on the stairs.

She merely nodded her response as she whisked past him.

And he smelled the gin.

The knowledge that Archie's mother was a soaker sickened him. Was that why Archie knew his mother would not fit in at Blankenship House? Could a lad of eight who had known no other life be wise enough to be ashamed of his mother? Poor lad.

Throughout the day, no matter what important documents he was being asked to peruse, Gregory could not remove his thoughts from Archie and his youthful mother. There must be something he could do for them.

"Do you bring your lunch here, Hopkins?" Gregory asked the solicitor's young clerk.

"Yes. Every day. Would you care to share it with me?"

"It's very kind of you to offer, but no. However, I have a . . . a small business matter I would like to propose to you."

Hopkins arched a brow.

"Could I impose on your cook to prepare three lunches each day? I'm willing to pay five pounds a month for such a service."

Hopkins started coughing. "Five pounds! 'Tis almost as much as I earn in a month! Can I be persuaded you are in earnest?"

Gregory's gaze was unwavering as he nodded. "I'm in earnest. I wish to know the urchin and his wretched mother have one good meal each day."

"For that kind of money, they can have a feast," Hopkins exclaimed.

Gregory patted the man's shoulder. "That's my hope." Then Gregory produced five sovereigns from his pocket and counted them out for Hopkins.

He went into Willowby's inner office and worked with the solicitor for several hours. He had known his father was rich, but he'd had no idea his father possessed such vast holdings of property. And money in several banks. Not to mention the stocks. No wonder his father desired that Gregory put his wild days and rakish ways behind him before he could be fit to manage such vast estates.

Throughout the tedious business with Willowby, a nagging worry over the lad beset Gregory. Despite assurances that the lad and his mother would not go hungry, Gregory was still troubled.

But he did not know what else he could do. He would have to talk it over with Glee.

* * *

Glee had not dressed for dinner when she came rushing down the stairs the minute Hampton opened the door to Gregory. Taking both of Gregory's hands, she studied him under lowered brows. "My poor Blanks," she said soothingly, "you look so very tired."

He unconsciously brought one of her hands to his lips and kissed it. "I am tired. Devilishly so."

She slipped her arm into his. "Come, let's go to the library and sit before the fire. A glass of sherry is just the thing to relax you."

He sat on the silk damask sofa near the fire while Glee poured him a glass of sherry.

"Thank you, my dear," he said when she handed him the glass.

She sat beside him and smiled. His gaze swept over her. She really was a taking little thing. And so cognizant of what it took to make him happy. He sipped the smooth sherry and settled back, happy to be warm at last. Willowby's office had been devilishly cold, but here warmth from the blazing fire permeated the entire library and spread contentment over him.

"I do so like it when you call me *my dear,*" she said. "By the way, you'll get the opportunity to call me any number of endearments tonight."

"Tonight?" he asked with disappointment. "I thought we weren't going out tonight."

"Oh, we aren't. It's just that Felicity and Thomas have come to Bath, and I've invited them for dinner."

Gregory scratched his head. "Did we know they were coming?"

"Heavens, no! They just decided rather on the spur of the moment. It's my opinion Felicity means to keep a watchful eye on me—you know, assure herself you're treating me properly. She'll want to see you lavish affection upon me, of course."

"Of course."

"I daresay she wants to see for herself that Mrs. Ennis is out of the picture."

Gregory gritted his teeth. He rued the day he had taken the lavender-eyed beauty to his bed. Just as maddening as Glee's far-too-frequent references to Carlotta was Glee's complete lack of jealousy. He would have liked it if Glee were just a little jealous. "The lady in question is ancient history."

Glee affected a pout. "Poor Blanks."

"Why do you call me *Poor Blanks?*"

"Because you've had to give up so much. I know Mrs. Ennis must have meant a great deal to you."

"I've told you any number of times I don't wish to discuss the woman. She's nothing to me."

Glee slid her hand along the side of his face. "You've had a most fatiguing day. I declare there's nothing more tiresome than sitting and looking at figures all day. I vow, 'tis more exhausting than digging in the garden." She glanced up at him and smiled. "Though I daresay you've likely never dug in a garden in your life."

"My lack of skills is only exceeded by my propensity to get in scrapes."

Glee scowled. "You've been listening to that wretched Aurora for too long."

He could not help but smile at the fiery little woman who was his greatest champion. Some good things came along with this marriage. Unfortunately, he would not be allowed to partake of most of them. Before he knew what he was doing, he lifted Glee's tiny hand and pressed a kiss into it.

She smiled. "What was that for?"

"For your loyalty," he said throatily.

"I told you I'll always be your best friend. In that respect I shall be a true wife to you, even if we aren't married in the real sense."

He couldn't get a read on her. She *did* care for him. She always had. She had even told him she enjoyed kissing him. He laughed to himself when he remembered her vow to improve her kissing. He could not see any need for improvement. Just thinking about pressing his lips to hers aroused him. Which wouldn't do at all. Nor would it do any good for Glee to fall in love with him, as Carlotta had done. The only thing constant about his affections was their inconstancy. And it wouldn't do at all to hurt Glee. Precious little Glee.

Her eyes shone as she watched him. "You must allow me to tell you what I've had Cook prepare for our dinner. There's to be a magnificent roast beef, stewed eels, plum pudding, buttered lobster and many vegetables, though I know you're not overly fond of vegetables."

"With all of my favorite foods, I shan't have to eat any of the vegetables. It sounds like a very good meal indeed. I must commend you on your household management. You're doing a fine job." If only he knew what she had done with the blasted earrings.

"I daresay there's room for improvement. By the way, dearest, did you see Archie today?" she asked.

A grim line settled on his lips. "I did. I saw his mother, too. She's barely older than you, and she's skinny like him. I have reason to believe she prefers gin to eating."

Glee winced. "Her poor son."

"The thing of it is, I don't know how I can help them."

"The crowns you pay him are of some help," she consoled.

"Yes, the lad told me he makes more in a single day than his mother earns in a month."

"That's terrible, but you must console yourself that people of that class *do* know how to economize, to get their money to last."

"But," he said, "people who live for their gin are a different breed altogether. It's my understanding they're given to focusing their entire lives on their drink."

"Oh, dear."

He tussled her hair. "I'm sure you've no experience with soakers."

"Only George," she said with resignation. "Before he married."

Gregory laughed. "Your brother was not a soaker. He drank to excess when he was young and with friends. A real soaker is one who drinks with or without friends. One who *has* to drink every day. One who becomes quite ill when not allowed to drink."

"Oh, dear. How does one go about changing a soaker?"

"There are many who say it cannot be done. Once a drunk, always a drunk. I understand some of them have the best of intentions but somehow cannot seem to help themselves."

"We must think of something, Blanks."

He nodded and rose. "We'd best get ready for dinner."

She stood and tucked her arm into his.

As they climbed the stairs, he asked, "Will you need help unfastening your jewels?"

She stiffened. "Patty can help."

So his wife did not need his assistance, he reflected bitterly. Was it his presence that repulsed her or her guilt over the earrings?

* * *

"A very good dinner, my love," Gregory said to Glee, who sat at the opposite end of the table from him, candlelight casting shadows on her lovely face. He had scarcely been able to remove his eyes from her all night. As the light flickered off her creamy chest and her elegant neck, he found himself longing to kiss a trail along her milky flesh.

She looked up at him and smiled.

Only a blind man could have failed to notice how fetching his wife looked tonight. She wore an emerald gown made of the sheerest silk that hugged the graceful curves of her body. Her eyes matched the green gown perfectly.

Because of his contentment with Glee, it had not been difficult to praise her, to toss her lovelorn looks, or to murmur endearments—all for the benefit of her sister, of course.

In fact, that sister's husband served ably as a role model for Gregory, for he clearly worshipped his wife.

When the first course was removed, along with Felicity's untouched eel, Thomas Moreland had lowered his brows. "Is anything the matter, love? I see you did not eat the eel."

"Everything's perfect, my sweet," she answered. "It's so perfect, in fact, that I cannot begin to eat all of it. I must save room for the buttered lobster. You know what a particular favorite it is of mine."

Her husband smiled, but his worries apparently mounted again during the next course. "I declare, my love," he began, "your color is off. You're so very pale. Are you feeling quite the thing?"

Felicity tossed back her head and laughed. "Honestly, Thomas, if you won't stop your wretched worrying over me, I swear I'll never bear you another child—and I know you want several."

Gregory's glance swept to Thomas. He wished to

gauge Moreland's reaction. Would the man honestly desire that his cherished wife go through birthing again? And again? Until he lost her?

"I know you keep assuring me of your hardiness, my love, but I do so worry," Thomas said.

There had been a time when Gregory would have thought it unmanly for a man—especially a big, strapping man like Moreland—to be so completely besotted over a woman, but now Gregory was beginning to learn that such deep affection was as much a part of life as cutting teeth. He'd just seen bloody little of it in his life.

While a bit too much in love with his wife, Moreland did make a rather good pattern card for Gregory to copy. After all, he must convince the Morelands—and Jonathan—of his love for Glee.

"Did you find anything amusing to do today, my love?" Gregory asked Glee.

She nodded. "Thanks to your considerate friends—Timothy and the twins—I was able to go to the Pump Room this morning."

"Was there a terrible crush there?" he asked.

"Enough. Felicity signed the book, so I daresay Winston Hall will be converged upon tomorrow."

"I hope my friends had the good manners to take you for a turn about the Pump Room?"

"Timothy had the good manners to fetch my water, but I had to settle for Mr. Jefferson to walk me about the chamber."

Anger boiled within him. Why would that scoundrel not leave his wife alone? Was the fiend bent on getting even with him because of that nasty business with Miss Douglas?

Glee set down her fork and directed a glance at her husband. "You will be pleased to know all three of your friends warned me not to become too friendly with Mr. Jefferson. They said you wouldn't like it above half."

Only with the greatest restraint was Gregory able to keep his voice from trembling with anger. "They were correct."

She pushed her turnips about her plate with a fork and did not meet his gaze. "I daresay Mr. Jefferson's a bounder, but I fail to see what harm it would do for me to speak to the man. I declare, it would cause more suspicion were I to cut him or avoid him entirely."

"You must trust me on this, my dear. I only want what's best for you." Now he was beginning to sound like the besotted Thomas Moreland!

"You must listen to your husband on this matter," Felicity said firmly.

After dinner Glee and Felicity retired to the saloon and sat next to one another on a silken sofa.

"You look so lovely, my pet," Felicity said, covering her sister's hand with her own. "Marriage must agree with you."

Glee swallowed. "I've never been happier." In spite of the fact her husband neither loved her nor wanted her, Glee truly was happy. Being with Blanks every day, greedily accepting any affection he might choose to cast her way, filled her with love.

Also, she liked being mistress of a house, being married to a man of means. But most of all, she just liked being with Blanks day in and day out. Had she the choice, she would not hesitate to marry him again.

"I confess," Felicity said, "I never thought anyone could love a man as dearly as I love Thomas, but I believe you care for dear Blanks in the same way. And I think he loves you as Thomas loves me."

"That would be my fondest wish, but Blanks has a

great distance to go before he'll love me that much.
Don't forget Thomas loved you, and only you, for the
six long years he was off in India, dreaming of coming
home and winning your love. Then the poor man had
to patiently wait another half-year before you finally
realized you had fallen in love with him. And now . . .
to tell you the truth, Thomas is quite obnoxious in his
devotion!"

"How dare you say my precious husband is obnoxious!" Felicity chided playfully. Then she leaned toward Glee and whispered, "To tell you the truth, I'm
just as obnoxious over him. He's not always the mushy,
moon-eyed lover. He's wise and strong and good-
hearted while maintaining the admiration of other, less
powerful men."

"You don't have to convince me. I've seen him when
he's in one of his kingly modes."

"And I've seen a tremendous change come over
Blanks," Felicity said. "I know it's only been two
weeks, but he seems so much more mature."

Being with Blanks every day, Glee had been unable
to detect a change in him, but now that she thought
on it, she realized Felicity was right. He was more
mature. Hadn't she called him an *old stick* any number
of times? Marriage truly had changed him. He backed
away from the pranks he would have heartily endorsed
only weeks before. He was taking his responsibilities
with his father's estate quite seriously, even though it
was tedious. And he grew troubled over those who
were less fortunate. She smiled to herself. Blanks was
changing. For the better.

His father, bless his everlasting soul, had known her
beloved Blanks better than Blanks knew himself.

"Marriage does seem to have matured Blanks,"
Glee agreed. "He even assures me he no longer keeps
his mistress."

Color hiked up Felicity's face. "I wish you wouldn't talk about such matters, but I daresay a pleasured man has no need to seek another bed." She looked up at Glee and smiled. "So it must be that you are properly warming your husband's bed, pet."

"Properly?" Glee said with a sly smile. "I was hoping it was improperly!"

Felicity smiled into the fan she held over her blushing face. "I daresay you've changed even more than your husband."

"Well, I *have* become a woman."

She heard the sound of the door closing and turned her head to see Blanks enter the saloon and walk toward her, a smoldering look in his eyes.

"Yes, you have become a woman, my love," he said, as he walked to her and bent to plant a light kiss on the back of her neck.

A tingle raced down her spine. 'Twas such a simple little gesture on his part, yet it unraveled her tight control. She smiled up at him. If this was how he was going to act in front of her sister, Glee prayed Felicity would come to Blankenship House several times a day.

The two men sat across from them.

"My sister was just saying how much more mature you seem," Glee said to Blanks. "You know, Blanks, I believe your father would be proud of the man you've become."

He stiffened for a second, then his slow smile came. "Do you think so?"

"Undoubtedly. I, too, am very proud of you, my dearest." Whether her husband liked it or not, Glee loved to voice endearments.

Tired from their journey, Felicity and Thomas did not stay late. After seeing them to the door, Gregory and Glee mounted the stairs together, hand in hand, as was their custom.

When they came to Glee's door, she looked up at him. "Shall we practice my kissing?"

He began to laugh. "It's more fun when it's unplanned. Spontaneous. You'll have to wait until I'm again struck by the impulse to kiss you." By Jove, but it was bloody difficult not to take her in his arms this very minute and crush her to him. But he had to be careful. Glee's heart was too fragile to toy with.

He pressed a kiss on top of her lovely head. "Good night, sweet Glee."

"Good night, dearest."

He smiled all the way to his chamber. Stanley had waited up for him and helped him undress.

Then Gregory collapsed onto his bed. It had been a tiring day. He was glad Glee had not made plans to leave the house this evening. That was one thing about the girl who was his wife. She seemed to have an instinctive knowledge of what he wanted and what he didn't want. She really was the perfect wife.

He thought of laying a trail of kisses down her slender neck and to the sweet valley between her breasts. And, sweet heavens, but he wanted her. He tried to tell himself it was just that he had been without a woman for too long. Which he undoubtedly had. It had been three months. He could not remember ever going that long without a woman. The trouble was, he didn't want another woman.

He wanted Glee. And he would never take her.

NINETEEN

As much as she loved her sister, Glee was glad Felicity was so much in her husband's pocket. For Glee had most enthusiastically abandoned her former ways and embraced the notion of being one of the bucks. Making the rounds of the milliners and mantua makers and linen drapers with her perfectly feminine sister now seemed as dull as watching grass grow.

'Twas much more fun to accompany Blanks and his friends, to fly through town on her phaeton, and to dress shockingly at the Pump Room.

Her shiny red phaeton gave her no end of pleasure. Though it had been her fondest hope to be "the woman in red," Blanks had forbidden her to wear the shocking red gown when driving in the equally shocking scarlet phaeton. So today she wore black. Not the modest dress of one in mourning, but a sensational one that allowed great expanses of her chalk-white skin to show.

Driving on the Pulteney Bridge, she came abreast of Appleton and brought her rig to a stop. "Would you care to race?" she challenged, shooting a smile at him.

His brows drew together. "Don't think Blanks would like it above half, Pix."

"La! I allow him complete liberty and he reciprocates."

Appleton's eyes shifted. "You wouldn't career through the streets of Bath?"

"Heavens, no! I would never forgive myself if someone were to get hurt. I was thinking about the road from here to Winston Hall."

Appleton bit his lip as he nodded. "Very well."

"Shall we wager?" she asked, a hopeful smile lighting her face.

He shook his head emphatically. "I refuse to take your money. Besides, I know for a fact, Blanks don't hold with you wagering."

"But my dear Timothy, Blanks need not know everything."

"I ain't going to let you win the race, and I ain't going to take your money."

She pouted. "Blanks does say how talented a driver you are. Four-in-Hand Club and all that. At all events, the race will be good experience for me. Shall we go?" She actually stood up, the reins drawn into her gloved hands.

"You first," he said.

With a flick of the crop, she was off.

He followed, and soon passed her. Which fired her fury. Her horse was capable of going as fast as his. And her rig was just as well made as his. She did not like being left behind by him. She flicked the ribbons and brought down the crop on the chestnut's flank. It spurred ahead and came parallel with Appleton's phaeton and a length behind his gray.

Appleton turned to look at Glee with a devilish grin.

Her hair had come unfastened and streaked behind her like a flapping flag in all its coppery glory. She grew simultaneously hot, then cold, and wished for her cloak while alternately happy that she wore none.

He pulled away again, and she furiously flicked the ribbons, which resulted in her gaining distance. But not enough. She lagged two lengths behind.

The passing scenery blurred by. Woods and cottages and lanes disappeared soon after they came into her vision. On foot, the distance between Bath and Winston Hall seemed so very long. Even in a carriage it had. But in a racing phaeton, the trip whisked by.

Appleton came to a stop at the avenue that led to Winston Hall. A few seconds later, Glee pulled up. "How fortunate that you did not allow me to wager," she said in gasping breaths.

He ran a hand through his windblown hair and chuckled. "You did admirably. Now, should you like to call on your sister?"

Realizing how disgraceful she must look with her hair flying loose, she said, "I think not. My sister would likely not countenance such an action as I've just taken part in. She's a bit old-fashioned, you know."

"Then canter back to Town with me. We can plot our scheme for tonight's assembly."

She and Appleton conspired throughout their trip back to Bath and parted near the Abbey, their plans for the evening finalized. It had been decided that Appleton would write the notes, for Glee feared Miss Eggremont would recognize her handwriting from the many times she had signed the book at the Eggremonts' residence.

She had just started down Milsom Street when a man in brown began waving at her. On closer examination, she realized the man was Mr. Jefferson. She stiffened as she tugged the reins.

Her phaeton had not come to a complete stop, but it had slowed enough for him to grab on and hoist himself up onto the seat beside her.

She flicked him an angry glance. "I don't recall inviting you, Mr. Jefferson."

"Be that as it may, I wanted to see you this morning. I've just left the Pump Room, where I was most disappointed not to find you."

Her head held high, she continued driving down Milsom Street. "Surely you could not have expected me to kiss you in the Pump Room?"

"No, not there. Please turn around to Sydney Gardens. There is a small grove there where we can perform the deed."

Her hands began to tremble. "I will not!"

"If you hope to regain possession of your earrings, you will do as I say."

She gritted her teeth. "You really are odious!"

"I only wish to return the earrings to their rightful owner."

She drove on in silence for several minutes. Perhaps she should go to Sydney Gardens with him. If he was correct about kissing her in a place where they wouldn't be seen . . . *"If* I should be persuaded to go to Sydney Gardens and allow you to . . . to kiss me, will you then return my earrings?"

"Of course."

"And you promise not to tell anyone about the kiss?"

"On my honor as a gentleman."

"Methinks you are not a gentleman or else you would not have taken my jewels." She rounded a corner and directed the phaeton back down Gay Street, toward Sydney Gardens.

"If it comes between honor and my desire for you, Mrs. Blankenship, then I am no gentleman."

Her eyes widened. "Just as I thought! How do I know I'll get my earrings back?"

"I'm rather afraid you'll have to trust me."

"Perhaps I'll tell my husband to fetch the earrings, after all."

"And have him think you gave me the diamonds as a lover's gift?"

She turned to look at him through narrowed eyes. "My husband would never believe that."

"It would be your word against mine. Don't forget, I have the earrings and you don't."

Blanks would know of the man's dishonesty, but she dared leave nothing to chance. Her position as Blanks's wife was far too precarious. "I've decided to give you one kiss." Her heart drummed madly. What if he tried to kiss her with open mouth? Or worse. What if he . . . tried to take liberties with her body? She would make sure they were far enough away from the crowds that they wouldn't be seen when they kissed, but not far enough away that her screams could not be heard if he proved to be untrustworthy.

During the ten-minute drive to Sydney Gardens, her hands trembled and she shivered. The sun that had earlier negated a need for a cloak now hid behind gloomy clouds. How she wished for a cloak! It could have served another purpose besides warming her. It could have covered her daring decolletage from the wicked Mr. Jefferson's hungry gaze. For the man would not remove his eyes from her. When she chanced a glimpse at him, the hunger in his eyes terrified her. If only Blanks would look at her like that!

Because the sun had all but vanished, few people milled about the crisscross paths of the park when she crossed the fields that were beginning to turn green. She turned onto the bridle path. She had never before noticed there was a wooded area that sloped away from the rest of the park. It was truly a place where they would not be seen.

She fervently hoped no one saw her. Her hair still

hung loose. Vast amounts of her skin were exposed. And she was alone with a man who was not her husband. Not a proper picture at all.

To make matters worse, she was riding in a scarlet phaeton that was sure to attract attention. If she could only get through the next few minutes, she would take care to amend her wayward ways. As much as Blanks liked racy women, he was sure to fume over her scandalous behavior.

Despite the chill which sent goose bumps down her back and arms, her cheeks grew hot as she turned down the lane to the thicket of trees.

Then she felt it. The scoundrel had the nerve to lay his warm hand on her exposed shoulder!

She swatted it. "How dare you! Your handling of me, sir, was no part of our bargain."

"Forgive me. I couldn't resist. You're so lovely."

She spun around to face him, her eyes shooting daggers. "And so taken," she quipped.

"Ah, yes, Blankenship."

They were surrounded by trees on either side of them. Only the road behind them was exposed to the park. She came to a stop and turned to him, her shaking hands still gripping the reins. "Kiss me, quick."

He scooted even closer to her and drew her to him even as she tried to push away.

"I can't kiss you properly if you won't cooperate," he snapped.

"I am cooperating—I just won't have your arms around me."

"But my dear, that's all part of kissing. Has your husband taught you nothing?"

"My husband, if you must know, is an excellent teacher." Then, still gripping the reins, she went flying into his arms and lifted her face to his for a kiss.

She thought she would cast up her accounts when

she felt the heat of his lips come down on hers. She silently counted to ten—very quickly—then pushed him away just as he was attempting to open her mouth with his tongue. "That's quite enough!" she shrieked as she stood up, took her crop, and swatted her chestnut, pulling the reins to turn the phaeton back to the park.

Gregory was leaving his solicitor's on horseback when, from the corner of his eye, he saw a bright red phaeton whisk down Gay Street. And sitting next to his wife was a man who looked dangerously like Jefferson. There was nothing for him to do but to follow her. Thoughts of poor Miss Douglas's fate at Jefferson's hands choked Gregory with fear. Not Glee. Not his sweet, innocent Glee.

As he drew closer he was able to confirm that it was, indeed, Jefferson who sat beside Glee. And she looked as if she had just taken a tumble in the hay. If it had been any other woman, he would feel sure that's what had just occurred. But not Glee. She wouldn't ever . . . She had promised. His chest tightened and he began to tremble.

He'd not felt such a retching feeling in the pit of his stomach since his father died. And he had only himself to blame. If only he had exposed Jefferson over the business with Miss Douglas, but he'd been too sensitive to the woman's reputation. A mere cut by London society had done little to suppress Jefferson's wanton ways. Gregory also felt guilty that he'd given Glee so little affection she was forced to seek it from a man of Jefferson's ilk.

He cursed the day he had agreed to marry her, but he knew he would never have been able to stand by

and allow Jefferson to take liberties with the girl.
Whether she was his wife or not, he would have cared.

When he saw her phaeton disappear into the woods,
he was prepared to intercede. Roiling, blinding anger
swept over him and filled him with rage as he spurred
forward with life-or-death speed. Then he saw Jefferson lay a hand on Glee's bare shoulder, and he grew
sickened. And so full of loathing he wanted to kill
William Jefferson. He jabbed his booted feet into his
mount and cursed it to go faster.

His heart pounded and his head swam as he watched
Glee's phaeton roll to a stop. Then Jefferson pulled
Glee into his embrace and kissed her.

Spurring his mount to a sprint, Gregory came to a
sudden stop at what he witnessed next. Glee stood up,
took the reins and turned around, leaving the thicket
with blinding speed.

Not wishing to be caught following her, Gregory
slipped in between some tall yews until Glee was out
of sight. He was still trembling all over and in a quan-
dary as to what to think. His wife had clearly kissed
Jefferson. Then it appeared she had pushed him away
and hastened to get back to safer ground. What was
going on?

He sat there on his mount for several minutes, his
head buried in his shaking hands. So this wretchedness
was what being married had brought him. Hang it all!
He had a good mind to get foxed.

Glee grew worried when Blanks had not returned
home in time to go to the assembly. She fought the
urge to send notes around to Timothy and the twins,
inquiring about her husband. After all, she had promised Blanks their marriage would not prevent him from
doing exactly as he had done before their marriage.

She hated going off to the assembly without knowing if Blanks had come to harm, but Felicity and Thomas had planned to collect her—and Blanks—in their carriage. She could not allow Felicity to know of her worry or to know how powerless of a wife she was. There was nothing for it but to ride along with Felicity and Thomas and pretend to be happy.

Her decision made, she called for Patty to assist her in getting ready for the ball. "We must make haste," Glee urged. "Felicity will be here any minute."

Feeling a curious mixture of anger and anxiety over Blanks, Glee ordered Patty to fetch the red dress. She had no sooner put it on when Hampton—from the other side of the chamber door—announced that Mr. and Mrs. Moreland had arrived and were ready to go to the assembly.

Patty fastened a red plume in Glee's hair, then Glee, without taking even a glance in her mirror, was out the door and hurrying down the stairs.

Felicity, wearing a sky-blue gown and a scowl on her face, watched as Glee came down the stairway. Glee had unconsciously worn the dress to get back at Blanks but had quite forgotten that her sister was sure to disapprove of so daring a gown.

"Oh, dear," Felicity said, "Blanks will allow you to wear that?"

"The thing of it is Blanks is not here so he cannot object," Glee said cheerfully, taking a shawl Hampton proffered and wrapping it around her shoulders.

"Where is our brother tonight?" Felicity asked. "I thought he was going to accompany us."

What would she tell them? Were she to say she did not precisely know where he was, Felicity would think it odd for a new bride to be so ignorant of her husband's whereabouts. Glee chose to avoid a direct answer. "I'm sure he'll join us when he finishes." She only hoped Felicity did not ask what Blanks needed to finish doing.

Felicity's good breeding prevented her from further inquiry. "Then I'm glad we decided to fetch you, for I wouldn't like going to our first assembly back in Bath and not have you for company, pet."

Glee slipped her arm into her sister's and walked with her to the front door. "I assure you I wouldn't care to miss tonight's assembly. Blanks's chums have planned some rather lively activity."

In the carriage, Glee enlightened Felicity and Thomas on the twins' and Appleton's lark at the last assembly but did not reveal what tonight's prank was.

When they arrived at the assembly, Glee's heart sank to see that Appleton and the twins were there. Without Blanks. She had assured herself he was with them. If he was not with them, where was he? Her heart thudded and her stomach dropped. Was he with another woman? With Carlotta?

She was happy for the opportunity to dance the first set with Appleton. Though he rarely danced, his gallantry induced him to step in for his missing friend. "I say, where's Blanks tonight?" he asked as they strolled onto the dance floor.

"That's what I was going to ask you. Have you not seen him this evening?"

He shook his head.

"Then I'm not precisely sure where he is. I daresay he'll show presently."

"I'm sure you're right."

As they left the dance floor at the end of the set, she saw Blanks. Though he appeared in formal dress and looked devilishly handsome, she could tell instantly he was in his cups.

And blazing anger flashed in his eyes when he met her gaze.

TWENTY

Appleton guided Glee directly to her husband. "Just filling in 'til you got here, old fellow," he said to Blanks as he handed Glee over.

Blanks ignored his friend and addressed Glee. "You are to dance with no one but me, madame," he said with barely controlled anger, his speech altered by the drink Glee smelled on his lips.

Glee and Appleton exchanged puzzled glances, then she took both of Blanks's hands. "I shall be delighted to dance with you, dearest. I've been so terribly worried about you."

Their further conversation was prevented by the appearance of Felicity and Thomas. "Good to see you, Blankenship," Thomas said.

Felicity presented her hand to Blanks, and he obliged by pressing his lips to it but gave her no greeting.

Glee's pulse raced as she watched her husband. His perpetual smile was absent and his eyes smoldered with fury. He left little doubt that he was angry with her, but she had no inkling what she had done to provoke such anger. "Come, dearest," she said, linking her arm through his, "let's take a turn about The Octagon so you can tell me all about your meeting with Mr. Willowby today."

"And you, my dear," he said mean-spiritedly, "can enlighten me about *your* day."

She continued to hold his hand as they pressed through the throng of carefree merrymakers in silken finery. Then they came upon William Jefferson, who presented her, then Blanks, with a wicked smile.

Blanks shocked Glee by barking, "A private word with you, Jefferson."

Jefferson's black eyes danced. "At your service, my good man."

Glee squeezed Blanks's hand as they continued toward The Octagon, Jefferson following on their heels. When they reached The Octagon, Blanks disengaged his hand from hers. "What I have to say to your . . . *friend* is nothing a lady should hear."

'Twas as if she had suffered a sudden thrust of knife. *Blanks knew about the kiss.* She began to tremble. "I beg to be allowed to stay, for I fear your conversation will not be without reference to me."

Blanks's lips twisted into a cynical smile. "Suit yourself, madame."

She hated to hear herself so curtly addressed as *madame.*

They entered the dimly lit Octagon but were not alone. A number of couples strolled the perimeter of the gallery room. Glee followed Blanks to the center of the chamber, where he came to a stop and faced Jefferson with a murderous glare. "I don't choose to tread on my wife's reputation," Blanks slurred, "but I give you warning that if you ever again seek to dance with my wife or to see her in private, I *will* call you out."

Jefferson tossed his head back and laughed. "Must you sound so maudlin? I assure you there's nothing more than a mild flirtation between Mrs. Blankenship and me. And truth be told, the flirtation has been rather one-sided."

Glee's heart drummed madly as Blanks tore into Jefferson, twisting the man's silken lapels in his big hands and thrusting his face nose to nose with Jefferson. "Keep your filthy hands off my wife or I'll kill you."

Terror-stricken, Glee watched the two men, one enraged, the other frightened. Then her eyes darted to the others who shared the chamber. They could not have heard Blanks's threats, but they could bear witness to his angry grip on Jefferson. And scandal was the last thing Blanks needed. Not with Jonathan fishing for any sign that his brother's marriage was in jeopardy. "Blanks, please," she said with trembling voice, "others will see you."

Blanks let go of Jefferson's coat and whirled at Glee. "You should have considered that before you met your lover in broad daylight in a phaeton that everyone in Bath recognizes as Mrs. Blankenship's."

Glee shifted her gaze from Blanks to Jefferson and spoke firmly. "Do as my husband says and leave us alone."

His eyes wide with fear, Jefferson nodded, spun on his heel, and left the Assembly Rooms altogether.

"He's not only a dishonorable lout, he's also a coward," Blanks said. Blanks curled his hand around Glee's arm until she winced with pain.

"Please, Blanks, don't make a scene. You've got to remember Jonathan."

"You certainly didn't," he said in guttural voice.

"I can't deny that I acted with complete impropriety, but you must believe there's nothing between Jefferson and me. You cannot know how much I loathe the man."

The pain on Blanks's face startled her when he spoke. "You told me you'd not have an affair."

"You'll have to take my word for it, Blanks. I have not had an affair—and I never will." Her voice softened. "Hurting you is the last thing I'd ever want to do."

"I think we'd best leave," he said angrily.

"But we can't. People will talk. The best thing to do is to stay at the assembly and convince everyone of how happy we are. We can't afford for anyone to suspect there's disharmony in our marriage."

"But there *is* a great deal of disharmony."

How those words hurt her! Especially when a harmonious marriage was what she desired most in the world. "That's for only you and me to know. To others, we must appear deliriously happy."

"You expect me to look happy when I saw my wife kiss another man? When I've threatened to kill that man?"

"Just for a little while, Blanks," she pleaded. "We must dance one set together, then we'll go home. You've drunk too much, and I need to put you to bed."

He twisted her arm even harder. "I had good reason to drink."

Yes, he did. He had seen her kiss Jefferson. Glee wanted to tell him the circumstances that led her to bestow the kiss on the loathsome man, but she could not bear to hurt Blanks by allowing him to think she valued *his* earrings so little she could wager them in a card game. Better for him to think her merely careless in her choice of friends. "I cannot disagree with you, but please, come dance with me. Just one set."

She watched his glassy, reddened eyes as he nodded.

As they were leaving The Octagon, Glee saw Felicity swiftly pass through its other side to the Bennett Street exit.

When Glee and Blanks reentered the ballroom, Appleton came rushing up to them. "Something quite dreadful's happened," he said.

Glee arched a brow. "What, pray tell?"

"I gave the note to a servant and asked him to deliver it to the lovely blonde in blue. I meant, of course, Miss Eggremont, but the idiot presented it to your sister."

Glee's eyes widened. "Oh, dear. I suppose that means Miss Eggremont is also wearing blue."

Appleton nodded.

"I shall run and tell Felicity about the mix-up in our hoax," Glee volunteered, then left the ballroom in order to fetch her sister.

Appleton, who was now joined by the twins, apprised Gregory of what had transpired.

"The lot of you are five and twenty years of age," Gregory scolded. "When will you stop behaving as if you're just down from Oxford?" Perhaps he should have taken Glee to Sutton Hall. Bringing her to Bath had proven disastrous.

"I believe the pot's calling the kettle black, old boy," Appleton said. "We ain't the ones three sheets in the wind."

"I think Pixie's right about you," Elvin said to Blanks, shaking his head. "You, dear Blanks, have become an old stick. Even if you are bosky tonight."

"I'll thank you to address my wife as Mrs. Blankenship!" Gregory did not at all like the manner in which his friends cavorted with Glee. They were a very bad influence on so young and impressionable a girl.

His three friends cowered, nodding at him.

Then Thomas came up to them. "Have any of you fellows seen my wife? I seem to have lost her."

"She's meeting Thornton at the Bennett Street entrance," Elvin said.

Thomas's brows drew together as his puzzled glance shifted to each member of the group.

"It's all very simple, Moreland," Blanks explained. Then he proceeded to inform Thomas of the *childish prank*.

"Who, may I ask, is Thornton?" Thomas demanded.

"Nobody you'd want to know," Appleton said. "A braggart if ever there was one with nothing whatsoever to make him so highly value his worth."

Blanks watched Glee and her sister reenter and cross the ballroom.

Relief on her face, Glee addressed Appleton. "Mr. Thornton hasn't arrived yet. There's still time to deliver another note to Miss Eggremont."

"He'll do no such thing!" Gregory snapped.

Glee shrugged and lifted her unhappy gaze to Appleton.

"Daresay," Appleton said, "it's far too childish a prank for men of five and twenty to commit."

The orchestra began to play a waltz, and Glee turned a smiling face to her husband. "Shall we dance this set together before we have to leave, dearest? I know how very fatigued you are from your tedious day."

Despite the fury which still raged within him, he realized Glee was right to put on a good front. In his wrath, he had almost lost sight of the reason why he had married Glee in the first place and the necessity that compelled him to appear happily wed. Silently, with an almost imperceptible nod, he offered her his arm and they strolled to the dance floor.

When the orchestra began, he held her stiffly and made no effort to converse with her. A pity he'd had so very much to drink. It caused his steps to falter and him to use Glee to prevent himself from falling flat on his face. His drinking also released his tongue from the inhibitions placed on it by society.

"I know I promised not to meddle in your affairs, Blanks—"

"Then don't."

He felt her tremble beneath his touch. "I don't mean to meddle," she said feebly, "I only ask that when you have made plans with me—such as we had for to-night—you send around a note telling me you'll not come. I declare, Blanks, I thought something dreadful had happened to you."

"Then you would have been a very rich widow, madame. Your brother saw to that in the marriage contracts."

"I wish you wouldn't call me *madame*. It sounds so . . . so stern, and I beg you not to try to make it sound as if I married you for your fortune."

He slowed his step and looked down into her face. "Did you not?"

She stomped her foot. "I did not! I admit I like the idea of being married to a wealthy man, but that's not the reason I married you. I married you because . . . because I thought we were the best of friends."

He detected a whimper in her voice. She was about to cry. He needed to get her out of this room before she made a scene. "Come, *my dear,* it's best that we go home."

She drew a long breath. "Yes, let's."

He took her hand and began to wind through the dancers far more erratically than he would have were he sober. Once out of the room, he procured her wrap, then they left the building.

"Bloody hell, it's raining," he muttered. "Stay here. I'll call a hansom."

"It's not raining very hard. I don't mind getting wet."

He looked at her slender figure in that abominable red gown with only a thin shawl over her bare shoulders. "I do mind. I shouldn't like to be blamed if my wife were to come down with lung fever and die."

The chit burst out crying. "But you'd be far better off—and much happier—with me dead," she whimpered between sobs.

He backed her into the brick wall under the portico and, with his arms, pinned her against the front of the building. "Don't talk like that. I shouldn't like it all if you were to die," he said in a gentle voice. "I would lose my dearest, most exasperating friend."

She raised up on her tiptoes and hugged him. "Oh, Blanks, I feel so terribly wretched that I've made you angry. I promise to be a good wife from now on."

He pulled away from her embrace. "You can start by not wearing that deuced red dress."

She giggled, and he stepped out onto the puddled pavement and signaled for a hansom.

Since Blankenship House was but a few blocks from the Assembly Rooms, they were soon home. And a good thing, Gregory thought. His bed beckoned. He had grown unaccustomed to getting foxed. Since he had decided to marry Glee, his life had tamed considerably. In fact, his friends were right. He *was* becoming an old stick.

He slipped when he tried to get out of the carriage and his knee slammed to the street when he fell. The next thing he knew, Glee had leaped into the wet street and stooped to help him up, her skirts soaking up the water that ran through the streets. "Are you hurt?"

"Of course I'm hurt," he barked.

With the aid of the hansom driver, Glee helped Blanks to the front door, where he grabbed onto the wall and pulled coins from his pocket, which he then thrust at the driver.

Glee opened the door, and Hampton came scurrying to meet them. He looked at Gregory, but his expression did not reveal that he found anything out of the ordinary in Gregory's altered behavior.

"Please help me get Mr. Blankenship up the stairs," Glee said. "He's taken a fall and hurt his knee."

"I don't need any help," Gregory snapped.

"Yes, you do," Glee said, turning back to Hampton.

The unfortunate butler did not know who the master was in this situation. He gazed from one to the other.

Then Gregory stepped forward and grabbed onto the bannister. "I can manage."

Glee raced up the steps to put her arm around Blanks's waist. "Lean on me," she said. He faced her and began to laugh. "Think you to help me when I'm more than twice your size?"

She shot him a defiant glance. "I'm stronger than I look." Then she turned back to poor Hampton. "Thank you, Hampton, but Mr. Blankenship and I will be able to manage now."

When they reached the second-floor landing, Blanks said, "I daresay the entire staff will know tomorrow that the master's been in his cups."

"I daresay you're right," she said, biting her lip as she struggled to walk to his chamber with her arm around him. He was not walking well at all. And his blasted knee hurt like the devil.

Glee opened the door to his bedchamber, then turned back to assist him into the room that was lit only by the fire in the hearth. He hated to admit that leaning on her slenderness really was of assistance. When he got close to his bed, he collapsed on it.

"I'll call Stanley," she whispered.

Gregory snatched her forearm. "But I thought you said you were going to take me home and put me to bed."

"And so I have."

He stared at her, at the fire flickering on her face. At her eyelashes that were still wet from the night's rain. At the foolishly absurd picture of her trying to lift him from the muddy street. At her undeniable loveliness. "Are you not going to undress me?" he murmured.

"That, my dear Blanks, is why I'm going to fetch Stanley."

His hand trailed down her arm and grasped her hand. "You're not behaving very wifely."

She sat on the bed beside him and with a gentle hand swept the wet hair off his forehead. "What do you mean?"

Bloody hell! Did she have no idea how such an intimate gesture would affect a man? Especially a man who'd been without a woman for so long? "Isn't a wife supposed to share her husband's bed?"

She spoke softly. "It . . . it wasn't part of the bargain, but if that's what you want, I will."

He ran his fingers through her radiant hair. "That's what I want," he whispered huskily.

TWENTY-ONE

Of course, it was the liquor speaking. Blanks didn't really want her. Most likely, he wouldn't even remember this night tomorrow. But she could not let this hungered-for blending go unfulfilled. If she could not possess his heart, she would take consolation in his body. She trembled from the sweet anticipation of being physically loved by Blanks. As she lowered her face to his, love surged through her like warm honey.

That first kiss was soft and gentle, with his arms closing around her, blanketing her in his warmth. The next kiss was far more intimate, more passionate. Their mouths opened hungrily, and she drew in the taste of his brandy-flavored tongue. Unaccountably, her breathing grew ragged, and his matched hers, breath for breath.

This intimacy consumed her, pulsing through her body an intense desire to be utterly possessed by the man she loved with all her heart. Her hands glided over the hard muscles of his powerful back, then moved to the front of him, where she slipped her hand into the gap between his shirt buttons. She thrilled to the feel of the hot flesh of his chest and the sound of him groaning with pleasure. Fleeting thoughts of their wedding ceremony flashed through her mind. She and

Blanks belonged to one another, body and soul. She shivered with delight. Tonight his god-like body belonged to her. And she belonged to him. Completely.

"Lie beside me," he crooned huskily into her moistened ear.

Her breath caught as she raised up, then spread herself like warm butter beside him. His arms came around her, urging her closer, so close that she could feel the drumming of his erratic heartbeat. And could feel his man's swell throbbing against her low in the torso.

His hands caressed her back, then her hips, sweeping her up into the maddening rhythm that joined them. She could not think clearly. Her thoughts were like shooting stars, soaring through a vastness that knew no boundaries. She would almost channel the thoughts into words when another, brighter star would streak through her endless pleasure-fogged brain. Through the blur of thoughts and powerful emotions shone her need to feel her flesh against his flesh. She began to unfasten the buttons of his shirt, slowly, seductively, one by one.

With a single, gentle hand he began to lower the bodice of her gown. She felt the rush of cold air cover her breasts. And heard the sharp intake of her husband's breath. He settled his hands on each side of one breast, handling it as if it were a tender piece of fruit.

Then she felt his warm mouth close around one nipple, and she thought she would go mad from the spiraling sensations he aroused within her.

"That wretched dress has to go," he whispered with a groan, trailing his hand down the length of her, leaving a path of tingling flesh.

As much as she wanted him to take her this very moment, to feel him inside her, she would have to briefly draw away from him. In essence this was their true wedding night. And the red gown was no part of it. She thought of the fine ivory lawn night shift she'd bought in the hopes of one day wearing it for Blanks. She would have to force herself away from him to go to her chamber and make herself ready for this most special of nights.

With a final hungry kiss, she slipped from the bed. "I'll come right back to you, dearest," she promised.

He grasped her hand, kissed it, and spoke with a thick tongue. "Hurry, love."

She crossed the soft carpet of his chamber, went through their connecting dressing rooms and came to her own chamber, which was lit only by the fire in the hearth. In the linen press, she found the lawn. Then she shimmied out of her red gown, allowing it to puddle on the floor. She stood there, naked and unashamed, stunned by her need for Blanks. She slipped the lawn over her head, then went to her dressing table where she reached for a bottle of perfume. She dabbed some scent on her neck, glancing in the mirror. Pins still secured her hair. Wanting to feel Blanks's fingers trailing through combed-out hair, she removed all the pins and brushed out her hair before returning to her husband.

When she entered his chamber she heard heavy breathing. Very heavy indeed. Like a sleeping man. With dread, she walked to his bed and gazed upon him. He lay on his back, his arms spread to each side of the bed, his white shirt unbuttoned to reveal his bronzed chest glowing with firelight and its dark hair trailing to his waist. Her hungry gaze traveled to the tussled hair on his head, then to his closed eyes. She drew closer. He was sound asleep.

"Blanks," she whispered as loud as one could whisper.

Nothing.

She sat beside him and ran a gentle hand over his brow.

Nothing.

"Bloody hell." 'Twas an expression exclusive to males, but it exactly summed up her deep, retching disappointment.

Tense with her denied desire, Glee returned to her own chamber and drew off the lawn. It would be worn only for Blanks. She bent to scoop her red gown from the floor, then changed her mind and allowed it to stay where it was. She would prefer Patty and the servants to think it had been thrown off in the heat of passion. She dressed herself in a heavier night shift, pulled back her covers, and climbed onto the bed.

At her immediate recollection of lying with Blanks, her eyes moistened. She had woefully lost what might be her only chance to truly be Blanks's wife. In more than name.

She was consumed with a deep, painful emptiness where she had thought to find fulfillment. Always, she had hoped for this night. She had thought—indeed, longed for—the day to come when she would receive Blanks's seed . . . to bear his child . . . to intertwine their lives so closely they meshed into one.

And now she had nothing. She began to weep.

His chamber was no longer in darkness, Gregory thought as he lay there, not wanting to move and bring back the searing pain in his head. He began to lift a leg and realized he still wore the shoes he had worn to the assembly the night before. Lying on top of the bed instead of in it, he was bitterly cold. The fire had gone out, and he wore but a thin shirt—and it was unbuttoned.

Such were the aftereffects of too much drink. He

remembered storming to the nearest public house in his rage at seeing Glee kiss the devil Jefferson. He remembered drinking all afternoon and into the night, when he had gone home and hurriedly changed for the Assembly Rooms. There had been a scene at the Assembly Rooms. He'd told Jefferson he would call him out if he ever touched Glee again. Then, with a wave of some unknown emotion, Gregory remembered coming here—to this very room—with Glee.

He bolted up in his bed. Good Lord, he had tried to seduce her! He closed his eyes and tried to remember exactly what had happened. He had said she wasn't obliging in her wifely duties . . . then she consented to make love with him.

How could he have forgotten? The taste of her. The feel of her eagerly pressing against him. The softness of her exposed breasts. But, try as he might, he could not remember feeling himself within her. He glanced down at his breeches. He had not removed them. Had he, he would be nude now. Which meant . . . the act had not been consummated. Foxed as he was, he must have bloody well passed out! He laughed a bitter laugh.

Relief washed over him as he fell back into his pillows. Thank God he had not impregnated her. Maddening as she was, he did not care to lose her.

A stabbing pain shot across his brow as he lay there thinking of Glee. Making love to him was not part of their bargain. She had his name, his fortune at her disposal. Why, then, had she willingly chosen to give herself to him? Did she feel obliged by wifely duty? Did she consent in order to assuage her guilt over kissing Jefferson? Had she consented because . . . she cared for him more deeply than she admitted?

Damn! Being married was a most complex affair. Now he was faced with deciding how he would act when he next saw her. Should he allow her to believe he remembered nothing? Should he apologize for his behavior? Perhaps he should warn her never to give in to his drunken demands.

Closing his eyes as if to ward off the pain, he inched his way off the bed and slowly crossed the room to ring the bell for Stanley. His wretched head hurt like the devil. So did his blasted knee. 'Twas enough to keep a man sober for the rest of his life. His valet would know to bring his special elixir. With that, a shave, and clean clothes he would be ready to face his wife. And today, he vowed, he would drink nothing stronger than water.

An hour later—still not feeling quite the thing—he left his chambers and was making his way down the hall to the top of the stairs when he heard his wife's voice at the bottom of the stairs.

"You're to deliver this letter to Mr. William Jefferson at the Paragon Building," she said.

Gregory came to a dead stop. His unsettled stomach flipped. As fuzzy as his memory was of what had happened the night before, he could have sworn Glee told him she would not see Jefferson again. Surely Jefferson would not be stupid enough to meet with a woman whose husband had threatened to kill him. Gregory's soaring rage and all its violent sparks returned.

Shaking with anger, he tore down the stairs and limped past Glee, who was standing in the foyer beside a demilune table, thumbing through the day's post. She looked up at him, color rising in her cheeks.

She looked nothing like the vixen she had appeared last night in the scant scarlet dress. Today, in a pastel sprigged muslin day dress, she looked like the old Glee, the innocent girl who had been his bride. Not the seductress she had been the night before.

"Any ill effects from last night?" she asked with concern.

"A great many, if you must know." He drilled her with an angry gaze. "Why, may I ask, are you sending messages to Jefferson?"

Her eyes widened. "I . . . I wanted to . . . to urge him to heed your ultimatum, of course."

He nodded, then continued on to his library.

Glee had the good sense not to follow him. Had she, he would have thoroughly vented his anger on her.

In his library, he drew open the draperies to allow more light into the room, then sat in a red leather chair behind his massive walnut desk, and with trembling hand penned a note to the Bow Street Runners in London. Since he obviously could not trust his wife to stay away from Jefferson, Gregory would have to impose his will on her without her assistance.

As soon as he had drafted the letter, a rap sounded on his library door.

Was that blasted Glee coming to use her charms to coax him from his anger? "Come in," he snapped.

Hampton presented himself. "Mr. Appleton to see you, sir. May I show him in?"

"Yes, do. And here, post this letter for me."

Gregory got up to greet Appleton. He owed his friend an apology for the way he had acted at the Assembly Rooms the night before.

He bowed when Appleton entered the library. "So glad you've come, old boy. I fear I owe you an apology for my abominable behavior last night."

Appleton smiled and dropped into the chair nearest Gregory. "It's your poor wife you owe the apology."

At least he had refrained from calling her *Pixie*. Still, Gregory could not like Appleton butting into his marital affairs. "What happens between my wife and me is no concern of yours."

"Be that as it may, I don't like seeing her get her head snapped off when she cares so deeply for you."

Glee care for him? He burst out laughing.

"What's so humorous?"

He couldn't tell Appleton the reason for his bitter mirth, no matter how close they were. "I was merely thinking how adorable my wife is when she's in one of her deeply-attached-to-me modes."

"I think you're deuced lucky to have her for a wife."

Gregory sent Appleton a quizzing glance. "You mean you no longer abhor the idea of marriage?"

"Well, I wouldn't want to be like Sedgewick. The man lives and breathes for that wife and babe. It's different with you and . . . Mrs. Blankenship. She allows you complete liberty. She told me so yesterday when we was racing phae—" Appleton clapped a palm to his mouth.

Gregory's brows drew together. "You raced with my wife?"

" 'Twasn't a real race."

"Where did this *faux* race take place?"

"On the road from Bath to Winston Hall. And we didn't wager. Told her as how you wouldn't like it above half."

Gregory rolled his eyes. "Then I can deduce that my wife wished to wager?"

"She ain't been out much. She doesn't know it ain't the thing."

"Then I must rely on your good character to steer her away from any such behavior." Gregory leaned forward. "And to keep her away from William Jefferson."

Appleton's eyes narrowed. "Depend upon it. The three of us have already warned her about the bloke."

"And her reaction?"

"She heartily agreed with us about his low character."

"That is reassuring news, to be sure."

"Speaking of news, I wanted to let you know me brother's in town. He signed the book at the Pump Room this morning. And the demmedest thing . . . I saw Miss Eggremont glance over the book, then she comes up to me like we were the oldest and best of friends. *You must make me known to your brother,* she purred. All because he's Lord Appleton, if you ask me."

"I don't doubt it at all. She's rather a schemer." Gregory was perversely pleased at Glee's perception of Miss Eggremont's unflattering character. A pity her perception did not extend to Jefferson.

"A pity our joke on Miss Eggremont last night was not successful," Appleton said as he got to his feet. "I really must go visit with me brother. I wanted to assure myself you weren't still mad at me."

Gregory smiled and stood up. "Never that, old fellow."

After Appleton left, Gregory sat at his desk, staring out the window and wondering how long it would be before he could expect the runner.

TWENTY-TWO

"Hello, Timothy," Glee said as she brushed past him in the hallway, neither meeting his gaze nor slowing down.

He turned around to look after her. "Good afternoon, P— . . . Mrs. Blankenship."

Glee had been too upset to wait for a groom to bring around her phaeton. Running along to the livery stable would save time.

Her phaeton was hitched and ready when she arrived at the livery stable a block away, and the groom assisted her onto the box. Trotting off, she had no idea where she was going. She wanted only to be by herself, to think on the baffling occurrences of the past day.

She crossed the River Avon at the Pulteney Bridge, cantered down Great Pulteney Street, and found herself once more at Sydney Gardens. Unlike the day before, the sun now brightened the sky, and many people took the air in the park. 'Twas so dissimilar to yesterday's dreariness. A pity her spirits were so low, for she would have excessively enjoyed a drive on a day like this.

She turned into the gardens and, with flushed cheeks, thought about the intimacy that had occurred between her husband and her the night before. Why, he had actually put his mouth to her breast! And, with a liquid surge low in her belly, she remembered feeling *that* part of him pressing against her. She had been so close to truly belonging to him.

It couldn't have just been the liquor he'd consumed that made Blanks desire her. Was it not said that liquor brought out the truth? On the other hand, liquor released inhibitions. That much she knew from her own experience drinking wine. Or arrack tea. And she knew for a certainty that, when in their cups, gentlemen went to molly houses. As a girl she had secretly read a letter Timothy Appleton wrote her brother when he was up at Oxford which referred to the night they were in their cups and visited a molly house.

Blanks's behavior today gave her no indication if he remembered last night or not. She had thought she would be able to tell by his words or mood what his reaction to last night was. Did he—or did he not—remember? If only she could have told. Were she to guess, she would say he *did* remember and was angry with her because of her seductive ways. He certainly had not been angry last night! It had been the first time she had truly felt as if she were his wife.

Then again, if he was so foxed he had passed out, he could have been too bosky to remember anything.

A pity it would be inappropriate to quiz him. Or would it? she thought boldly, turning her phaeton around to leave the park. Perhaps it *was* something she ought to discuss with him.

Not now, of course. She had set fire to his fury one too many times in the last day.

She recrossed the River Avon and directed her phaeton along Upper Borough Walls and past Queen Square, unclear what her destination was. She grew repentant every time she thought of Blanks's raging anger. If only she had never kissed the disreputable

Mr. Jefferson. And why had she been so dim-witted as to write him a letter this morning?

She had been so focused on her hungered-for union with Blanks she had given no thought to him discovering that she had written to William Jefferson. And the letter was so pitifully harmless! She merely demanded the return of her earrings. She yearned to wear them for Blanks, to show him how much they meant to her.

Now her temper seared. Why had the wretched William Jefferson not returned her earrings? She had kept her part of the bargain. She had kissed him. A terribly dull kiss, to be sure. Not like with Blanks. She thought of the potency of Blanks's heated kisses. Why had William Jefferson been so eager to claim so innocuous a kiss? He knew she loathed him, yet he still demanded the kiss. It was as if he took perverse satisfaction in embarrassing and angering Blanks. The odious man!

She turned onto Royal Avenue, then trotted along the Royal Crescent, then through Crescent Fields. The sight of an unaccompanied woman driving a bright red phaeton garnered a great deal of attention. Everywhere Glee turned, curious stares followed her. She could not be faulted for trying to impress Blanks with her forwardness. Today, of course, she looked quite simpering in this virginal dress. Why had she not worn something more flamboyant? A pity Carlotta had already claimed purple as her own.

Glee's temper scorched at the thought of Carlotta. She would wager Blanks had never gone to sleep waiting for Carlotta to change clothes! Then a wicked thought struck her. Perhaps Carlotta wore nothing at all when she became intimate with Blanks. Fury pounding in her breast, Glee felt certain she loathed Carlotta as much as she loathed William Jefferson.

Glee had so very much to learn about pleasing Blanks and no idea of where to start.

Another matter causing her consternation was Blanks's complete reversal since they married. To please him, she had tried to be fast, then he acted as if he did not like fast women. When she knew better. The unwavering Blanks persisted in acting as if he were her brother. He grew angry when she addressed his friends by their Christian names. He would not allow her to wager. He forbid even the mildest flirtation with William Jefferson. And he abhorred her seductive red dress at the same time he delighted in removing it!

The offending red dress, though she had never told him, she had copied exactly from one of Carlotta's purple creations. And he most assuredly had liked it on Carlotta Ennis. Try as she might, Glee could not please the man she had married.

All of her battle strategies had failed. It was time to bring out a new arsenal. But what?

She drove on mindlessly until she found herself on Broad Quay, the street where Blanks's solicitor's office was located. She came to a stop in front of Mr. Willowby's office and saw Archie sitting on the steps to the building. He looked up and recognized her, a smile covering his thin face as he leaped to his feet. "Can I be of assistance to ye today, madame?"

"You certainly can. Oblige me by taking these reins, first." She handed him the reins as she climbed down from the phaeton, then she turned to him. "Mind my rig and there'll be a crown in it for you."

He smiled cockily at her as she swept toward the building. She had to climb to the third floor before she located her quarry. There, she found the young woman who had to be Archie's mother.

The woman looked up at Glee with inscrutable hazel eyes, then went back to mopping the wooden hallway.

"I wondered if I could have a word with you," Glee began, walking up to the woman. From three feet away, Glee could smell the gin.

The woman stopped mopping and propped her thin frame on the mop handle, hitching a brow in Glee's direction. Blanks had been right. She was not much larger than her son. And she did so look like little more than a child herself.

"I'm Mrs. Blankenship," Glee said. "My husband is a client of Mr. Willowby's and has done business with your son on, I believe, several occasions."

"The bloke what gives me boy all them crowns?"

Glee nodded. "In fact, my husband offered your son a job as a groom, where his room and board would be furnished, in addition to making a decent salary."

"And what did Archie say to that fine offer?"

"He said he couldn't leave his mother."

A slow smile crossed the woman's dirty face. "More likely, the lad wonders why 'e should work six days a week for a small salary when 'e earns such grand fees from yer 'usband already."

"But my husband has other residences. He's not always going to be in Bath."

"A pity," the woman said, picking up her mop again.

"What's your name?" Glee asked softly.

"Me name's Mildred Agnostinio. Mrs. A., they calls me."

"Agnostinio's Italian, is it not?"

Mildred nodded.

"But certainly your lad's not Italian. He's as fair as you."

"Mr. Agnostinio was me second 'usband."

"But . . . you could hardly be more than twenty, and you've already been married twice?"

"I'm three and twenty," she said proudly.

"You had Archie when you were but fourteen?"

The woman's eyes went cold.

Glee decided to press on. "Where do you and Archie live?"

She shrugged. "What's it to you?"

"My husband and I would like to offer you a position in our household. You would have a fine roof over your head, all your meals, and a . . ."

"A decent compensation," Mildred snapped. "It so 'appens I make a decent salary right where I am."

"And you live in a fine dwelling?"

"Where we live suits us just fine. We can go and come as we please and don't 'ave to answer to no one."

"If you won't care for yourself, can't you at least care about Archie?"

Mildred lifted her chin. "Archie's free to go live with yer 'orses, if that's what 'e wants."

"But all he has is you," Glee whispered somberly. "You can't wish for him to be lonely. He's only a child."

"Me Archie's older than 'is years."

"Because he's had to take care of you all these years. How long have you had your drinking problem?"

The woman whirled at Glee. "Leave me alone. Yer just like all them other do-gooders. I'm 'appy the way I am. Archie's 'appy." Then she picked up her pail and thundered down the stairs.

Glee followed. "Mrs. Agnostinio? Would you mind if I ask Archie once more if he would like to come into service with us?"

"For all I care, ye can take him," she snapped.

Oh, dear, this interview had not gone at all as Glee had planned. She silently followed Mildred down the stairs but made no more attempts to engage her in conversation.

Glee left the building, reaching into her reticule for coins for the lad. "Here, Archie," she said, placing five shillings in his grimy palm. "You've done another fine job. You know, my husband still would like you in service to us. Have you given it any more thought?"

He studied his shoetops. "Me mum needs me."

Glee ran a steady hand over his head. "You're a good lad, Archie."

All the way back to Queen Square, Glee thought of Mildred Agnostinio. The woman obviously was letting her obsession for liquor rule her life. And ruin her life. That was the only explanation for why she would turn down the security of a position in their household, where she would be expected to keep regular hours, to be clean—and not to smell of gin.

If only she could be persuaded to give up her gin. But Blanks was probably right. Some people could never give up their drink.

She must talk it over with Blanks. He was older and had seen more of life than she had. He would know what to do.

Blanks looked up from his correspondence as Glee sailed into the library.

"Oh, Blanks, I'm so happy you're here, for I most particularly wanted to talk to you." She slid into a chair across the desk from him.

His pulse sped up. Was she going to speak of the intimacy that occurred between them the night before? When confronted with it, he would not be able to lie and deny knowledge of it. But how, in a gentlemanly way, could he explain his behavior? He looked up at her. She looked so impossibly innocent. It was hard to believe this was the same woman who had offered him her body the night before. She wasn't the innocent she appeared. He knew without a doubt she had not only kissed Jefferson but had also sent him a letter this very morning. He fleetingly thought of Carlotta's warning. *Glee's not the innocent you think her.* His stomach knotted. Surely Glee *was* innocent. Gregory was most vexed with her. No matter how sweet she looked today. He arched a single brow. "Yes?"

"I talked with Archie's mother."

"May I ask why?"

"To offer her a position in our household, of course."

"Of course. And what was the woman's response?"

"What do you think it was?"

"She turned it down."

"I knew you'd understand, and you're quite right about her turning it down. How did you know?"

"Her propensity to drink. To soakers, their entire lives are ruled by the bottle."

"Is there not something we can do?"

He shook his head. "I wish there were, my dear, but the only person who can help a soaker is himself or herself. They have to *want* to give up the drink."

Glee nodded thoughtfully. She really was such an innocent, he thought. Her youthful idealism collided with harsh reality.

"It's my opinion," she said, "that Mrs. Agnostinio— that's her name, you know—and Archie have no real place to call home."

"You are most likely right."

"You'd think the offer of a fine roof over their heads would be attractive."

"To most people who live on the streets, that would be the case. But not to one whose life is ruled by the obsession for liquor."

"If she doesn't care about herself, you'd think she'd care for her poor son." She looked up from staring dejectedly into her lap. "You were right about her being young. She gave birth to Archie when she was but fourteen."

Gregory winced. "I doubt if she was even married."

Glee's mouth dropped open. "Oh, Blanks, you must be right! That's why she didn't answer when I quizzed her about being married twice. She was ashamed to admit Archie had no father."

"Poor lad," Gregory murmured.

"There must be something we can do."

He got up and moved to her, lifting one of her delicate hands and stroking it tenderly. "I wish there were, but I'm afraid all we can do is continue helping the lad as we are now."

"But they're so thin! I worry about them not getting enough to eat. And Mrs. Agnostinio is likely to take Archie's money and spend it on drink."

"I've already thought of that and have made some small provision for them to get at least one good meal a day."

Her emerald eyes danced as she looked up at him. "You have? Oh, Blanks, that's wonderful. You're such a good man. I'm glad I married you."

It was impossible to stay angry with the maddening wench when she spoke to him like that. And when she possessed such compassion. He rather thought he, too, was glad he married her. Even if she drove him quite mad.

TWENTY-THREE

Gregory had just finished giving instructions to the Bow Street Runner who had arrived from London when Hampton announced Lord and Lady Sedgewick were calling.

Dismissing the runner, Gregory bounded from the library and happily greeted George and his wife. "Are you staying at Winston Hall?" he asked.

"Yes, Felicity insisted," Dianna said. "Where, pray tell, is my sister? I cannot wait for her to show me the house now that you've settled in."

"I believe Hampton's knocked her up to tell her you're here," Gregory said.

Glee's footfall sounded on the stairs, and Gregory looked up at his wife's smiling face. He would have to remember to play the part of the adoring husband in front of her brother. "Dianna's most anxious for you to conduct a tour of our house, love," he said to her.

Unable to contain her joy, Glee ran up and hugged Dianna and George. "It's so very good to have you back in Bath. Where's the baby?"

"She's with her nurse at Winston Hall," George answered.

A disappointed look crossed Glee's face. "Then you

won't be staying with us? I declare, I shall be most vexed with Felicity for hoarding you."

"But there's so much more room at Winston Hall," Dianna defended.

Gregory moved to Glee and settled his hand about her tiny waist. "I daresay Wellington could have put up his whole army in its many chambers."

"I am persuaded the house tour can go along without Blanks and me," George said. "Blanks will have to enlighten me on the current amusements in Bath." He clapped a hand on Gregory's back.

Glee put her hands to her hips. "I should have known my brother would show up in time for the racing season."

George shot his sister a wry smile. "Surely you didn't think I'd come here just to see my sisters."

Blanks lifted Glee's hand and pressed a kiss on it. "George and I will run along to the library, my sweet."

The women sauntered down the foyer in front of George and Gregory, exclaiming over the paintings and the newly painted walls. Gregory was glad he had George to divert him from such deadly dull matters as decorating.

In the library, he poured George a glass of port, then another for himself and dropped onto a sofa opposite George. "You've picked a most interesting time to come, old boy. Not only are the races due to begin, but a bang-up cockfight's to be held day after tomorrow."

"You don't say! Haven't been to one in an age."

"Does it not get tedious living in the country?"

"I must confess I do miss the sporting pleasures the city affords me, but other than that, I've no complaints. There's nothing quite as satisfying as having one's own family and being able to continue on the same land one's ancestors have possessed for centuries. You must be anxious yourself to return to Sutton Hall and start a family."

If only he could be more like George. His father would have been proud of him. He regretted that while his father was alive, he gave him no source of pride. And since his father's death, he had done nothing which would have pleased his parent, save getting married. A pity he wanted no part of marriage. And family. And all those things George had so eagerly embraced. "In due time," he answered.

George settled back and studied Gregory. "I trust my sister is behaving herself?"

Gregory burst out laughing. "Your sister, dear friend, needs a good spanking."

George's brows shot up. "What's the minx up to?"

"For starters, she insists on addressing my friends by their Christian names."

"In public?"

Gregory nodded ruefully. " 'Tis a constant source of anxiety that others will think her . . . well, rather fast, if you must know."

"But you're her master. Can you not just tell her to stop doing that?"

"Ordering a lady about, I'm afraid, does not come naturally to me. However, I have expressed my displeasure a number of times."

"If that's your only problem in a fortnight of being married, I'd say it's not too bad."

"But that's not the only problem. As much as I adore your sister, she vexes me to death. There's also the matter of the phaeton."

"What phaeton?"

"The phaeton Glee purchased herself—without my knowledge, mind you—a high-perch phaeton which she proceeded to paint bright red."

"And she trots about Bath in it unescorted?"

Gregory nodded. "And that's not all. She has taken it into her mind that as a married lady she must dress in the most shocking fashion."

"She looked rather demure today," George defended.

"I cannot disagree, but I must tell you today's gown is not typical. Your sister has taken a propensity to wearing dresses that expose a great deal of flesh. And the colors aren't at all the thing. No pastels for my wife!"

George shuddered. "I'm afraid that sounds rather like Carlotta."

Gregory leveled a stern gaze at his friend. "But Carlotta was *not* my wife."

George cleared his throat. "Dianna informed me Glee knows all about Carlotta. Could Glee possibly be wishing to emulate the woman she may view as a rival?"

That would explain Glee's behavior. *If* theirs was a love match. But Glee was not in love with him. And she had no reason whatsoever to be jealous of Carlotta Ennis. Comparing Glee to Carlotta was like pitting diamonds against tarnished brass. "I've hardly seen Carlotta since I declared my intentions to marry Glee, and I've conveyed as much to my wife, as painful as it is to speak of the matter to her. Unfortunately, she brings up the subject with far more regularity than I'm comfortable with."

George set down his glass and frowned. "Demmed sticky situation, to be sure. But I'm reassured you've given up Carlotta. I had my doubts that your love for my sister was as great as is hers for you."

Glee love him? She must be a better actress than he had given her credit for. The idea of Glee being in love with him curiously pleased him at the same time it vexed him. Odd, too, that this was the second time in as many days that he had pondered the possibility that Glee could love him. It wouldn't do at all for Glee to fall in love with him. His resolve against falling in love would only bring her pain, and—as troublesome as she was—he would not wish to see her suffer in any way.

Sitting face-to-face with her brother only impressed upon Blanks his foolishness—and selfishness—in marrying Glee. She did deserve a husband who loved her as George loved Dianna and Thomas loved Felicity. "And how, my dear brother, is marriage treating you?" Gregory asked.

"As you must have already learned, it's extremely satisfying."

A lump in his throat, Gregory watched his contented friend, regretting that his own cold heart, unlike George's, was incapable of loving. Of course, he could never reveal such a dark secret to Glee's brother. "My only regret is that I waited so long to marry," he lied.

George's smile widened. "My feelings exactly. Now about Glee's fast behavior, mark my words, she's doing it to spite you because of Carlotta. In Glee's eyes, you've never been attracted to proper ladies. Trust me, I know how my wayward sister's mind works."

Almost anyone would be able to understand Glee better than Gregory. It seemed everything she did ran contrary to the ordinary. But, really, she couldn't be jealous of Carlotta! The assumption that Glee thought he loved Carlotta was utterly illogical because it was founded on the ridiculous notion that Glee was in love with him. Which was absurd. "A pity I don't in the least understand how my wife's mind works. I daresay if I did, it would save me a great deal of grief."

George nodded sympathetically. "Enough talk of my perplexing sister. You must tell me all about the cock-fight day after tomorrow."

Some time later, their discourse was interrupted by the appearance of their wives.

"Come, Blanks, let's go to the Pump Room with Dianna and George so they can sign the book. Bless them, they came here straightaway after arriving in Bath," Glee said.

"And if they hadn't," Gregory said, "I daresay you'd have boxed your brother's ears."

Glee met Blanks's gaze with dancing eyes. "But of course! How well you know me, my love."

"Would that I did," he mumbled, rising and offering his wife his crooked arm.

At the Pump Room, they met up with Felicity and Thomas. "Blanks was telling me of the cockfight day after tomorrow," George said excitedly to Thomas. "Are you going?"

Felicity watched him for a reaction. Thomas, who had not been born to wealth, was much more serious and bookish and less sport-mad than his male counterparts who had been born to privilege.

"I haven't been to one in an age," Thomas replied.

"Exactly as I was telling Blanks!" George said. "How fortunate that we've arrived in Bath in time for it."

"Yes, quite," Thomas said without enthusiasm.

"If our husbands are going to talk of cockfights, I am persuaded that we ladies shall have to leave them and take a turn about the room," Felicity said.

Glee and Dianna joined Felicity for the stroll. "Does not my sister look well now that she's a married lady?" Felicity asked Dianna.

"I declare, there's a marked bloom in her cheeks. I daresay she's never looked lovelier."

Felicity smiled. "I vow, Blanks feels the same. He's so attentive."

If only they knew. Glee was shocked that anyone could find bloom in her cheeks. It seemed to her she perpetually moped over her failure to capture Blanks's heart.

Dianna slipped her arm through Glee's. "How, dearest, are you enjoying being a married lady?"

"I've never been happier," Glee said. Which was partly true. While she had never been happier, she also had never been more downcast. 'Twas a most curious mixture of emotions that being married provoked in her. "Blanks is such a treasure."

"It's been my observation," Felicity said, "that marriage has evoked a most pronounced change in Blanks. He's nothing at all the hedonist he was before his marriage. And he's infinitely more mature. You wouldn't believe how zealously he tries to protect Glee and her reputation, and he's terribly jealous of any attention she may bestow on another man."

"Such is love," Dianna said wistfully.

If only they knew. It was certainly not jealousy that spurred Blanks's feigned devotion. "We are all so terribly fortunate to have married men we love so unabashedly."

A glow came over Dianna's face. "Indeed we are."

"You, my sisters, are the best recommendation I know of for love matches," Glee said. "I used to think that after the first blush of love wore off that husbands and wives were at daggers drawn with one another. But, if anything, I believe you seem to love your husbands— and they you—more each passing month."

"I've been blessed twice," Felicity said. "Both of my marriages were love matches. After Michael was killed, I never thought I'd ever love again. It puts me to the blush to say I love Thomas more fiercely than I ever loved Michael. I declare, I'm the most fortunate woman on the face of the earth."

"No, I am," Glee and Dianna said at exactly the same time.

All three women broke into laughter.

Glee's laughter was short-lived. She lifted her smiling face to see William Jefferson, standing alone near the door, watching her with smoldering eyes. A scowl settled on her face. It would give her no end of pleasure to cut him direct. Especially in front of Blanks. It had been twenty-four hours since she had written him to get her jewels back, and she had heard nothing.

What if, she thought happily, he had brought her earrings today? No, that wouldn't do at all. She could not be seen with the man. Blanks was angry enough to call him out. And she would never do anything that might jeopardize the safety of her beloved husband.

They walked past Jefferson—who, thankfully, made no effort to engage them in conversation—and rejoined their husbands, whose circle now included the twins.

"Where's Timothy?" Glee asked Melvin.

"He's been every minute with his brother since Lord Appleton arrived," Elvin said.

An amused grin slid across Blanks's face. "My dear, have we not decided that your calling my friends by their Christian names might give some people the wrong idea?" He tossed a martyred glance at Glee's brother.

"You see what a stickler my husband's become since he became a married man?" Glee said to George with mock indignation.

George smiled. "If I find any fault with Blanks, it's that he's not heavy-handed enough with you, pet."

"But your sister's right, Sedgewick," Elvin said. "Blanks has become a different man since his marriage. In fact, Pixie's much more fun to be around than he is."

"Who's Pixie?" George asked, a puzzled look on his face.

"That's what we call Gl—er, your youngest sister."

George roared in laughter, then attempted to stifle it as he turned to Blanks. "I see what you mean, old fellow." Then George directed his attention upon his sister. "Really, pet, a married woman—or a single woman for that matter—does not carry on in so familiar a manner with men. Why, I'd take Dianna over my knee and spank her if she behaved in such a ragtag fashion."

To this, Felicity and Glee broke out laughing.

"What's so funny?" George demanded.

"First," Felicity said, "I cannot in my wildest imagination picture Dianna ever acting without the greatest amount of propriety."

"And, secondly," Glee said, "you could never be so angry with my dear sister that you would ever turn your elegant wife over your knee."

Glee glanced at Dianna, expecting her to share in their mirth, but Dianna's face had gone white. "What's the matter, Dianna?" Glee asked with concern.

"I don't feel altogether well."

George hovered over his wife, voice and brows lowered in concern.

"Oh, dear," Glee said. "Allow me to fetch you some water. The water here's said to be quite a restorative." Then Glee dashed off to the fountain.

As she strode there, from the corner of her eye she saw that Jefferson shared her destination. She vowed to completely ignore him. She couldn't be the cause of Blanks getting killed in a duel. The very thought sent her stomach plummeting.

"A cup of water, please," Glee said to the attendant as Jefferson came to stand at her left. She acted as if she did not see him.

To his credit, he also ignored her. Until she was about to step away.

"I believe you dropped this, madame," he said, holding out a folded-up piece of paper for her.

Her cheeks hot, she set down Dianna's water and tucked the note into her reticule to read later. Then she took up the water and started back to Dianna when she fleetingly met Blanks's heated gaze. She glanced away quickly so she would appear not to have seen him. She could not be angered that he distrusted her so greatly when she was near Jefferson. Blanks had justification. She only hoped he had not seen her accept the piece of paper.

As she drew closer to Dianna, Glee realized her sister-in-law was quite ill. Not only had the color drained from her face, but she also began to tremble as if she had been broadsided with a blast of frigid air. "Here, dearest," Glee said, handing her the water and laying her arm around Dianna's shoulder. "I declare," Glee said with worry, "you're burning with fever."

George's brows dropped as he lowered his worried face to Dianna's. "Come, my love," he said gently, "we must get you home to bed. I'll have a doctor come."

"I was fine an hour ago," Dianna said feebly.

"But you're quite sick now," Glee insisted.

Thomas stepped forward and offered his carriage to take them immediately back to Winston Hall.

Glee watched after them as they left the Pump Room. She worried about her upset brother as much as she worried about his stricken wife. "I hope Dianna's affliction passes soon," she said, tucking her arm into Blanks's. "Come, dearest," she said somberly, "we had best go home, too."

She was anxious to get to the privacy of her chambers so she could read the note from the odious William Jefferson.

TWENTY-FOUR

Gregory directed a stern glance across the breakfast table at his wife. "Oblige me by not even asking about us smuggling you into the cockfight. I daresay if you found pugilism offensive to your feminine sensibilities, a cockfight—with its fatalistic outcome—is tenfold more bloody."

Glee looked suitably repentant. "I am cured, dearest heart of mine. I have neither the desire to dress as a boy nor the urge to see man or beast beaten to death. Who do you go with today?"

"Since the twins will be riding with Appleton and his brother, I shall take my carriage over to Winston Hall to collect Thomas and George."

"I don't believe Thomas shares your interest in cockfighting."

Gregory shrugged. "You're most likely correct. It's my understanding that as a younger man he was single-mindedly frugal. Were you not the one who told me he worked as a groom and saved every farthing he earned in order to seek his fortune in India?"

She nodded. "So my dear brother-in-law's youthful education in the pursuit of fun and sport has been sadly neglected. A pity he only has one of the largest fortunes in England to show for his wasted youth!"

"Why do I feel as if you malign me because my fortune is only inherited?"

"But, my dear husband, you have earned your wealth by having to put up with me for a wife!"

He could tell by her mischievous smile she spoke with levity. "Keeping you out of the briars is rather a full-time occupation, to be sure." He rose and scooted his chair back up to the table. "What will you do today?"

"I have . . . errands throughout the city that will require my attention."

He moved to her and brushed his lips against her cheek. "I'm depending on you to behave yourself, my sweet." He swept from the room and through the house to his waiting carriage.

At Stanton Hall he disembarked from the carriage, and a footman let him into the great house, where a butler announced him to Thomas.

From his library, Thomas dashed into the marbled foyer to greet him. "If you'll have me, I'll join you, but I'm afraid Sedgewick won't be able to make it."

"So he's caught whatever it was that caused Lady Sedgewick to become ill at the Pump Room yesterday?"

"Not exactly," Thomas said, his brows plunging. "My sister is no better today, and George is terribly worried about her. He sat by her bed all night."

Just then George descended the sweeping staircase. "There you are, Blanks. Sorry, old boy, that I won't be able to come to the cockfights today."

Gregory walked to the foot of the stairs to meet him. "Lady Sedgewick's not any better?"

George shook his head grimly. "I'm devilishly worried about her. It's not like her to be so sick."

Gregory was at a loss to understand why having a sick wife would keep a fellow from one of his favorite pursuits. It was not as if he were having to travel for days to see the cockfight. For God's sake, he'd be back in two hours' time. But it was not Gregory's lot to question George's motivation. "You've had the doctor?"

"Yes. He bled her and feels certain she'll be back to normal in a few days—after the fever has run its course. But the long and short of it is I can't possibly leave her. I'm far too worried. I shouldn't enjoy the fights for worrying about her."

Gregory turned to Thomas. "Are you as upset about your sister as her husband is?"

"No one's as upset as her husband is," Thomas said with a chuckle. "At least I'll never regret allowing her to marry George. No man could cherish her more than he does."

George clapped a hand on Gregory's back. "I'd better hurry back to Dianna. I don't like to leave her alone."

Once he had mounted the stairs and was no longer within hearing distance, Gregory asked, "Is Lady Sedgewick really that gravely ill, or is George merely overreacting?"

Thomas shrugged. "She *is* awfully sick."

"Then perhaps you'll want to stay here as well?"

Concern etched on his face, Thomas nodded.

During the short drive to the cockfights, Gregory pondered the vast change that had come over George since he married Dianna. It was as if a different being had taken possession of him. Why, George loved cockfights better than almost anything. He had once ridden a hundred miles to see one. Before today, Gregory would have had no compunction about wagering on the unlikelihood of George missing a cockfight because of his wife's fleeting illness.

But when it came to sitting useless at the bedside of his cherished wife or to seeing a cockfight, Dianna won. Hands down.

Gregory lifted the curtain of his coach and looked out at the countryside. The sun was high in the blue sky and daffodils spread their yellow glory indiscriminately along the roadside. It was a beautiful day to be alive. Then why, Gregory asked himself, did he feel so wretchedly lonely? It wasn't just that George and Moreland had stayed behind. It was so much more. George's love for Dianna had enriched his life. Filled it. That's what marriage was about.

They were there for each other in the good times as well as the bad. He sighed. Glee's sister was adored by Thomas Moreland. Her brother cherished Dianna. By God, that's what Glee deserved, too.

Yet she had given it all up to help him secure his fortune.

Glee had been furious when she had read Mr. Jefferson's letter. Instead of having her diamonds delivered to her at Blankenship House, he apprised her of the fact they would be waiting for her at the Paragon Building—in his chambers—when she cared to call for them.

If she was not so afraid that Blanks would catch her trying to send another letter to Mr. Jefferson, she would have immediately written back to him demanding they be sent to her.

After sleeping on it for a night, Glee decided she would fetch the diamonds, after all. Only this day, she would dress extremely primly. It was one thing to dress the vixen for her beloved Blanks, but quite another to have the beastly Mr. Jefferson gawking hungrily at her!

She had Patty bring out a black woolen gown she had worn for her father's mourning, and she dressed in it for the trip to the Paragon Building.

Another problem was that any number of respectable people she was acquainted with also lived in the Paragon Building, and it wouldn't do at all for any of them to see her entering a bachelor's chambers. Perhaps she could merely wait at the door while a servant fetched her earrings. But that would not do, either. The longer she stood in front of Mr. Jefferson's lodgings, the more likely her chances of being discovered there.

After careful consideration, she decided to take Patty with her. What could look more respectable? Surely a woman with an assignation with a lover would not bring along her maid.

Glee did not care a fig what people thought of her or her reputation, but she cared dreadfully for Blanks's. First, she could not jeopardize his inheritance by flaunting their unconventional marriage. But, more than anything, she could not allow Blanks to think she loved another. Even if he did not love her, she could not bruise his pride in such a manner.

Though he had never admitted it, she knew Blanks's sensitive emotions had suffered a lifetime of battering from the despicable Aurora. And Glee would spend the rest of her life making up to him for it.

With Patty in tow, Glee set off by foot for the Paragon Building. She had tied her black cap to her head with yards of black lace she hoped would conceal her face from onlookers.

They walked the several blocks to the Paragon Building and, seeing no one she knew loitering about, she mounted the steps to the building. Just inside the

double front doors, she found a directory that told her
Mr. Jefferson's quarters were in Number 8.

With her stomach turning, she began to climb the
stairs to Number 8.

"But, Miss Glee," Patty protested, "ye can't go to
a single man's establishment."

"I know that!" Glee whispered. "That's why I've
brought you along, silly."

"What will Mr. Blankenship say if he finds out?"

"It is my profound hope that he never finds out. I'm
only going to be there long enough to fetch my earrings that Mr. Jefferson most ungallantly took from me
after I lost to him at whist."

"You mean Mr. Blankenship doesn't know about the
earrings?"

Glee shook her head. "He'd just purchased them for
me, and I couldn't allow him to think they meant so
little to me that I could wager them in a meaningless
game of cards."

Winded, Patty held onto the banister as they came
to the second-floor landing. "I supposed that was the
only thing poor Mr. Blankenship's ever bought ye?"

Glee nodded ruefully. "And they're ever so precious
to me."

"All right, gel, but let's hurry and be done with it."

They approached Number 8 and Glee knocked timidly.

A moment later a male servant opened the door,
took an appraising look at Glee, and cocked a brow.

"I believe you have a package that belongs to me.
I'm Mrs. Blankenship."

He swung open the door. "Please come in. Mr. Jefferson's been expecting you."

Glee and Patty entered the narrow hallway and followed the servant to a small, dark drawing room where
the man instructed them to sit down.

* * *

In less than one hour, Gregory lost a hundred pounds at the cockfight. After saying his farewells to the Appleton brothers and the twins—all of whom also lost substantial sums of money—Gregory climbed into his carriage for the short ride back to Bath.

Though his friends had been their usual boisterous selves this day, he had only halfheartedly joined in their merrymaking. Ever since he had left Winston Hall, he had felt deuced low.

He supposed Glee and his friends were right. He *had* become an old stick. Glee had married him because she thought they would have such great fun. But he was turning out to be . . . Good Lord, he was turning out to be exactly like his father! The pursuits of his not-too-distant youth now seemed intolerably frivolous. Cockfights no longer held the allure they once had. Neither did gaming. Or womanizing.

Fact is, it seemed to him Thomas Moreland and George were the happiest, most well-rounded men of his acquaintance.

As his carriage pulled up to Queen Square, Gregory saw the runner standing in front of his house. Why was the runner not watching Glee as he had been so firmly instructed to do? Gregory's chest tightened. Had something happened to her? Gregory leaped from the carriage before it came to a stop. "Where's my wife?" he demanded of the runner. The man had clear instructions to follow Glee at all times—and never to show himself at Blankenship House. Something was dreadfully wrong.

"I came here straightaway, sir," the runner said breathlessly. He stepped closer to Gregory and lowered his voice. "You said as how Mrs. Blankenship was never to go near Mr. Jefferson . . ."

"Yes? Speak up, man!"

"Well, she's at his house this very minute."

Gregory issued an oath. "Come," he demanded, running to catch his carriage. "To the Paragon Building," Gregory ordered the driver.

During the short ride to Jefferson's lodgings, the runner apprised Gregory of what he had observed during the past forty-five minutes.

"I don't believe you have to worry about your wife being up to mischief, sir. She's got her maid with her, and . . . she's dressed in heavy mourning."

All Gregory could think of was poor Miss Douglas and the fate that had befallen her at William Jefferson's hands. If Jefferson laid a hand on his wife, Gregory would take pleasure in killing him. Gregory's heart beat ferociously. His palms were clammy. He felt as if his very life were in danger. Poor Glee was such a babe. She did not deserve to be a pawn in Jefferson's game of vengeance.

He pounded the top of the carriage, signaling for the coachman to drive faster.

"You say my wife was on foot?" Gregory asked.

The runner nodded. "And I ran all the way back to your house, sir. I wasn't there a minute when you drove up."

"Thank God," Gregory said in a trembling voice.

The carriage skidded to a stop in front of the Paragon Building, and Gregory leaped from it and hurried up the steps. "What number is it?" he called to the runner.

"Number 8. Second floor."

Gregory shot to the stairwell and ran up the stairs. When he came to Number 8, he did not knock. He stormed in. "Where's my wife, Jefferson?"

TWENTY-FIVE

Gregory ran down the hallway, checking each room for Glee. In the drawing room, he found Patty with her mouth gagged, but he didn't stop to unbind her. If she was gagged and bound, so was Glee, and he had to find her before that devil defiled Glee's innocence.

Gregory called to the runner. "Untie my wife's maid." Then he bounded up the stairs and threw open the first door he came to. And there stood Glee, her mouth bound, her watery eyes wide with fear, as she backed into a corner to get away from Jefferson. Gregory's fury exploded so thunderously he barely registered his relief that she was still clothed.

In a single stride he grabbed Jefferson and rammed Jefferson's head into the plastered wall. In the second it took Jefferson to recover, Gregory crashed his fist into Jefferson's face. "So help me, I'll kill you," Gregory threatened through gritted teeth.

Jefferson lunged at Gregory, but Gregory ducked to evade the hit, while Jefferson went flying onto the top of his bed. Before he could get up, Gregory had swung his weight on top of him and proceeded to pummel the sides of his head.

Footsteps sounded outside the room and a scuffle ensued. Gregory spun around to see the runner pounding Jefferson's man servant. The servant was no match for the runner. Soon, with the servant nursing his wounds in the hallway, the runner entered Jefferson's chamber.

Jefferson eased himself up on his haunches like a dog. The blood on his face trickled to his blue satin spread.

"Be a good man and untie my wife," Gregory ordered the runner.

Gregory walked around the bed, away from Glee, and stood with his back to the door, staring daggers at Jefferson. "I thought after the business with Miss Douglas you were completely without principle. Now I know you're without a soul. Damn you to hell, Jefferson!"

Jefferson collapsed back on the bed. "Take her and go. You don't have to worry about calling me out. I'll leave England at once."

The man was a coward, too. He knew he couldn't best Gregory on an even field, and he likely knew Gregory's fury was so great he would not shoot to wound, but to kill.

Released from her bindings, Glee flew to Gregory and flung her arms around him, weeping. "I . . . I..just wanted to get your earrings back from him," she sobbed.

Gregory scooped his wife into his embrace. All his anger at her melted under the sheer relief he felt at this moment.

"Take them," Jefferson uttered, waving toward the desk. "They're in my desk."

Gregory put Glee at some little distance from him and bent to kiss her forehead, then offered her his handkerchief.

After she wiped her tears, she walked to the desk and found her earrings in the top drawer. She clasped them in her hand and walked to the door, where Gregory met her before slamming the door behind them.

By now Patty had been released of her ties and she flew—crying—into Glee's outstretched arms. "I'm so very glad Mr. Blankenship came when he did," she managed betweens sobs. "I declare Mr. Jefferson is a fiend."

Gregory turned to the runner. "See that the maid gets safely home. I wish to speak privately with my wife in the carriage. And . . ." he paused, meeting Patty's thankful gaze, "I hope we can depend on your discretion."

Patty nodded solemnly. "I couldn't love Miss Glee more if she were me own sister."

Before they departed, Glee hugged Patty once more.

In the carriage, Glee broke into sobs again. Gregory scooted closer and settled his arm around her. "It's all right, love."

"How can you call me love when you must think me horridly wicked?"

"You're not wicked," he said softly. "Foolish, perhaps, but never wicked."

She buried her face into his chest. "Oh, Blanks, I'm so terribly sorry. I *did* love your earrings so. No gift has ever meant more. But I lost money to the vile Mr. Jefferson at whist that night at the Assembly Rooms and nothing would appease him but that he would have my earrings. He told me I could have them back if I would kiss him."

Now he understood Glee's peculiar actions that day he had observed her in Sydney Gardens. "The kiss I witnessed."

She looked up at him, nodding, great tears sliding down her cheeks. "Then the beast wouldn't return them. I . . . I didn't want you to think I didn't cherish them. I was dreadfully anxious to get them back. That's why I came here today."

"And he tried to ravish you." Gregory tightened his hold on her. "It's not your fault, sweetness. The man was only trying to get back at me because I somewhat exposed him for the vile creature he is in London. He hates me so much he wanted to wound me in the worst way."

"What happened in London?" she asked. "I perceive it has something to do with a Miss Douglas."

He frowned. "Miss Douglas's brother was a friend of ours who was killed in the Peninsula. Appleton and I—along with George—promised to look after her." He stopped and bit his lip. "We failed miserably."

"What happened to her?"

"Jefferson promised marriage but failed to deliver on the promise when Miss Douglas became . . . You needn't concern yourself."

A moment later Glee said, "He got her with child, did he not?"

Gregory nodded solemnly.

Glee sighed. "Well, Blanks, at least we have succeeded in convincing the *ton* ours is a love match," she said with an insincere laugh.

He settled a kiss on the top of her head. "Apparently so."

She saw that his knuckles were bleeding. "You're hurt! Oh, Blanks, I should never forgive myself if you were to get hurt saving your foolish wife from Jefferson's clutches. I was so terrified when you were fighting. I was afraid he would draw a knife on you. He's such a wicked man."

"Had there been a knife in his bedchamber, I have no doubt he'd have used it on me."

"How did you know to find me? And rescue me?"

"Since I'm far more well acquainted with Jefferson's character than you, I hired a Bow Street Runner to follow you, with instructions that William Jefferson was a dangerous man. So when he saw you enter Jefferson's building, he came straightaway for me."

"Thank goodness. But I thought you'd still be at the cockfights."

"As it happens, I didn't have to take Thomas and George home because they didn't come. Thank God they didn't," he said throatily. "Had I returned them to Winston Hall, I'd have been too late . . ." Emotion choked his voice.

"Oh, Blanks, you're my knight rescuing me from the evil dragon. You're the bravest man I've ever known."

"I wouldn't say that. I merely protect what's mine."

She snuggled up to him as they drove from one end of Bath to another. He had told the coachman to drive anywhere and not stop until he told him to. Gregory, cradling a whimpering Glee to him, oddly did not want the ride to end. He could not remember ever feeling such utter contentment.

"Did you say my brother did not attend the cockfight?"

"I did. He didn't."

She sat up ramrod straight. "George miss a cockfight? He must be at death's door."

"Not him. Dianna, and I daresay that's worse as far as George is concerned. He's most devoted to her."

Glee's face went white. "Dianna's at death's door?"

"No. No. She's merely suffering with a fever that the doctor assures George will go away, but George is beside himself with worry. Thomas said George didn't leave her side all night."

"I must go to Winston Hall," Glee said.

Gregory conveyed the new direction to the coachman.

At Winston Hall, Glee brushed past the butler, who opened the door to them. "I've come to see my sister."

At the sound of Glee's voice, Felicity came running from the drawing room.

"How is Dianna?" Glee asked, her brows drawn together.

By now Thomas had joined them at the foot of the stairs. "I wouldn't know," Felicity said, directing a glance of mock outrage at her husband. "Thomas will not allow me to go near her room—because of my condition."

Glee smiled up at Thomas. "Thank you, Thomas. I feared Felicity would force herself into the sickroom, and that wouldn't do at all—because of her condition." Glee started up the stairs. "I'm sure George could use some relief—and I daresay Dianna needs a level-headed female. I'm persuaded Colette is utterly useless at a time like this. The French are so given to vapors, you know."

Gregory put out a hand to block Glee's progress. "I don't know if I like the idea of *you* going to the sickroom, my dear."

Glee turned back and gazed at him with wonderment on her face. "Oh, Blanks, my darling, that's the nicest thing anyone has ever said to me." Impulsively, she threw her arms around him and kissed him briefly. "But you must know, I am *never* sick. Tell him, Felicity."

"Glee does enjoy excellent health. She's never even had a headache."

Resigned to his wife's decision, Gregory watched her climb the stairs. Then he realized he was not behaving that differently from George. He really did care for Glee. Of course, he wasn't in love with her as George was with Dianna. They had neither shared a bed nor the creation of a child in their image. Like George and Dianna. And like Felicity and Thomas.

Soon George joined them.

"How's Lady Sedgewick?" Gregory asked.

"I'm persuaded she's better. I got her to drink some water."

"Why don't you try to grab some sleep?" Thomas asked, concern in his voice. "She'll be in good hands with Glee."

George shook his head. "I can't. I know I should, but I'm still too upset. The poor lamb is never sick. I'm wretchedly worried."

Thomas clapped a hand on his back. "She'll be back to normal tomorrow. Mark my words. 'Tis just a passing fever."

"I hope you're right."

Gregory felt utterly helpless to offer succor to his lifelong friend who was dangerously close to weeping. "Then how about a game of billiards before you return to your vigil?"

"I suppose I could," George said wanly.

Gregory insisted that George and Thomas play the first game, and he would play the winner. He took a seat on a high stool and watched. It was obvious George's heart was elsewhere. He could hardly make a shot, and normally George was uncommonly good at billiards. He was likely trying to get the game over without delay so he could return to his beloved's bedside. Poor fellow.

Thomas won handily, and George was all too happy to return to Dianna.

Getting to his feet, Gregory said, "Perhaps I won't play the winner, after all. I'm determined to get that wife of mine out of the sickroom. She's vexatious enough when she's well."

Truth be told, Gregory's fear for Glee—even now

that he had rescued her—was acute. He did not at all like not having her near. As long as he was with her, he knew she was all right.

Good Lord, he was turning into George!

He watched as George went upstairs. A moment later, Glee came down, a smile on her face. "Dianna awakened and spoke to me. She's ever so much better now. And she's not nearly as hot as she was yesterday. I believe the fever has broken."

"Thank God," Felicity said. "Maybe now that brother of ours won't behave as if we're hosting a wake."

Glee turned to Gregory and rolled her eyes. "If Dianna hadn't been so terribly ill, I believe I'd laugh myself sick over George's ridiculous behavior."

His arm around Felicity, Thomas said, "I see nothing ridiculous in George's behavior. I daresay I'd be just as bad if Felicity were that sick."

Gregory copied. After all, he had fine examples. He placed his arm gently around Glee. "Me, too. If it were Glee, that is."

Glee looked adoringly into Gregory's face. "Now that's twice today you've said the sweetest thing to me. I declare, I don't deserve you, love."

"It's I who don't deserve you," Gregory insisted.

The ride back to the town house was not nearly as comforting as the ride there for Glee sat up straight in the seat beside him. He thought he liked it better when she snuggled against him.

At the town house Hampton greeted him at the door. "Your brother has arrived in Bath to stay with you, Mr. Blankenship. I took the liberty of having his things placed in the gold room."

Gregory came to a dead stop, briefly shifting his puzzled gaze to Glee. "My brother?"

"Yes, sir. He gave me his card. *Jonathan Blankenship,* it said."

Gregory gathered his composure. "What a pleasant surprise."

His words were uttered in the nick of time, for Jonathan, on hearing his brother's voice, came from the library. "Hope you don't mind me not letting you know of my arrival," Jonathan began.

"Since when is my brother not welcomed happily into my home?"

"We're so very glad you've come," Glee said, dipping a curtsy. "Why, just this morning Blanks was telling me how much he would enjoy a visit from you." She tucked her arm into Jonathan's. "How long will you be staying in Bath?"

His eyes shifted from Glee to Gregory. "My plans are rather indefinite."

TWENTY-SIX

This was Glee's chance to make amends for all the grief she had caused Blanks. For however long Jonathan was to stay here in Bath with them, she would see to it he was completely convinced of his brother's devotion to her—and of her devotion to his brother. Her glance flitted to Blanks's bleeding knuckles. Oh, dear. How would they explain them to Jonathan? Could he have received them at the cockfight? Or perhaps he assisted the coachman in dislodging the carriage wheel from a muddy mire at Winston Hall. She bit at her lip. Neither scenario seemed probable. Then an idea struck her.

"Jonathan, you will hardly recognize your brother for he has changed so drastically." She strolled alongside of her brother-in-law as they made their way to the library. "This morning Blanks risked his life to protect me from the most wretched cutthroat who tried to steal my earrings. Show him your knuckles, darling," she said to Blanks.

He frowned. "Jonathan does not wish to look at my bleeding knuckles."

Jonathan's furtive gaze slid to Blanks's mangled hand as they came into the library and dropped onto silken sofas. Glee and Blanks sat together on one; Jonathan faced them on another.

"A cutthroat in Bath in broad daylight?" Jonathan asked incredulously. "I've never heard of such. And I thought Bath the safest city in all of England."

" 'Tis entirely my own fault," Glee explained. "I should never have worn the earrings in daytime. It's just that they were so very special, being the only gift Blanks has ever purchased for me." She glanced up at her husband and smiled. Blanks slid her an insincere grin.

"Did you actually fight the man?" Jonathan asked his brother.

Glee detected a wisp of pride in the smaller, fairer brother's voice.

"I daresay it was an unconscious reaction to him threatening my wife," Blanks said.

Jonathan glanced from his brother to Glee, who gloried in her husband's unexpected admission.

"But he bested the beast," Glee said with pride. "The man raced off on foot, and I daresay we won't be threatened by him ever again."

"That'll teach him not to toy with my brother. No one who knows of Gregory's prowess with his fists would dare challenge him."

"I thank you for your confidence in me, but I cannot admit to being as skilled as I once was. Out of practice, you know."

"I hope you are, dearest," Glee said, stroking the sleeve of Blanks's brown jacket. "I shouldn't like it at all if you went about jeopardizing your life. Now that you're a family man, you'll simply have to change your ways."

Jonathan's mouth dropped open. "A family man? Surely . . ."

Smiling mischievously, Glee shook her head. "I

have no reason to believe I'm increasing—yet," Glee said.

Relief washed over Jonathan's countenance.

"Have you come from Sutton Hall?" she asked her brother-in-law.

"Yes." He directed his gaze at Blanks. "Mother sends her best."

Blanks failed to acknowledge Jonathan's comment.

I'll bet she does, Glee thought. "I should love to see Sutton Hall," Glee said wistfully in an effort to smooth over the awkward silence.

"I daresay it's yours for the taking, Gregory," Jonathan said.

Blanks nodded. "In good time. My poor wife was so tired of being buried in the country when we wed that I promised her a Season in Bath."

"He's so very good to me," Glee added.

"Yes, I've heard," Jonathan answered grimly. "A new phaeton, a sizable wardrobe—not to mention the house and carriage. It's a wonder there's any money left."

"Be assured our father's estate can easily afford such insignificant purchases," Blanks said.

"I don't think the finest town house in Bath an insignificant purchase."

Blanks looked somberly at his brother. "No, but it's a fine investment, you must admit."

"And, delightfully, large enough to afford you your own suite, dear brother," Glee reminded. "We're so very happy you've come. Though many lively events are planned tonight, if it is agreeable to you, I'd just as lief stay here with you tonight and enjoy a cozy evening at home. Besides, my brother and his wife will not be out tonight, owing to her sudden illness, which I pray is nearing its conclusion."

"As do I," Jonathan said without conviction.

Glee smiled at him. "Now, you must be tired after your journey. Why don't you go up to your chambers and rest? Dinner will be served at five."

After Jonathan left the library, Gregory got up to close the door, then came back to sit beside Glee. "You realize the gold room is next to mine?"

"Yes?"

"That will make Jonathan acutely aware of our . . . marital arrangements."

He watched Glee's face until the impact of his statement dawned on her. "Oh, I see." Then her face brightened. "I'll just have to sleep with you while he's here."

God, but she was such an innocent! Did she think a man and woman could sleep together innocently? He, for one, would have a most difficult time lying beside Glee and not want to gather her in his arms. And once she was held against him, he would be powerless to stop at a chaste kiss.

The events of the night he was foxed intruded on his thoughts. An innocent she might be, but Glee was also a woman of extraordinary passion. He had already awakened it once. The next time he feared he would indulge her passion to its natural fulfillment. Sweet heavens, he must force himself to think of something else.

"Enlighten me, please, on why you told my brother the outrageous story of the cutthroat robber?"

"I knew he'd inquire on the nature of your wounded hands, and I thought the cutthroat tale would emphasize your gallantry toward me. You must admit, my story wasn't really far from the truth. If the vile Mr. Jefferson is not akin to a cutthroat robbing my diamonds, I don't know who is. And you did fight with him to protect me. So there you have it."

Gregory burst out laughing. "I suppose you're right, my dear. How resourceful of you."

That night at dinner Gregory sat back and watched his little wife making it her mission to show Jonathan how remarkably Gregory had changed since his marriage.

"You know, Jonathan," she began, "I think your father must have been an extremely wise man."

Jonathan set his fork on his gilded plate. "He was, but how did you know?"

"As you must know, I'm aware of the . . . unusual terms of your father's will."

"About Gregory's marriage?"

"Just so. It's my belief your father knew what solidness lay beneath Blanks's devil-may-care exterior. That, of course, is what motivated him to draw up the peculiar will. And by doing so, he forced Blanks to mature at a far greater rate than he would have, given his own natural inclinations. You must ask Blanks's friends, Mr. Appleton and the twins. They'll confirm that Blanks no longer pursues his former interests. You know, the gaming and drinking and . . . womanizing. He's settled down into marriage every bit as admirably as my brother has."

A curious sense of pride washed over Gregory as he listened to his wife and watched the intent expression on her youthful face. She had even refrained from calling Appleton Timothy! If he *had* to have a wife, he could not have found one better than Glee. Even if she had vexed him half to death.

"I find your brother's transformation most admirable. However, a similar metamorphosis in my brother remains to be seen, Miss, er, Mrs. Blankenship."

She tossed him an impatient glance. "You're to call me Glee. After all, you're now my brother."

"Forgive me," Jonathan said. " 'Twill take time."

A room-brightening smile flashed across her face as she replied, "We have forever." Then she sent Gregory a warm glance.

Oddly, a feeling of utter contentment swamped Gregory as he peered into her smiling eyes.

"It's my belief," Jonathan said, "that our father desired Gregory to take an active role in managing the estates, and I've yet to see evidence of that."

"Oh, but he has, Jonathan. He spends long hours every day at Mr. Willowby's office learning all about your father's various holdings."

"Gregory?"

"Yes. I told you he's vastly changed. It wouldn't surprise me one bit if he were to take possession of Sutton Hall and focus all his efforts not only on continuing its success but also in improving that which your father left."

Good Lord, what was the chit getting him into? Where did she come up with such outrageous ideas?

Jonathan's brows lowered. "I daresay that's what our father had in mind."

"I hope your mother won't feel she's being usurped," Glee said.

Jonathan was silent for a moment. "I daresay she'll have time to prepare for it."

"It may come sooner than you think," Glee confided. "Once we have children, I shall want to retire to the country with them."

Gregory nearly choked on his wine. How did Glee manage to come up with such fiction without a moment's hesitation? He settled back in his chair and watched her, an amused grin on his face. He should have charged admission!

"I cannot picture Gregory being content in the country," Jonathan said, shooting a glance at his brother.

"You must admit," Glee responded, "he has never been made to feel completely at home at Sutton Hall."

Stunned that his mere slip of a wife had the courage to bring up a subject never before openly broached and had the perception to understand feelings Gregory himself had never before voiced, Gregory watched her with glowing pride.

Jonathan shrugged, then looked at Glee sheepishly. "You refer, of course, to the estrangement between my brother and my mother."

"I do because Blanks won't."

Sweet heavens, but she had guts! Gregory was only beginning to discover the depth of Glee's character. She was neither the frivolous noblewoman nor the practiced flirt he had been prepared to accept as his wife. Though they had been married less than three weeks, he was gripped by the profound conviction that he and Glee were united by something far stronger than a vicar's words or his mother's emeralds, that they were bound to each other by some unseverable lifeline which was as vital to them as drawing breath.

He was almost paralyzed by the stark realization that for the first time in his nearly four and twenty years there was another being who shared all that he was. Not just his riches, but also his tortures. This was perhaps the most profound moment in his life.

He was at a loss to analyze his emotions for they were curiously at odds. While one part of him wished to rejoice over the near-physical sensation of being so close to another being, the other side of him wished to erect a shell around himself. He'd never had such a feeling of camaraderie with anyone before as he now shared with Glee, and he wasn't sure he liked the idea of another person penetrating what had been uniquely his for all his life.

Jonathan took a long drink from his wineglass, set it down, and leveled a guilty gaze at Gregory. "Well, it seems the cat is finally out of the bag."

Gregory held up both hands, palms facing his brother. "Not by me. My youth is not a topic I discuss with anyone. Not even my precious wife." *Precious? Why had he selected that word?*

"I have always felt rather guilty that Mother played such favorites," Jonathan admitted.

Gregory shrugged. "It's only natural. You were her own son. I've always understood that."

"Truly, Blanks has never complained," Glee said. "But as his wife, and as an observer of human behavior, I've been able to deduce a number of things about my husband's life that I would not be privy to through him. One of the observations, of course, being the words and deeds of your very prejudiced mother. But I assure you, her actions have not made Blanks resent you in any way. He loves you the same as he would were you full brothers, rather than half brothers." She lifted the wine bottle and poured more wine in their glasses.

"I'm deuced uncomfortable with this conversation," Gregory said. "Tell me, Jonathan, what amusements do you hope to find in Bath?"

"The usual, I suppose. When in Bath, what is there other than the Pump Room and the Assembly Room and musicales?"

"You missed a bang-up cockfight this morning," Gregory said.

"I'm not into the sporting life as you are, dear brother. In fact, I've come to tell you I've written a piece that's been accepted by the *Edinburgh Review.*"

Gregory's brows arched. "Liberal?"

"Yes. Actually, it's an attack on primogeniture."

"An apt topic for one who has been denied a fortune because of primogeniture," Gregory said.

Jonathan smiled. "Now, we're really letting the cat out of the bag."

"I know our father very well meant to get around primogeniture with the peculiar stipulations of his will. He thought me unfit to manage his estates, and he understood I was possessed of a deep aversion to marriage. Therefore, his estates would go to the esteemed son who was better qualified to see to their continued prosperity."

Jonathan glared at Gregory. "I *am* the better qualified."

"Be that as it may, I am married now, and the estates are mine. Our father did not reckon on my good fortune in finding so worthy a life's mate." Gregory flashed a smile at Glee.

"Nor did I, quite frankly," Jonathan answered.

Gregory grinned at Jonathan. "Then you'll simply have to be patient and see for yourself."

"This seems a most odd conversation for the two of you to be having," Glee said. "Like with daggers drawn—but most amiably."

"I'm more comfortable now that you know where I'm coming from," Jonathan said. "It's comforting to know you bear no malice toward me."

"Your malice is not toward me, either," Gregory responded. "You merely covet the money and lands that are in my possession, and I don't even believe your motive's selfish. Your motive is your desire to see that our father's work does not go to ruin. Which I assure you, it won't."

"I warn you, I'm willing to do anything in my power to keep that from happening."

Gregory flashed a grin at his brother. "As I would expect."

"You two may be amiable enemies, but I don't at all like this talk." Glee turned to Jonathan. "You must tell me about your writings. I didn't know you were in possession of such talents."

"My brother's most serious-minded," Gregory said.

Jonathan addressed Glee. "Yes, Gregory's forever telling me I don't know how to enjoy myself."

Glee laughed. "Now he's changed so drastically, he's telling his friends they spend far too much time in idle pursuits. It's my belief Gregory has a lot more of his father in him than you think."

Good Lord, could she be right? Always, it had been Jonathan who was most like their father. Serious. Frugal. Disinterested in sporting and drinking and gaming and womanizing. Could Glee see what he himself had never been able to see? Was he becoming more like his father?

After the sweetmeats were laid and consumed, they retired to the drawing room, gathering around the game table where they drank port and played loo, with no mention being made of the antagonism between the brothers.

Gregory knew Glee had drunk too much wine when she began calling him Blanksie. It was time to put her to bed.

In his bed.

TWENTY-SEVEN

His arm around Glee, Gregory climbed the stairs just ahead of Jonathan. His footstep never faltered as they passed Glee's chamber door. At the door of his room, he stopped and, with his arm still resting on Glee's shoulder, bid his brother a good night.

"We really are so very glad you've come to stay with us," Glee repeated to Jonathan. "Tomorrow I shall take you out in my phaeton—only I'll let you drive it."

"I'll enjoy that, though I daresay having my own stable is a luxury I shall never be able to sustain."

"Then you should ask your brother to increase your portion. He's rich."

If Gregory did not quickly shepherd his foxed wife into his room, she might bloody well give away his fortune.

"Then where would be the challenge?" Jonathan asked Glee with levity and a twinkling in his green eyes. "Having been brought up with no expectations, I've learned to be satisfied with less."

Glee directed a mock scowl at her husband, then glanced back at Jonathan. "But I daresay you could keep a phaeton."

"Perhaps," Jonathan said. Then he took Glee's hand

and barely brushed it with his lips. "Thank you for the hospitality. I shall look forward to tomorrow's drive."

Once in his own chamber, Gregory looked around. A fire blazed in the hearth, and a lone candle burned beside his bed, casting a yellow pool on the green velvet spread which covered his full tester bed. Though nothing was changed, the room seemed different. He told himself he was merely unused to coming here with Glee. This was his private domain, yet here she was taking her rightful place for the sake of convincing Jonathan their marriage was no sham.

Though Glee was in her cups, she was not so bosky she could not dress—or undress—herself. "I'll just step into my dressing room and slip on a night shift," she told Gregory.

Regarding his own sleepwear, Gregory did not know what he was going to do. Normally he slept in the buff, but that would hardly do tonight. Perhaps he could just remove his coat, shirt and shoes and sleep in his breeches. The idea sounded devilishly uncomfortable.

As he began to remove his jacket, then his shirt, in his mind's eye he began unconsciously to picture Glee doing likewise. Having previously seen her very satisfactory breasts, he knew their pleasures only too well. Pleasures he could not allow himself to indulge in tonight. Yet completely against his resolve, he began to become sexually aroused.

Frowning, he kicked off his shoes and removed his stockings, then climbed beneath the coverings on his bed and sat there to await Glee. The door to his dressing chamber creaked open and he watched as Glee came through his dressing room, then glided into the bedchamber. Beneath the fine white linen of her nightshift he could see her soft curves. Firelight danced in her auburn hair as she moved toward him—not as a girl but as a woman. There was no shyness about her as she met his gaze with smoldering eyes and with uncommon grace moved toward the bed.

She came to the opposite side of the bed and slid under the covers. She was so close, he could feel her warmth and was conscious of every breath she drew.

"Should you wish to kiss me good night?" she asked in a breathless whisper.

He groaned. *Did a greengrocer have vegetables?* "My dear, if I allowed myself to kiss you, I'd be unable to prevent myself from wanting to taste other pleasures I'd wish you to offer. And that, my lovely wife, was not part of our bargain."

"Oh, dear."

He blew out the bedside candle, then lowered himself fully onto the bed. He lay there in the darkness listening to the crackle of the fire, the whistle of wind beyond the windows—the unchanged breathing of his wife. The room seemed filled with the floral scent that was peculiarly Glee's. Yet the fragrance was light. Like Glee herself.

"Perhaps we should talk," Glee suggested. "Jonathan might be listening to assure himself we truly are together."

"We could."

"How are your knuckles?"

"They're not bothering me."

"Good."

Now there was another long silence.

"Blanks?"

"Yes?"

"What about just a little kiss?"

It must be the port she had drunk. She knew so little of men's appetites she couldn't possibly realize how an innocent kiss could lead to something much deeper, something that could strip her of her own innocence.

He willed himself to think of her as George's flighty

little sister, a girl who had agreed to marry him merely to become a woman of means.

But that portrait of a mercenary Glee was completely inaccurate. She had shown him tonight she was neither immature nor superficial. Like granite, she was substance itself. She possessed a great deal of understanding of human behavior—especially his. 'Twas almost as if she *were* his other half.

"I can't kiss you," he said, "for then I'd be powerless to stop myself there."

She turned to him and he felt her warm breath when she spoke. "I shouldn't mind if you didn't stop with a kiss."

Good Lord, but it must be the port! Surely she could not comprehend what she was saying. "You can't know what you're offering."

She drew even closer to him, so close her leg brushed against his. "But I've said it before, dearest, and I knew what I was saying then, too."

He could not trust his voice to be free from the hunger which blazed within him. He turned to her, capturing her in his arms as she moved against him, fitting herself to him as his lips came down on hers, hungrily, in an explosion of passion. He parted her lips, devouring her. She not only seemed not to mind, but from the passion of her reaction, she seemed as eager as he.

He settled a final nibbly kiss on her sweet lips before lowering his face to kiss her neck, as his hands worked frantically to slide the nightshift past her slender shoulders. Then his lips trailed over the bare skin where the shift had hung, his hands gently stroking her uncovered breasts, lifting them, kissing them with his wet, open mouth.

When his mouth closed over her nipple, she gave a soft moan of pleasure. He wanted to hate himself for the depth of his greed for her, yet how could a union so blessedly sanctioned be wrong? Glee, his cherished wife, was the only person who had ever delved beneath the careless facade he revealed to the world. It was fitting that she share in this ultimate, irrevocable bond.

Besides, he had never been affected so profoundly by a woman before. The very sound of her voice, her evocative scent, and especially the feel of her rounded slimness—each of these drove him mad with desire. But together they rendered him as powerless as Samson.

His hand glided over the smooth flesh beneath her shift. It skimmed over her stomach and fanned out over the softness of her hips before he began to caress between her thighs and felt the heady pleasure of her raising her hips and grinding into his hand. As his finger probed her wetness, she parted her thighs, whispering provocatively.

Good Lord, but she was intoxicating! His breathing harsh and labored, he rose to remove his breeches. "Are you sure you mean to go through with this, love?" he asked in a husky whisper.

"Oh, yes! Please."

His breeches removed, he settled himself on top her, one leg on either side of her. "It may hurt the first time," he whispered.

"I don't care, dearest." She cupped her hand to his face in so tender a gesture he could have fallen to his knees and worshipped her.

He eased himself gently into her, prepared for her to cry out in pain. But she did not. He dared to go a little deeper and she responded by rocking into him, hungrily, then frantically. He had thought to go slow, but she wanted—indeed urged—the shattering, mind-numbing pleasure of their frenzied mating.

He exploded into her sleek warmth and as she shuddered beneath him she cried out his name. Only she did not call him Blanks. She crooned *Gregory,* making his name sound almost reverent.

Her arms tightened across his bare back as if she did not want him to pull away.

Not putting his weight on her, he rested deep and low within her.

"Oh, Blanks," she whispered huskily, tracing circles on his back. "Can we do that again?"

He chuckled softly, then placed her face between his hands and bent to kiss her gently. "I'm reasonably sure I shall be able to oblige you, my sweet."

"Could we have the candle on the next time? I should like to see your body."

His Glee was no girl but a sated woman. A woman of undeniable passion.

Where Blanks was concerned, Glee knew no pride. He had only to admit his desire in order for her to eagerly beg that he take her. And now that he had, she still knew no pride. Only the debilitating pleasure of being possessed by him. Even if she did not lay claim to his love, she had enough. Lying beneath him, joined in this most intimate manner, brought more happiness than she'd ever thought to capture in a lifetime.

In the soft candlelight she watched her hands move slowly, firmly over his magnificently muscled torso, then sweep down to cup his solid hips. Her face nuzzled into his musk-scented chest, she listened to his reassuring heartbeat, then lifted her mouth to his again. She tasted the port they had drunk, and she quivered with a sated contentment.

They made love again. Unlike the first time, this time there was no pain. Only nearly unbearable pleasure.

Afterward, he collapsed beside her, pressing her to him, whispering endearments.

"Oh, Blanks, I told you we'd have great fun if we married."

He gathered her into his solid embrace and chuckled. "Then it's grateful I am you persuaded me to hear your suit."

"Not nearly as happy as I am, my love, even if you do persist in reminding me that *I* was the one who offered for *you*."

He fell asleep, nearly dazed from the unequaled pleasure her actions and words had given him.

But when he awoke at dawn and glimpsed her sweet face in slumber beside him, her shoulders bare, he tried to rid his mind of the deep contentment—even love—she provoked.

A gnawing fear gripped him. He bolted up in bed and looked down at her. Her long lashes brushed against her beloved face. She seemed so youthful and innocent still. Now he realized she was more precious to him than his own life. It was impossible to love more deeply than he loved her.

And he feared he may have impregnated her.

If he should lose her now, he would die.

He slipped from the bed, bitterly angry with himself for not remembering his greatest fear, for assuaging his own need at the cost of what could be his beloved wife's life.

He quietly dressed, then left the bedchamber, carefully easing the door shut behind him. He wanted to be away from Glee for he could not think clearly in her mesmerizing presence. He felt like riding his horse as fast as lightning in a fruitless effort to purge Glee from his mind. If only he could undo what he had already done. He could never again allow himself to so blissfully indulge in what she so freely offered. For losing her would be unbearable.

TWENTY-EIGHT

At first Glee thought it was still night, for the heavy velvet draperies in Blanks's room blocked the light from entering the chamber. She stretched out, as contented as a waking kitten, her naked body writhing beneath the covers of her husband's bed. Her smile widened as she remembered every blissful minute spent in Blanks's arms the night before. His complete possession of her swamped Glee with an overpowering sense of well-being.

Faintly aware of Blanks's musk scent, she opened her eyes and turned to his side of the bed, only to be deeply disappointed to find him gone. Clutching the sheet to her breasts, she sat up and looked around the chamber for signs of him. "Blanks?" she called, thinking he might be in his dressing chamber.

There was no response.

Disappointment swept over her. She had rather fancied the idea of languishing in his bed again this morning, of once more feeling him so closely entwined with her it was impossible to tell where he left off and where she began. For they had been that close.

Then, too, if Blanks were here, he could help her extricate herself gracefully from his chamber. She should die of embarrassment were Blanks's valet to discover her in such a state of undress. She fell back into the soft feather mattress, a smile curving across her lips. It pleased her that the servants knew her husband had finally exercised his conjugal rights. Now she really understood what it was to be Mrs. Blankenship.

But how to get dressed?

First, she must find the shift Blanks had removed in the heat of passion. She looked for it on top of the bed. It was not there, nor was it on the floor nearby. She lifted the covers high into the air and finally found her shift beneath them at the foot of the bed and swiftly slipped it on.

Then, she crossed the room and walked through Blanks's dressing chamber to her own, surprised that the sun was high in the sky. It must be close to noon. Why hadn't Blanks wakened her?

Patty heard Glee and opened the dressing room door. "Allow me to help you dress," she said. "I've selected the rose muslin."

Glee sighed. "An excellent choice since my brother-in-law is here. Blanks would not at all like me to dress flamboyantly in front of his brother. Where, by the way, is my dear husband?" She shrugged out of the night rail.

Patty slid the rose muslin gown over her mistress's head. "His valet said the master left at dawn to go riding."

Glee's brows lowered. "And he hasn't returned yet?"

"I daresay he's off with that solicitor of his again." Patty handed Glee's stockings to her.

Leaving me to entertain Jonathan. Glee sat down to put on her stockings and shoes. "And what of his brother?"

"He's at the breakfast table as we speak."

"Then I'd best hurry down and make him feel at home."

Once dressed, Glee hurried from the chamber and raced down the stairs without even glancing into the looking glass.

"Good morning, Jonathan," she called cheerfully to him as she strolled into the bright morning room. "What poor hosts you must find us!"

"Not at all. I'm rather slow to start in the morning myself." His glance skimmed her, then over her shoulder. "Where's your husband?"

She caught her breath as she poured herself a cup of coffee. "The servants tell me he left dreadfully early this morning. I never heard him leave myself." She especially liked telling him that part. "I daresay he's gone to Mr. Willowby's. You'll learn I didn't exaggerate when I told you how seriously Blanks takes his responsibilities as head of the family. He's a completely changed man. If you like, we can drive by Mr. Willowby's office when we take our drive in the phaeton."

He shook his head. "No, I wouldn't want Gregory to think I don't trust him—although I don't."

She peered at him through narrowed eyes. "While I admire your candor, I abhor your sentiments."

He blotted his lips against his serviette. "Which I find admirable. It's never been a secret to me that you're deeply in love with my brother."

She laughed. "I suppose not, since the first time I met you I blathered about having loved Blanks all my life, which is quite true, though I try to pretend otherwise to Blanks. You must know how fleetingly his affections have been engaged in the past. I believe his interest wanes upon conquest." She leveled a stern glance at Jonathan. "I mean to keep him a satisfied lover until the end of our days."

"A noble—though impossible—goal, my dear sister."

"Obviously you cannot begin to understand what great maturity has come over your brother," she said, rising from the table. "Are you ready?"

He stood up and proffered his arm.

As they strolled from the house, she lifted a smiling face to Jonathan. "You must know I want to dislike you because you mean to undermine my beloved husband, but I find I cannot. Because you're his brother, Blanks loves you. And if my husband loves you, I must."

The phaeton was waiting for them as they left the house.

Jonathan stood back and squinted at it, shielding his eyes with a flat hand as if the bright hue would blind him with its brilliance. " 'Twould be rather difficult to go unnoticed in this." An amused smile on his face, he turned to assist her in climbing on the box before he hopped up and took the ribbons.

"You sound exactly like your brother," she said with feigned displeasure. "In fact, you'll find that Blanks becomes more like you—and your father—with each passing day."

"So you keep telling me," Jonathan said with a frown. "I fail to see how a leopard can change its spots." He drove toward the Royal Crescent.

"Has it never occurred to you that the spots were merely acquired as an armor to shield him from the abuse your mother so readily administered?"

Jonathan laughed. "I cannot believe my brother has need to possess armor. A more confident person than my brother I have never known. He's been blessed with extraordinary good looks—and certainly received all the height in the family. He's bright and athletic and loved by all who know him. I assure you my brother has no Achilles' heel."

Now she laughed. "How little you know him if you believe that. What you say *is* true when Blanks was away from Sutton Hall, but throughout most of his life—at Sutton Hall—he was needled by a stepmother who perpetually complained about him, converting her husband to her way of thinking. Which left Blanks feeling that nothing he could do would ever please either of them. So why not be a thorn in their sides?"

Jonathan looked incredulous. "Gregory told you this?"

"Of course not! I've figured it out on my own, but I know I'm on target."

"I think you're daft!"

"How much, my dear brother, you sound like Blanks."

"Good. Then we're in agreement on at least one thing."

"I don't mean to be mean-spirited toward your mother, as I'm sure you could not have a mother more devoted than Aurora is to you. It's just that she has absolutely no affection toward Blanks, and you cannot deny it."

Swallowing, Jonathan refused to meet her gaze. "I cannot deny it."

"I dare you to analyze it from Blanks's perspective. All those years he heard nothing but how worthless he was. Was it no wonder he began to believe it himself?"

"You make a most convincing point," he conceded as he drove around a stopped delivery cart. His voice grew soft. "I envy my brother the champion he's got in you."

"I am persuaded that you, too, will find a woman who will love you as I love Blanks," she said.

"You may be confident, but I'm not. In fact, I'm not at all ready for marriage."

She thought of how similar Blanks had felt—until she forced him into marriage. "I daresay most young men are of your thinking—until Cupid's arrow snags them as it did my brother—and Blanks," she added uneasily.

He drove past the fine town houses on the crescent, commenting on them, but Glee's thoughts were elsewhere. Her heart raced as she tenderly remembered the feel of Blanks within her, the agonized sound of his voice as he huskily whispered his satisfaction into her ear.

Mixed with her overwhelming desire to renew what was begun last night was a deep, retching disappointment that she had not seen Blanks's face when she awakened this morning. Why had he left her? Was he not as delighted as she? Her heart began to drum, low and menacing. Was Blanks not as full of bliss as she? Surely he was. He had to be.

A somberness came over her as they continued their ride, Jonathan commenting on the unity of Bath's classical Georgian architecture. "Yes, you're so right," she would say. Or, "I have often thought the very same thing myself." Or, "I do so agree with you."

This continued until they reached the foot of the city and she cast a glance down Broad Quay to see if Blanks could be at Mr. Willowby's office. If he had gone riding, he'd be on his magnificent bay, not in a carriage or phaeton. With great relief, she saw Archie holding the reins to Blanks's bay in front of Mr. Willowby's office.

The thought of being so near Blanks sent her heart racing. "Oh, look, Jonathan! Blanks *is* at Mr. Willowby's. Let's stop and say hello to them."

He reined in and rounded the corner, pulling to a stop in front of the office building.

Her heart stampeded at the thought of facing Blanks for the first time since he had taken such thorough possession of her. She blushed as Jonathan helped her down. Then she bent down to Archie's level. His cheeks were pink from the sun. "Good afternoon, Archie. Can you manage caring for my husband's horse as well as my phaeton?"

He puffed out his slender chest. "Ye can count on me."

"Good," she said, patting his blond head. "We shan't be long."

In Mr. Willowby's office, Glee introduced herself and Jonathan to the clerk and asked him to inform her husband of their presence.

The clerk passed into the interior office where his employer was conversing with Blanks, then Blanks came bounding from the office, a smile on his face. His glance flicked to Jonathan first and he bowed; then, with unbelievable softness in his dark eyes, he met Glee's gaze. "Hello, my dear."

She stepped forward and gave him her hand. He kissed it tenderly. "I trust you are well today, dearest?"

How she loved it when he called her that! A smile broadened on her face. "I've never been better," she said softly.

Blanks dropped her hand and looked away from her quickly. He cleared his throat. "So what do you think of the scarlet phaeton?" he asked his brother.

"It has a very fine ride," Jonathan said.

"And the appearance?"

"Your wife tells me my opinion of it exactly matches your own."

Blanks laughed. "It must be as Glee says. The older I get, the more I resemble Father."

"So she keeps telling me," answered Jonathan, a martyred expression on his face.

Blanks met Glee's gaze again, this time with no nervousness. "Have you talked to Mrs. A. today?"

"Not yet. Should you like me to?"

"There's no harm in trying," Blanks said.

She moved away.

"Wait!" he cried.

She turned back, a quizzing look on her face.

"I'll come with you." He turned to Jonathan. "We won't be a moment."

It took some time to locate Mrs. A. because she was cleaning inside a suite of offices on the first floor. Glee walked up to her as she was dusting a desktop. "Do you remember me, Mildred?"

Her eyes distrustful, Mildred glanced from Glee to Blanks. "What do ye want with me?"

"You know," Glee said softly.

Blanks stepped forward. "We're not free from worry over the life you provide for your son. Do you not think the boy deserves a full belly and his own bed to lie in every night?"

She smirked. "Yer the nob what pays for our supper every day?"

Blanks nodded.

"I thank ye for me son, but don't waste yer money on me."

"Food lacks the allure of liquor, I perceive," Blanks said.

She nodded.

"Then Archie may come to live with us in the not-too-distant future—since you have so little regard for preserving your own life," Blanks said to the lad's frail mother.

Glee gasped. How could Blanks be so insensitive? She raked her eyes over the thin woman with such a gaunt face. His words, unfortunately, were likely true. Though lean of years, Mrs. A. looked to be at death's door.

"I've talked to 'im about comin' to live with ye," Mrs. A. said. "As much as I 'ated the idea of me lad leavin,' I urged 'im to go live with ye, but 'e won't leave 'is mum. I'm all me boy's ever 'ad."

Glee's heart went out to Mrs. A. What a sacrifice she had been willing to make for the sake of her son. A pity she was not strong enough to make the ultimate, life-saving sacrifice of giving up her gin.

Glee's gaze settled on Blanks. He swallowed, and the muscle of his cheek tightened. The woman's words, oddly, must have had a profound impact on him. There was sadness on his face, but there was something else, too, something Glee was unable to understand.

"And you're still not willing to come into service with us?" Glee asked. Even from two feet away, the stench of stale gin could be smelled.

Mrs. A. turned cold eyes on Glee. "If . . . if I was a stronger person, I would. But I cannot and nevermore will be able to walk a straight and narrow line."

Blanks took Glee's hand. "Then it seems we've nothing more to say to you, Mrs. A."

Glee shot her husband a worried glance. He squeezed her hand before climbing back up to Willowby's floor.

In Willowby's office, Blanks apologized to his brother. "You must pardon my ill manners. I've been a dreadful host, but I shall make it up to you. Should you like to go to the Pump Room?"

Glee slipped her arm into Jonathan's. "Yes, really, Jonathan, you must sign the book."

"Of course, I should be pleased to go there," he said, "but I lack my brother's facility for making and keeping friends. I fear no one will care one way or the other if I'm in Bath."

"Pooh!" Glee said. "I don't believe you for a moment. You have far too many good qualities to recommend you."

As they left the building, Glee was struck over the fact that though Jonathan was coddled by loving parents, his confidence did not extend beyond Sutton Hall; however, Blanks had absolutely no confidence at Sutton Hall but a great deal of it away from there.

She watched with some degree of sadness as Blanks mounted his bay for the trip to the Pump Room, wishing he and Jonathan had changed places.

TWENTY-NINE

Once at the Pump Room, Glee basked in the thrill of Blanks's possession. She was unable to remove herself from his side or to prevent herself from gazing wondrously into his beloved face while touching, feeling him in every way she could.

The twins, dressed identically in buff breeches and chocolate-colored coats, happened into the lofty chamber while they were there and joined their little circle, bowing and issuing greetings to Jonathan.

"I must tell you our dear brother shall bring us a great deal of pride," Glee said to the twins. "Jonathan's an author! Very soon we shall be able to read his treatise in the *Edinburgh Review.*"

"You don't say!" Melvin said, turning to Jonathan. "What's the article on?"

"This first one's on primogeniture."

"Then there's to be more?" Glee queried happily.

Jonathan looked painfully self-conscious. "I've one under consideration on compulsory education."

"Can't say that I agree with that," Elvin protested. "Too devilishly expensive, and I daresay our class would be the one to foot the bill."

"I can't agree with you," his twin countered.

At this point Melvin and Jonathan struck up an animated conversation with one another.

It was also at this point that Glee glimpsed Carlotta enter the Pump Room alone. Glee edged even closer to Blanks, compelled to watch Carlotta. Dressed in regal purple velvet, Carlotta glanced at Blanks, colored, then strode to the other side of the chamber. Oddly, this was the first time Glee had seen Carlotta since she had wed Blanks. Had the widow left town in order to avoid meeting Blanks in public? She had been neither at the Pump Room nor the Assembly Rooms these three weeks.

Glee had wondered if Carlotta were terribly in love with him, but she had only to see the pained look on Carlotta's face to know how keenly the woman still loved him. And despite that she despised Carlotta Ennis, Glee felt a unique empathy for her. After knowing the pleasure of being bedded by him, Glee realized it would be no easy thing to purge Blanks from her—or Carlotta's—mind and body.

Seeing that Jonathan was engrossed in his conversation with Melvin, Glee looked up and met her husband's intense gaze. "Come, darling, I should love to take a spin about the room with you."

They walked some little distance, with Blanks making no effort to engage her in conversation. His face stern, he seemed as distant as the moon.

"A pity about Archie," Glee began.

He nodded, no expression evident on his inscrutable face save for his perpetual half-smile. "It's quite odd, really," he said, more as if he were thinking aloud. "I believe I'm actually learning from Archie."

"How so?" she asked, caressing Blanks's handsome face with her eyes.

"In some ways I find the lad far richer than I."

Glee's brows shot up. Whatever could her husband

be talking about? How could the wretched little boy be wealthy when he had nothing save the few shillings he earned from Blanks? Then, the realization struck her. *Archie was richer than poor Blanks.* For Archie possessed something Blanks never had: a mother. A mother he loved and who loved him. Glee could have wept for the lonely boy her poor Blanks had been.

On the other hand, she rejoiced that he had shared such a deeply personal revelation with her.

She squeezed his hand. "Yes, I see it. He is." Changing her tone, she continued. "I expect we shouldn't force ourselves on the lad. He really is vastly fortunate."

"We'll keep a watch over him and be there if the need arises."

"You really think his mother will drink herself into the grave?"

A muscle in Blanks's jaw twitched. "I'm certain of it. As much as it pains me to say it, she's one foot in there already."

Glee's eyes filled with tears. "Oh, Blanks, can we not persuade her to change?"

He patted her hand. "I'm afraid not, my dear. We can force nothing on her. Any change has to come from her, and I'm convinced she would rather feel her life slipping away than change its course."

Glee lowered her moist lashes.

Blanks smiled at her. "It appears you've made a conquest of my brother. I daresay he appreciates you touting his literary celebrity."

She shrugged. "I'm a bit out of charity with Jonathan, if you must know. After all, his sole reason for being in Bath is to find a means to strip you of your fortune."

"That's as may be, but I value his honesty. 'Tis more than his mother ever owned. Her great defense when maligning me was that *she was only interested in my good.*"

"Please don't talk about that horrid woman! I vow, Blanks, I detest her."

He laughed and lifted Glee's hand for a kiss.

Glee's glance caught Carlotta's as her face went white and she looked away. She *had* seen Blanks affectionately kiss Glee's hand. Warmth suffused Glee. She might not own Blanks's heart, but she possessed something very close to it. Color stung her cheeks as she thought of the closeness they had shared the night before. She could hardly wait for tonight!

Gregory, on the other hand, was trying to think of how he could prevent himself from tasting of Glee's pleasures that night. Not that he did not want to partake. Glee's very touch stirred him as no other woman had ever done. He told himself he should be content with strolling with her, feeling the pleasure of her arm touching his, hearing her sweet voice, drinking in the love he now believed she felt toward him. And though he returned her affection tenfold, he must deny himself her physical pleasures.

During his long ride in the country this morning, he had thought that becoming estranged from Glee would make it easier for him to deny her. But to cut himself off from her would be to rip out his heart. Even if he could never allow himself the luxury of making love to Glee, he could never deprive himself of her company.

She leaned into him, lifting her smiling face. "Think you Jonathan heard us last night?"

When she had called out his name? The evocative memory had the power to rob him of breath. *Gregory* had never sounded so sweet.

He looked down at her. There was no regret on her face, only a trusting love. "The walls are rather thick," he murmured, patting her hand. "I've . . . worried that I may have hurt you." He swallowed hard, unable to look at her.

"I'm a bit sore, but I daresay once I become accustomed to . . . you, there will be no more soreness."

She dared to hope for what he would be unable to give her. 'Twas like a rapier to his heart. "Would that I could die in your arms, my love," he murmured sadly.

"Don't be so morbid," she teased. "I really cannot bear to think of your demise."

Now he looked at her, long and hard. And he knew without a doubt, Glee loved him. Which made their abstinence all the more regrettable. "Nor I yours," he said bitterly.

He saw that Carlotta went to the fountain for a cup of water. His glance caught Glee following his line of vision, then she stiffened. He braced for the reference Glee was sure to make about his former mistress. He waited, but Glee said nothing. Could it be that previously Glee had not loved him, therefore had not been jealous of Carlotta? And now that she loved him she wished to avoid thinking of or discussing Carlotta?

"Since we've assured your fortune, you don't have to dance attendance on me in public, but I really hope you don't stop," Glee said.

A pity she was so sure of him. He would have to prepare her for the inevitable letdown. "You know I don't want children?"

Glee's hand gripped his arm. "Oh, Blanks, I hadn't thought . . . Do you think I could have . . . ?"

"I hope to God not," he said in a rueful voice.

She gave him an odd look. "It wouldn't be the end of the world, you know. I suspect, too, your father would have been pleased to know a grandson assured the unbroken continuation of his estates."

"Who says it wouldn't be the end of the world?" he demanded harshly. If Glee were to die on childbed, 'twould be the end of his world.

They reached the part of the room where they had started their walk, and Melvin and Jonathan were so engaged in their conversation, they did not see Gregory and Glee.

"Another turn about the room, my love?" Gregory asked.

"I should like it excessively."

They walked some little distance before either of them spoke again. "You have a most beautiful body, Blanks," she said with no trace of shyness.

"As do you, my love. A pity I shall have to abstain from its pleasures."

Her eyes widened, and a look of raw pain swept over her face as she looked at him, her fingers digging into his arm. "Surely you tease?"

"I wish I did," he said morosely.

She came to a stop and looked up at him with watery eyes. "I must know why you say that."

He swallowed and avoided looking at her, then shook his head.

"It's my inexperience," she said with shaking voice, a tear slipping from her eye. "Though I thought you well pleased last night."

He took both her hands and peered earnestly into her solemn face. "I've never in my life been more well pleased."

"You're saying that to spare me embarrassment."

He lifted her hands to his lips. "I'm saying it because it's true."

Now tears began to spill from her eyes. "Allow Jonathan to take my phaeton home—to keep it for all

I care! I suddenly find I must leave." Then she turned from Gregory and hurried from the room.

He fought the urge to go after her. It was far better this way. Let her adjust to the idea of a chaste marriage.

Tears clouding her vision, Glee stormed through the pedestrians who clogged the pavement of Bath. She neither spoke to nor made eye contact with anyone. All she could think of was how miserably she had failed as Blanks's wife. In one moment's time, her bliss had sunk to despair. Where had she gone wrong? Now that she'd found her world in Blanks's arms, she could never return to the loveless charade their marriage had been before.

If she couldn't lie with Blanks the rest of her days, she had no desire to live.

She made no effort to check the flow of her tears as she wove in and out of the stream of people. She thought back over all the words that had passed between Blanks and her at the Pump Room. Hadn't he said he could not bear to think of her demise? He had also paid homage to her body. Her heart nearly stopped. He said he wished he could die in her arms.

Then why had he decided he could not allow himself to renew their lovemaking? She remembered seeing Carlotta at the Pump Room. Could the sight of Carlotta have reminded him of what pleasures he was missing? But hadn't he told Glee he'd never in his life been more *well pleased*? The more Glee thought she knew Blanks, the more she realized how little she really knew about him.

When a knot of women stopped to peer in a milliner's window, Glee impatiently walked around them, splashing in a puddle on the street, not caring that she stained her dress and ruined her shoes.

She made it to Queen Square and ran up the stairs to her chamber, slamming the door behind her, locking it, and throwing herself prostrate on the bed.

The flow of tears had stopped, yet she continued to lie there for another hour, a gnawing emptiness stripping her of all feeling save a deep, lonely melancholy.

Finally, she rose and bathed her swollen eyes. Her inflexible husband had met his match in his not-to-be-dissuaded wife. Hadn't her determination secured Blanks for her husband? Blanks's denial of the most intrinsic human emotions only drove Glee to orchestrate the desired compliance. It would just take time, and she had already pledged a lifetime to him. She could wait while her ministrations wore away his resolve, much like chiseling a rock. She smiled to herself as she drafted a note to Winston Hall inquiring about Dianna's health, then she went to speak to Miss Roberts about dinner and paid a call on her friend, Miss Arbuckle.

At dinner Glee reigned over the table. Neither Blanks nor his brother would have been able to guess how fragile her nerves had been just hours before. For she gave no sign of it. She spoke solicitously to her husband. She complimented Jonathan on the success of his literary career. She and Jonathan spoke of Melvin and the many similarities between Melvin and Jonathan.

"He confided to me he has drafted a treatise on the extension of suffrage, and I agreed to look over it tomorrow," Jonathan said excitedly.

"So you see," Glee said to Jonathan, "your brother's set is not comprised solely of bloods."

"So it seems."

"Though it may come as a shock to you, dear brother," Blanks said with levity, "I've even been known to read the *Edinburgh Review* on occasion."

Glee watched with amusement as the brothers began to talk of liberal reforms and found a great many common beliefs.

After dinner they took the carriage to the Upper Assembly Rooms. "I hope you don't mind picking up my friend Miss Arbuckle," Glee said. "I daresay her mother is suffering the same complaint as Dianna and is unable to accompany her. So, I've offered to."

"How is your sister?" Blanks asked.

"The note I received before dinner said she was much improved. It is to be hoped she can return to the assemblies soon."

"Is Miss Arbuckle the lady who speaks only in monosyllables?" Blanks asked.

Glee frowned. "Only when she's addressed by gentlemen. I have found her speech quite animated when we talk of books. She shares my great love for them."

They collected Miss Arbuckle, and she sat next to Jonathan on the ride to the Assembly Rooms. In the dim carriage Glee watched the two of them, wondering how Jonathan would react to the timid miss. Unfortunately, Miss Arbuckle's dress was constructed of very heavy fabric and its neckline was rather higher than that dictated by fashion. Though plain, her face had a delicacy about it, but Glee decided the lady's best features were her piercing, black eyes. And fortunately, tonight she refrained from wearing the spectacles she usually wore.

Jonathan turned to the young woman and cleared his throat. "My sister tells me you are enamored of literature, Miss Arbuckle."

"Yes," she answered with no further elaboration.

"We are very excited," Glee said to Miss Arbuckle, "that Jonathan's to be published in the *Edinburgh Review.*"

Miss Arbuckle's eyes danced and she broke into a friendly smile. "May I inquire as to the nature of your article?" she asked quietly.

"Primogeniture, particularly as it relates to the crown."

"How very interesting," Miss Arbuckle said.

'Twas the most words Glee had ever heard Miss Arbuckle utter to a gentleman. For the remainder of the journey, Glee had no worries over Miss Arbuckle being neglected.

In fact, even at the Assembly Room, Miss Arbuckle and Jonathan—and later Melvin—sat in The Octagon and conversed on political matters.

The absence of Mr. Jefferson and Carlotta inordinately pleased Glee. Also pleasing her were the many attentions Blanks lavished on her throughout the night. They danced with each other for two waltzes, provoking a bittersweet memory of the intimacy that had bound them the night before. There was nothing to do for it, Glee decided. She would simply have to seduce her husband.

After they dropped Miss Arbuckle off that night, Jonathan said, "I find Miss Arbuckle to be the most well-informed young lady I've ever met. It's women like her who make one want to extend the franchise to women. In fact, she encouraged me to write an article on the very matter."

"I'm amazed that you actually elicited complete sentences from the lady," Blanks said.

Glee directed her attention to her husband. "You have to understand, Blanks, most young woman have been schooled to think of you as a rogue, and I daresay rogues hold no attraction for Miss Arbuckle."

Blanks grinned. "Decidedly none, I should say."

When they arrived back at Queen Square, Blanks helped Glee from the carriage but held her hand not a second longer than necessary. Even as they mounted the stairs to the second floor, he avoided touching Glee in any way.

They came to her door first. He stopped in front of it. "Good night, my love," he said, pecking the top of her head.

Fuming, she answered through gritted teeth. "Good night, dearest."

Closing her door behind her, she backed into it. Perhaps she would *not* seduce her husband tonight, after all. She was not about to stride through their connecting dressing rooms and demand that her husband bed her. She must force herself to muster a semblance of pride.

Instead, she shed her gown and donned a more substantial night shift than she had worn the night before and climbed into her bed, dousing the candle. She lay in the darkness, listening to Blanks stirring in his dressing room. She pictured his bronzed chest as it would look when he removed his shirt. She thought about the feel of his hands and mouth as they had devoured her the night before, and she remembered how his sinewy back and legs had felt when beaded with moisture as she stroked him with the gentle hands of a lover.

And she lay bereft in her bed, praying Blanks would change his mind and come to her.

THIRTY

Despite that he had been unable to sleep because of his debilitating desire for Glee, Gregory decided a trip to the booksellers was in order. He most definitely desired to purchase a copy of the *Edinburgh Review*.

Since the bookshop was only two blocks away, he walked. Every step of the way, Glee filled his mind and senses. Then another scent infringed on his thoughts. *Lavender.* He looked up and into the violet eyes of Carlotta Ennis as she walked toward him and met him with a solemn gaze. "Hello, Gregory," she said in that husky voice of hers.

"Good morning, Mrs. Ennis," he said stiffly, coming to a sputtering halt.

She edged up to him. "Do you mind if I walk with you for a spell?"

He shrugged. "I lay no claim to the public pavement."

They walked a block before she finally spoke. "When you . . . dismissed me, you said it was your desire to continue our . . . relationship after you wed. Do you still feel the same?" she asked.

His mouth went dry. His heart beat erratically. God, but he wanted, indeed needed, a woman. 'Twas all he could think of throughout the long night. But the woman he wanted was not Carlotta.

His silence spoke more eloquently than words could have.

She laughed a bitter laugh. "It's as I feared. You've fallen in love with your wife."

He gazed into her misty eyes and nodded somberly.

"Then it appears I've not only wasted your time, I've made an utter fool of myself," she said in a trembling voice as she turned away from him.

He hated to see her hurt, especially now that he knew what it felt like to crave a union that could not be.

She started to walk away, but he reached out to touch her arm. "Never a fool, Carlotta," he whispered in a low, remorseful voice.

Their eyes met and held for the briefest of seconds before she spun around and left.

With Jonathan at the ribbons of the phaeton, he and Glee were en route to pay a morning call on Miss Arbuckle. Glee was most pleased. Jonathan had stopped at the florist's and bought a nosegay of posies to present to the worthy lady. The day was lovely with cloudless cerulean skies, and despite that Blanks had not come to her bed the night before, Glee's spirits were high. Never one to accept defeat, she had confidence that, with time, she could bring Blanks around.

Then she saw the beautiful woman in lilac walking with somber grace along Quiet Street. Glee's stomach tensed. Next she was witness to her own husband stopping and talking to Carlotta Ennis before the two of them continued along the pavement.

Had Blanks driven a stake through her heart, Glee could not have been wounded more deeply. Unknowingly, she let out an anguished cry when Blanks, with a solemn look on his face, grasped Carlotta's arm after she spun away from him.

The man Glee had bestowed all her love upon had lied to her. He was still meeting his mistress.

Jonathan, following the direction of Glee's gaze and sensing the cause of her distress, quickly turned the phaeton onto Stall Street.

Glee was unable to check the flow of her tears. As painful as was the realization that Blanks still bedded Carlotta was the betrayal Glee suffered over her husband's lies. More than once he had insisted his relationship with Carlotta had been severed. By defiling Glee's trust he had wounded her more deeply than even his infidelity could have.

His face grim, Jonathan spoke. "So I perceive there's one area in which my brother shows no inclination to change."

As angry and anguished as she was, Glee could not betray the man she had married. To seek consolation from Jonathan would be to acknowledge the vulnerability of her marriage. "I will not allow you to malign my husband," she defended.

Jonathan cursed under his breath and angrily flicked the ribbons. "I cannot take you to Miss Arbuckle's if you're going to be a watering pot."

"Then I beg that you set me down at Queen Square," she said, sniffing.

He mumbled something unintelligible and turned at the next corner.

When he pulled up in front of the town house, she spoke to him, careful to shield her tear-stained face from his scrutiny. "By the way, it pains me that I'll not be able to be here for your entire stay. I have pressing duties to attend to back at Hornsby."

He nodded solemnly.

* * *

In her chambers, Glee and Patty hurriedly packed a valise and portmanteau for their return to the home where Glee was born.

"Will the master be going, too?" a surprised Patty asked.

Glee cleared her throat. "Not at this time, I don't believe."

Patty's brows lowered. "I declare, I hope he's had more notice of this journey than I have!"

Impertinent girl! What occurred between Glee and her husband was no business of Patty's.

With her packing complete, Glee penned a brief note to Blanks.

> *Darling,*
>   *It seems I've served the purpose of our marriage; so, now I am returning to Hornsby and releasing you of all responsibility toward me.*
>   *With deepest affection,*
>   *Glee*

Her heart pounding in her chest, she went into his chamber, to the room where their marriage had been so gloriously consummated. The very smell of the dark chamber evoked Blanks and all the love she felt for him. But she could not allow herself the luxury of remembering the magic that had occurred between them in this very room. Her eyes avoiding the bed, she propped her letter up on his desk, then fled from the room.

In the hallway, Hampton, in his characteristic expressionless delivery, informed her the carriage was ready. Her eyes watery, Glee wouldn't chance a last look at what had been home to her and Blanks.

Along with her maid and with help from the coachman, Glee grimly boarded the coach-and-four. Since it wouldn't do to weep all the way to Warwickshire, to distract herself Glee had carried along a volume of Sir Walter Scott, which she proceeded to read.

"I don't know how ye can read when the carriage is in motion!" Patty exclaimed. "I declare, it rattles me stomach somethin' awful."

Glee did not look up from the page. "I believe a number of people suffer from the same complaint, but my own stomach is affected neither by movement nor vapors. Mama always said my stomach was as strong as iron." Talk of her stomach made Glee wonder if she would ever have experienced morning sickness were she to have conceived a child. Poor Dianna had suffered terribly from the complaint. Felicity, being of the same blood as Glee, was never sick a day. Such thoughts had the effect of causing Glee to grow even more morose. If only she had been able to conceive Blanks's babe. 'Twould be something of Blanks to fill the aching void of his absence.

For she knew her departure from Bath would cement the irrevocable break with Blanks. She had served her purpose. Now Blanks would be free from the unwanted ties of matrimony.

Having purchased the latest edition of the *Edinburgh Review,* Blanks returned to the town house. "Have my wife and brother returned from Miss Arbuckle's?" Gregory asked the butler.

Hampton avoided eye contact with his master. "It appears Mrs. Blankenship had a change of heart. Not long after she left, she returned and ordered the coach-and-four be brought around while she and her maid rather hurriedly packed for their return to the country.

When he had heard *coach-and-four* mentioned, Gregory's heart tripped. Had Glee gone to Hornsby Manor? Or Sutton Hall? Had some emergency arisen that called for her attention? He'd miss her like the devil. "Did Mrs. Blankenship, perchance, leave me a letter?"

"I couldn't say, sir. I did see her leave your chamber shortly before she left. It may be that she left some type of communication in your room."

Nodding, Gregory hastened up the stairs to his chambers. His stomach oddly disturbed and his pulse erratic, he walked up to his desk and read Glee's letter.

Then he angrily wadded it up, cursed a blue streak, and threw the ball of vellum at the nearest wall. Did the minx have the effrontery to think he did not want her? Fury rocked him. Even if he weren't ever to bed her again, he had no desire to deny himself the pleasure of her company, as painful as it was to behold her without carrying his passion to its natural conclusion.

Good Lord, he thought, could Glee be angry because he refused to indulge in the pleasures of her body? His mind flashed back to her reaction when he'd told her there was to be no more lovemaking. She had expressed her unhappiness at her inability to satisfy him! He laughed loudly and bitterly now. Nothing in his wretched life had ever satisfied him so thoroughly.

And he had allowed the poor girl to think herself undesirable! That had to explain why she had left him. His first inclination was to hurry after her, to make her listen to him when he told her how highly he had valued their lovemaking. But, after more careful consideration, he realized her departure, though painful now, would be for the best in the years to come. Being with her day after agonizing day would only inflict nearly unbearable suffering upon him.

With a bittersweet ache in the vicinity of his heart,

he went down to his library, where Jonathan found him a half-hour later.

Gregory's head jerked up from the quarterly review when he heard angry footsteps outside his door. Then the door flew open, slamming into the wall behind it and rattling the paintings on the library wall.

Gregory's brows lowered as he watched his brother storm into the room and stride up to the desk where Gregory sat. Jonathan stood there, his eyes flashing angrily, his voice trembling with rage. "Of all the careless, conscienceless things you've done in your miserable life, you've now sunk as low as you can go."

A puzzled look crossed Gregory's pained face. "Pray, enlighten me. What conscienceless thing have I now done?"

"You haven't been married a month, and you flaunt your purple-hued mistress right in your wife's face!"

Gregory pounced to his feet, his hands fisted, fury in his voice. "I've done no such thing!"

Jonathan watched his brother through flashing, narrowed eyes. "I saw you and Mrs. Ennis. So did Glee. What was your poor wife to think when she saw you go after Mrs. Ennis and grab her arm?"

"Dear God!" Gregory groaned, shaking his head. "It wasn't at all what you think." He looked directly into his brother's angry eyes. "I give you my word, I severed the . . . alliance with Carlotta as soon as I offered for Glee. That's the truth."

"Then explain to me why you two were together today."

Gregory shrugged. "I know what it must have looked like, but it was an honest case of two people passing in the street."

"And you just happened to snatch her arm, with a worried look on your face?"

"I told you, it's not what you think," Gregory mumbled, collapsing back into his chair. "Are you sure Glee saw this?"

There was a curious mixture of anger and sorrow on Jonathan's face. "God, man, she wept."

The words struck a blow to Gregory's windpipe. Finally, he murmured, "So that's why she's left me."

"Can you blame her?"

Gregory shook his head somberly. "Perhaps it's best this way. I've been an abominable husband."

"Admit it, Gregory. You married her merely to claim your inheritance. There was never a real marriage."

"Without Glee, I don't care about anything. Take the money," Gregory said.

"I can't! It's obvious Glee's devoted to you."

Gregory looked up hopefully. "Devotion?" He had guessed she might be in love with him, but this was verification of his most ardent hopes.

"You're a bloody moron if you can't see how truly Glee loves you."

"But it was to be a marriage in name only. She said—"

"She talked you into the marriage, did she not?"

"How did you know?"

Jonathan laughed. "Because the girl was madly in love with you, you idiot!"

'Twas like brilliant blue skies ripping through black clouds. Dare he hope Glee really loved him? His hopeful heart began to drum with anticipation. "I'd like to believe it," Gregory said throatily.

"Are you in love with her?" Jonathan asked, disbelief in his voice.

Gregory met his brother's gaze solemnly. "So keenly it hurts."

Jonathan edged back onto the arm of an upholstered chair and lowered his weight onto it. "I believe you really are. Why else would you risk your fortune by confiding in me your plot to gain Father's fortune?"

Gregory shook his head bitterly. "Nothing matters anymore," he said in a low voice not devoid of pain. "Glee was—is—my life."

"Then go tell her, man!"

"But . . ." He couldn't tell his brother of the unnatural dread which filled him when he thought of burying himself into his beloved wife. "Perhaps it's better this way."

THIRTY-ONE

The first week of her return to Hornsby, Glee sulked in anger toward Blanks. On her eighth day she allowed herself to think less bitterly toward him. During one of her solitary rides through the estate she came upon the dome-topped folly which was reflected in the shimmering water of the pond beside it. This was the place where she had forced Blanks to marry her.

As with any memory connected to Blanks, she was free of shame no matter how brazen had been her pursuit of him. From the first, her battle strategy had been to spare no humiliation in her quest to snare his heart. She laughed bitterly, with the trees and the now-thick carpet of ruffled green grass her only audience. True to her pledge, she had drawn the line at nothing in her fervent drive to earn his love.

And it had all been for naught.

During the succession of empty days of hollow existence at Hornsby, Glee had relived every moment, every loving word or gesture that Blanks had bestowed on her. She came to realize had she the opportunity to do it all over again, she would not have changed a single thing.

As she perceived it, there were two reasons for her failure. The first, of course, was Blanks's affection for

Carlotta Ennis. The other was Glee's own failure to satisfy him sexually. What a fool she had been to imagine she could compete with so experienced a lover as Carlotta must be.

As Glee dismounted and led her horse around the columned perimeter of the folly, her memory of that rainy day she entrapped Blanks shot through her like a bullet. That was when her anger began to abate. Blanks could have revealed her wickedness to George that day, but he sacrificed his own happiness to shield her. 'Twas such an honorable act.

A man with that kind of nobility was deeply at odds with one who could lie so convincingly about Carlotta. With the ice around her heart melting, Glee told herself Blanks lied merely to spare her own feelings.

He was so gentle and loving. She thought of his efforts to help Archie and of his gallantry in declaring himself to her brother. So many acts of his kindnesses—and his protectiveness toward her—crowded into her mind, imbuing her with the love she had never been able to deny. Now she came to appreciate that despite her anger she had used an affectionate closing in her farewell letter him.

She almost came to regret that she had left, but she had finally accepted that she could never force Blanks to love her. And with no hope for his love, all she could want was for him to be happy. Liberated and happy.

Her eyes moist, she sighed. At least she would always have her precious memories of the three glorious weeks she had been Mrs. Gregory Blankenship.

Not a day, not a minute had agonizingly dragged by that Gregory's thoughts had not been invaded with memories of the angel who had been his wife. He took solitary rides through the countryside in a vain effort to purge Glee from his thoughts. He avoided the Pump Room and the Assembly Room and anywhere where someone might inquire about his wife. The wound was still far too raw for him to deepen.

His brother, who continued to stay at Gregory's town house in order to further his friendship with Miss Arbuckle, did not let a meeting go by that he did not needle Gregory about going after Glee. All of which made Gregory realize how much his brother meant to him.

One afternoon when his memories of Glee nearly overpowered him, Gregory felt compelled to return to her chambers. He had been picturing her in the emerald dress he loved her to wear, and he wondered if she had taken it to Hornsby. He rifled through her dressing room but saw no sign of the emerald dress. Instead, she had left behind the dresses he disliked so excessively. The scant red, the near-backless black, the copper metallic. Upon looking at them, he smiled to himself. That she'd left them behind curiously pleased him. It was as if her simple action were a silent concession to him.

As he fingered the soft silk of the red dress, George's words came back to him. Her brother had said he believed Glee desired to appear *fast* in order to attract him. Would that he could believe that.

But, of course, had she truly loved him, she would not have been able to flee.

That same afternoon he answered correspondence, read over the draft of his brother's next article, and perused and signed a sheaf of papers for Willowby. All the while George's words kept ringing in his ears. Could Glee really have meant to appear fast because she loved him?

Could she, he asked himself, have really loved him? Jonathan was convinced she did. Gregory even remembered his own assurances that she must care for him when she offered him her body.

If he could be convinced of her love, his own happiness would be as infinite as the air they breathed.

He thought of Glee's closeness to her sister, and was overcome with a need to ride over to Winston Hall and speak to Felicity about Glee.

When Gregory arrived at Winston Hall, he was pleased to learn George and Thomas had gone shooting. What he had come to learn concerned only Felicity. Or Felicity and Dianna, who was like a true sister to Glee.

When Felicity entered the drawing room where he awaited, her brow was creased with worry. That her lovely face so closely resembled Glee's made him physically ache for Glee.

"Tell me those nasty rumors I hear about my sister returning to Hornsby are not true," Felicity said.

Having risen to greet her and kiss her proffered hand, Gregory's lips thinned into a grim line. "I'm afraid they are."

"Oh, dear," she said, collapsing into a chair.

He could not help but notice her tiny waist finally had thickened to reveal evidence of the babe which grew in her womb. The thought caused him to stiffen. "Pray, how is Lady Sedgewick? I trust she has returned to good health?"

Felicity laughed. "Quite good, actually, though George coddles her unbearably. He still hasn't allowed her from her chamber. You know how he is where Dianna's concerned."

Gregory nodded solemnly. "I used to think it foolish. Now I understand."

Her face solemn, Felicity studied him.

"I've been wondering," Gregory began. "Since you're so devilishly close to your sister, I thought perhaps she may have confided in you. For example, George once suggested that Glee's endeavors to appear fast might be prompted by her desire to appear more attractive to me." He frowned. "Unfortunately, in the past I've been known to associate with loose women. Before Glee, you understand."

An amused smile crossed Felicity's face. "George told me the very same thing about Glee's outrageous dress, and I told him he was likely right. Dianna—this was before she became sick—said she was sure of it. In fact, Dianna said Glee admitted to her quite some time before your betrothal that she had always been in love with you." Felicity gave him a long, sympathetic look. "Is this, perhaps, what you came here to hear?"

His face lifted when he smiled at her. "Indeed it is." Then he got to his feet.

"Shall you go now to Hornsby?"

He nodded.

THIRTY-TWO

Gregory told himself he should wait for the morrow. He had only two hours of daylight left, but he was so thirsty to behold his beloved, he could not go through another night without seeing her. Champion would carry him in good stead, and the roads should be in good condition since no rain had fallen recently.

Thoughts of the laughter ringing in Glee's voice, of her floral scent, of the smoothness of her fair skin and the vibrant life of her cinnamon-colored hair—all of these thoughts sustained him throughout the long hours of his journey. Most of all, he cherished her for the true wife she had been to him.

He had come to understand so much of life because of her. Now he knew how the urchin Archie possessed far more than he ever had. Gregory could now empathize with George, who loved his wife quite possibly more than he loved himself. And Gregory had finally come to understand that his youthful wife knew his own heart far better than he had known it.

He grew so hungry to see her, his breath grew short and his hands trembled. He tried to rehearse what he would say to her, but none of the words he articulated seemed adequate.

Two hours after night had fallen, he rode up the

avenue to Hornsby Manor. Light shone in nearly every window of the sprawling manor house. He still did not know what he was going to say to Glee, but he knew he would speak his heart.

In front of the house, he dismounted and tethered his horse, then nervously approached the front door. The butler who answered the door raised a puzzled brow. "May I help you, sir?"

"I'm Mr. Blankenship. I've come to see my wife."

Sweeping the door open, the butler apologized profusely for failing to recognize "Miss Glee's husband."

As he stepped into the house, Gregory looked upward and saw Glee hurry gracefully down the stairs. She wore her emerald gown, and Gregory was convinced she had never looked more beautiful.

"Blanks! Is anything wrong?"

The sight of her in all her radiant beauty affected him profoundly. "Your family members are well," he said. Then to the butler, he added, "A private word with my wife, if you please."

"Very good, sir," the man said as he scooted off.

Glee came to the bottom of the stairs and froze in front of Gregory.

His hat in his trembling hand, he worshipped her with his eyes. "All your family is well, save me, that is . . . that is, if you consider me family."

A worried look flashed across her tiny face and her hand went out to him. With pain, he noticed she was not wearing his mother's emerald ring—their wedding ring. "Pray tell, what's the matter?" she asked.

"It seems you left behind in Bath something I was unaware I possessed."

"What?" she asked, her brows plunging.

"My heart."

Her watery eyes widened, but she made no move

from the bottom step where she had frozen. "What are you saying?"

He swallowed. "That my resolve never to marry, never to fall in love, has crumbled like yesterday's biscuits."

A light began to dance in her eyes. "Gregory Blankenship, are you trying to tell me you have fallen in love with me?"

"I am," he said solemnly.

She started to move forward, then pulled back. "But I thought you were in love with Carlotta Ennis."

"Never."

"But—"

"You saw me pass her in the street."

"You didn't exactly pass her. You walked with her!"

"I did. At her request. I want you to believe that was the first time I had seen her since I became betrothed to you."

"Really?"

"Really."

"I *wanted* to believe you wouldn't lie to me. I believe I was at odds to know which hurt me the most, your lying about Carlotta or your infidelity with her."

A muscle in his jaw tightened, and he spoke in a low, throaty voice. "I was never unfaithful to you, Glee."

"But . . . why did you grab Carlotta by the arm?"

"Having discovered what it was to love you, I knew something of the pain she must have been feeling."

"I see," Glee said thoughtfully. "She purposely met you on the street to beg that you take her back, and when you wouldn't, she berated herself."

"It seems my wife is a most adept student of human behavior."

Glee came down the final step and linked her arm

through his. "I hope you have come to realize how well I know you, my dear Blanks."

"Actually, it's something I've only recently discovered."

They strolled from the house and into the parterre garden behind the manor.

"Do you know, Blanks, since I've been back at Hornsby, I believe I've discovered something more about you."

"What's that?"

"The reason you don't want children."

His heart thumped. "And?"

"It all has to do with losing your mother on child-bed. Remember, you told me you hated your father for—essentially—killing your mother."

Good Lord, Glee *did* understand him better than he knew himself. He nodded.

"It's my belief that you fear to impregnate me—or any woman you value."

He came to a stop and nestled her face between his hands. "I can't ever risk losing you."

"But, my dearest husband, I've told you the women in my family are good breeders. And I've never been sick a day in my life. It's my belief I'll bear you a dozen healthy babes."

He settled his hands on her shoulders. "You're far too precious to me."

"Then you're willing to throw away our happiness because of a silly notion formed when you were a boy?"

They began to walk again. The smells of night and Glee's intoxicating presence comforted him as he sorted out his thoughts. Though his wife was five years younger than he, in so many ways she was wiser. His silly anxiety about the dangers of fathering a child *was* a holdover from his unnatural boyhood. More than he did, Glee realized true happiness would never come to them if they could not be united in every way.

After some time had passed and still he had made no response, Glee came to a stop and put her hands to her hips. "Gregory Blankenship, love of my life, I shall make a pact with you. *If* I should die with child-birth fever—which I assure you is highly improbable—you have my permission to do yourself in."

He tilted his head sideways, an amused grin on his face.

She grew solemn and slowly moved to him and enfolded herself in his arms. He looked down into her lovely face bathed in moonlight and he tightened his exquisite hold on her before lowering his lips to hers.

After the tender kiss, Glee looked up at him and spoke in a seductive whisper. "You do know that I've always loved you?"

" 'Tis just one of the things I'm learning about my extremely addictive wife."

Then he scooped her against him, savoring the feel of her.

"Blanks?"

"What, my darling?"

"Shall we go to bed now?"

"A very good idea, I should say."

If you enjoyed WITH HIS RING, be sure to look for A FALLEN WOMAN, the next book in award-winning author Cheryl Bolen's fabulous *The Brides of Bath* series, available wherever books are sold in August 2002.

Since her husband's tragic death in the Peninsula, Carlotta Ennis had hoped to attract a wealthy husband in Bath. Instead she made the ruinous mistake of loving a rake who was willing to seduce her, but not to marry her. Now that she has been so thoroughly compromised, she is certain no decent gentleman will ever marry her . . . until James Rutledge returns home from the war and offers his hand—though Carlotta is convinced it is out of duty, and not love.

After Carlotta's husband gave his own life to save him in the heat of battle, James had vowed to return the man's gift by providing for his wife and son. Though the lovely widow agrees to become his bride, James believes it is his fortune alone that she desires. Yet as near tragedy sends Carlotta into his arm, it also propels her to confess her deepest secrets. Will James let her dark past come between them, or listen to his heart's undeniable truth . . . that he's fallen in love with a fallen woman?